For N., T. and T.

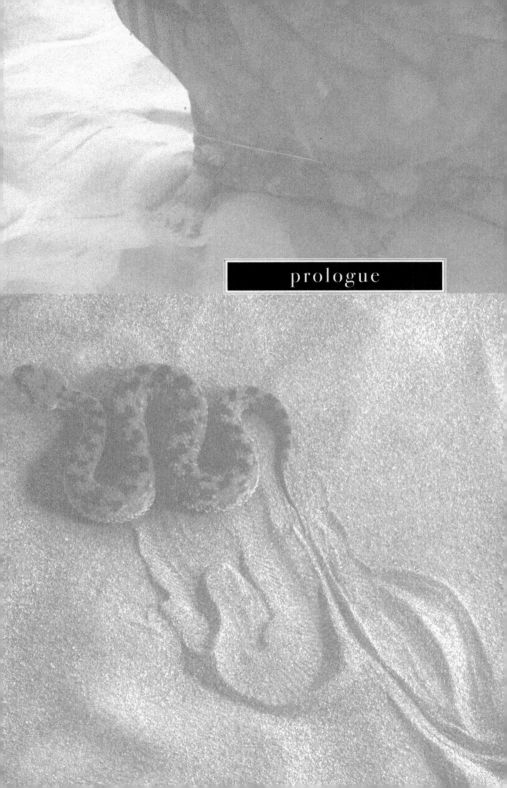

prologue

Sohrab

I t was because I had no father that I asked questions.
My life would have been different. My questions would
have been smothered by fatherly love. I would not have
sniffed out and chased truth like a dog after a rat. I would
not have learned to pick through webs of silences and evasions.

I came to know the delicate and the sharp sides of truth. I
learned that the most important truth can be all around, in the
eyes of loved ones, in the places we live, but might not be understood. I learned that sometimes no one *wants* to be reminded of
certain things.

If it were not for stubborn questions, slow minds and hearts
that were locked tight and secure, the truth about our family
would have remained hidden forever.

IMAGINE AN ALBUM full of photos, preserved, dated and
explained. Imagine that this is the album of truth.

If there were a first photo in this story, it would be of
morning, a beautiful, peaceful country morning in the tiny
kingdom of Lesotho, the film exposed on the day Sohrab, my
brother – *my half-brother* – not quite as fatherless as me, was

taken away by the Lesotho Paramilitary Police. If I were to write an inscription on the back of this photo, it would read: *This was a moment when a fatherless child needed his father. If ever there was a time when a dead father would be welcome back, this would be it.* The date would be 1986.

The scene looks perfectly normal. There are some clay-coloured *rondavels* and square houses that were built after the white missionaries came and explained to the people that houses without corners were against God. Although you cannot see this, the voices of the women at the river rise over the mutterings of the rock pigeons in the eaves of an old sandstone house. In the distance the mountain they call Quoquolosing glows in the early light, and all the rolling, parched land is the colour of blood and dawn. In a corner of this photo are three people: an old Masutho granny, no more than five feet tall; a little orange boy who looks like a goat herder from the desert; and an overgrown Indian girl in coveralls – that would be me. All three sit on a bench worn shiny by indolence, along the eastern wall of a house, backs to a glowering sun. Instead of facing the beautiful valley with its villages and rolling fields, we face a wall that is blank but for a large contingent of lizards clinging to the sandstone.

That is the photo. What cannot be seen is that, like the lizards, we only had space in our brains for the sensation of warmth that morning. What cannot be seen is what happened next as we sat warming our blood.

In the distance came the sound of a kombi as it turned off the main road and laboured along the treacherous drive that led to Dr. Patel's house. We glanced over our shoulders as this kombi stopped in the dirt. We swivelled around when we heard the motor shut off. The driver stretched where he sat, then the doors slid lazily aside and six Lesotho Paramilitary Police climbed out, straightening their berets and brushing crumbs from their tan uniforms. They were in no special hurry. One told a joke. Another urinated. Some pulled guns from the kombi, holding them by the tips of their fingers so that we were reminded of the way men hold soiled babies. We thought, *those guns must be delicate.*

We stood to watch them saunter to Dr. Patel's door, where they did not knock or call out *ko ko,* the friendly greeting that sounds like knuckles on wood. By this time, there was a familiar and unwelcome metallic taste forming in our mouths. It was the taste of fear.

A minute later the soldiers emerged holding Sohrab by the arms.

We had not seen Sohrab for some days. He was struggling to find his way to manhood, but the struggle was not going smoothly. He was barefoot and reminded us of a young, foolish and dusty dog. He did not resist the soldiers, which was wise. He may even have harboured some pride to be the object of their mission.

"Who is this rag and stick that looks like our Sohrab?" 'Mè Jane murmured.

But strangely, we remained rooted to our bench, like watchers of one of the faded films at the college library on Cinema Night. We had no influence over this story and little comprehension of it. Only when my mother burst out of the door and charged down the hill did we shake ourselves.

She was large, my mother, and her hair flew around her head like the snake hair of Durga, the mother of all things, as she descended on the soldiers of the Lesotho Paramilitary Police, Leribe Region. The soldiers fell back.

"Don't touch him," my mother commanded, then she took hold of Sohrab's arm to take him home. Sohrab, stupid proud dog-boy, idiot *tsotsi* that he was, pulled his arm away, meaning to remind everyone that he was not to be mistaken for a child, nor for the son of a mother. If I had been close enough, I would have clapped him on the head.

The Captain of those soldiers was calm. "'Mè Zara," he said, "we know who is somebody and who is not somebody. You should have taught your boy to run. You should have taught him to hide. Now it is too late."

"I am friends with the Interior Minister," Mother blurted out, which made one of the men guffaw.

By this time 'Mè Jane had made her way down and wrapped her fat arms around my mother and held her while Sohrab was swept away into the kombi and gone, leaving us to muddle and wonder if what we had seen was real.

We walked for the next hours on slanted earth, the apprehension of Sohrab having unbalanced us to the point that ordinary sights and sounds startled us. Speech was impossible. A gulf of frightened silence grew among us. There was nothing to discuss or dispute. We reckoned Sohrab was guilty of immoral and heinous activities: truancy, seduction, waywardness and, perhaps, worse.

We could only await the bad news in silence, words stunned from our minds.

The Thing

After Sohrab was taken away, that was it for a time. Nothing happened. We remained locked in silence. It was only later that we heard that Thabo Majara was dead, his throat slit like a lamb at Christmas. As for Sohrab, people said he knew much about that. They said Sohrab was the hand and Sohrab was the blade. Who was to know?

"These rumours are nothing but the scatterings of field mice," 'Mè Jane pointed out.

But we looked about when we heard these things, wondering. We thought Bushman knew something, but he only grinned the stupid grin of the innocent.

Well, those field mice must have carried their mess far, because it seemed they left this world entirely and wandered into the Not-Living Place, causing certain Things to hear the rumours about Sohrab.

What actually happened was this: one afternoon, when the shadows were long, we noticed a human figure on the face of the Lightning Cliff, suspended in air, its attachments to this world tenuous. It stood and sat, shifted this way and that, crossed and uncrossed its arms. It was an Old Thing, round through the middle, with skin that emanated a ghastly pallor. It looked familiar but our minds refused to give it a name. When I pointed it out to 'Mè Jane she could not see anything but rock. I kept pestering her about it until finally she put down her armful of washing and sighed and began to pray.

"*Modimo...*" she began in a parched voice, then she took up a broom and swept the air with great strokes and cried out, "Go away *Sethotsela*, Ghost-Thing!" and asked me if that made things better. Amazed, I told her it had; the Thing had taken notice of her broom and vanished.

I glanced at that spot on the Lightning Cliff on many occasions in the following days. I could detect only the slightest stain on the rocks.

"Who was it?" Bushman asked.

"A lost traveller," I speculated.

'Mè Jane peered over her glasses at us. She had refused to admit that she had seen the Thing. "You must not keep asking me that," she said stubbornly, but I had other approaches.

"I wonder," I said, "what God would do to someone who will not answer the question of a child..."

'Mè Jane looked at me and sniffed. A moment later she said, "Very well. Listen carefully." We could see that she was relieved to be talking. "What you saw was one of the Ancestors. It is someone who wishes to come back to our world."

I think I must have known that the Thing was Devkumar Uncle, though I said nothing to 'Mè Jane. I knew how his mind worked, living or dead. He would have heard the story of his son's detention. At first he would have done nothing. He would have tried to ignore it, maybe even turned it into a stupid joke. But at night, and when he was alone, it would have come back and bothered him. It would have bothered him more and more, until his eyes bulged and became red. Then he would be angry. His anger would be enough to make him poke his head out of eternity and return from the Other Place.

What a bad surprise he would have.

Since the day Devkumar died, Sohrab, his only real blood child, had hardly attended school and when he had, it had been a disaster. He had not remembered his father's wishes, had not trod the paths of mathematics or science or writing or machinery. Sohrab had become a dust-streaked urchin of the streets, a leader of dogs and a *tsotsi* of the worst criminal sort. If poor Devkumar Uncle knew, he would blame my mother. My mother would blame him back, then they would fight.

Meanwhile our mother had plunged deeply into some papers and refused to look at us. Dr. Patel, still burning with the humiliation of having his very house invaded by the police, even if they were the soldier-police, stayed out of view. The villagers from the valley eyed all of these goings-on and kept a safe and wary distance. All of which left 'Mè Jane and Bushman and me to sit on the veranda, our noses sniffing the air for fresh mouse leavings.

We said nothing. We observed the moving red curtain of dust sifting endlessly across the sky. Our hopes dried in the sun. Our thoughts shrivelled in the red dirt at our feet.

A MONTH AFTER Sohrab's detention, the popping of a motor broke the silence. Our eyes rolled around in dust-clogged sockets and we blinked and squinted and saw a battered car bouncing onto the college grounds.

"What do you see?" croaked 'Mè Jane.

I saw the car stop and a familiar figure climb out. I did not allow a single fibre of myself to twitch. If I could remain perfectly still and let my breathing become shallow then nothing strange would happen. This might have worked had I not wet the bench.

"*Modimo*, is that Mastah?" breathed 'Mè Jane.

"Of course not, 'Mè. He is dead."

'Mè Jane had shown me that we can deny time, forcing it to go back and try an alternate path. But a small thing like a wet frock and a rivulet of urine spreading along the grain of the bench can ruin everything.

Bushman came and stood beside me. He seemed to understand what was happening. "If you watch them too much they will think they are alive," he whispered. "Ignore it and it will return to its place..."

We closed our eyes so we would not see the Thing emerge onto the sunlit hillside.

At first there was no sound, then came a queer dead flopping sound like fish on the riverbank. Mercifully, the Thing making the sound must not have noticed us in the shadow of the roof. We heard it go around the side of the house, moving without a word, circling, searching for an opening into the Living World. At that moment my eyes fluttered open. I tried to control them, but they were insistent on seeing the Thing from the Other Place. They saw crumpled pants. They glimpsed the white shirt and the bald head that glistened with sweat. It looked like Devkumar Uncle except faded and worn down. This, I presumed, was the terrible effect of being dead.

It had poor eyesight not to notice us. But then, we were as motionless as the rocks in the cliff. It found no breach in our wall (except for one) and went on its way down the hill to its car.

We thought it was gone for good. A while later Bushman chuckled triumphantly because he thought we had offered it nothing and it had not found a voice.

I kept the matter of my unruly eyelids to myself.

WE HAD THE CHANCE to prevent that Dead Thing from returning. In fact we tried. At first we offered it no quarter. We refused to think about it or mention it. This meant that there were two big subjects that we could not mention: Sohrab and the Thing That Was Once His Father. But it is impossible, of course, for humans not to talk. And this Devkumar Thing had a death-grip on us. If our thoughts strayed for a moment, there it was.

"It smelled," I finally commented one day.

"Like the sea," nodded Bushman, then he shook his head and scowled because we had let down our guard.

We were shelling peas from the garden, shelling, chewing the sweet husks and spitting them on the floor.

Later: "What can it want?"

"To live...," he answered without hesitation.

We talked about it too much. And my eyes had opened and seen what they should not. So the Thing came again and caught us unaware. When we looked up we saw it clearly. Sunlight fell fully upon it where it stood at the doorway. In its hands were large, garishly-ribboned parcels. There was no chance for us to compose ourselves or direct our eyes away. It was too late. It fixed us with the toothy grin of a corpse. Then it knocked.

'Mè Jane glanced at me, took a breath and said very loudly, "Good gracious, Madam. It's Ntate Devkumar."

At that moment my mother was sitting at her workbench, painting a piece of broken glass. She started when 'Mè Jane spoke, upsetting a small tin of green paint.

"You must not call me Madam. You know how I hate that."

"But Madam...look who has come home!"

My mother looked at Devkumar Uncle and said, "Tell him to go away and take his...*stupid* possessions with him."

It was clear to us that the sight of it was too much for her. Her mind must have cracked along the seam between dream and sense. She began humming a song, "Amazing Grace," and she dipped her brush in the spilled paint on her workbench.

The Thing moved along the outside wall of our house until it stood before an open window where its head was framed like a picture. It moved its lips. At first there was only a parched scraping sound. But as we stared, we lent it certitude and life.

"Maybe I come later. You people so busy-busy and all..."

9

We lost the battle right there. After that the Thing was like a dog that had begged a scrap. It had no intention of leaving us alone. My mother's song ended and she stared at the shard of glass in her hand. 'Mè Jane invoked the spirits of the Ancestors and looked to Mother. And so deeply were we in the trance of the Thing that it could have danced the Death Dance through our house with hardly a challenge. But it did no such thing. It preferred to remain at the window and push its parcels, one by one, through the opening so that they plopped on the low wooden table where our bowl of shelled peas stood, tipping onto the floor and sending peas bouncing through paint and dirt and chips of wood and chewed pea husks.

"What are you doing here, Morena? Have you come back because we did not honour you?" 'Mè Jane cried out.

The Thing stared at her with wide, fishy eyes. "Honour me? What the hell this means? Did you forget me this much? What about greetings for father-lost, father-found? What about hello-mister-how-do-you-do? What about that? What the hell is the matter with this house?"

That was how Devkumar Uncle returned from the Dead Place. For a long time after that we had to contend with a Dead in our midst. It was real trouble, but we learned to get along and pretend everything was normal.

Of course, we had no real choice since we feared the wrath of the Dead more than anything.

That first day the Devkumar Dead Thing finally went off down the hill looking irritated. We gathered our peas and washed the paint from each one.

Later we saw the Thing at the shed, poking among the parts of cars left behind from its life. Before I had a chance to stop him, Bushman went straight to the shed and with that animal way of his looked it in the eyes.

"And who the hell this is?" demanded the Thing, but then suddenly it knew. It knew that Bushman was the baby that had taken its place in life when it had died. It knew and in that moment seemed to understand everything that had happened to us.

"*Bhut-baby,* isn't it." *Witch-baby.*

But Bushman merely grinned and dug in his sack and offered up a dead mahogany beetle in a candy wrapper.

PART ONE

lies and *secrets*

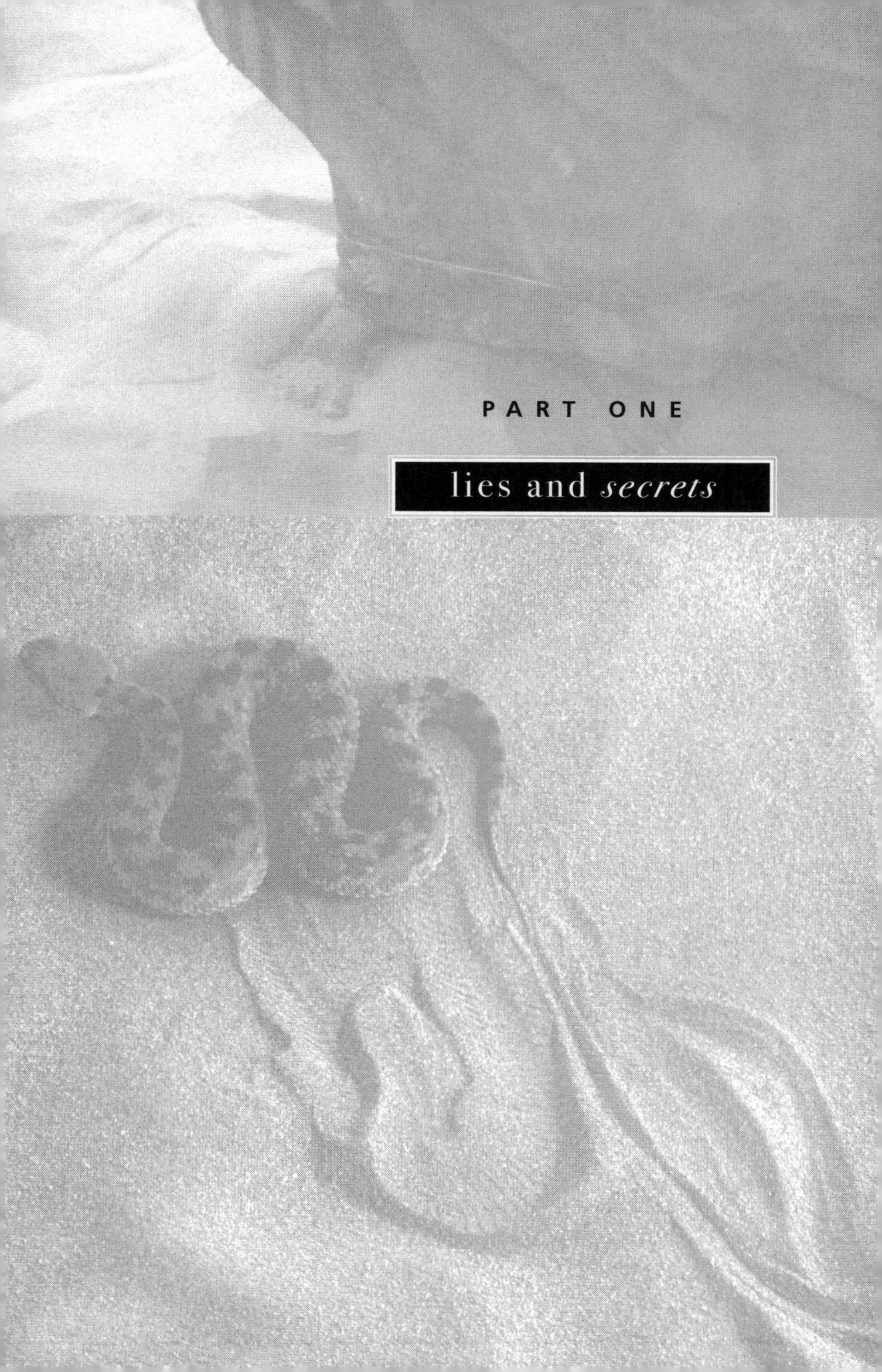

Origins

This photo captures the precise instant when lightning strikes the top of the rocky, red cliff behind our house. It is an afternoon shot, but dark because of the dusty clouds. On close inspection, the cliff has odd markings on the face.

Now taking a photo of lightning striking a cliff may seem lucky, but lightning struck that place many times and almost every day during summer and for this reason it was called the Lightning Cliff. It was high enough that in the days of the Ancestors those suspected of bad sorcery were brought to the top and thrown down by chiefs, to die on rocks at the bottom. Sorcerers are crafty though. As they die they can cast spells. During the course of our little lives, we were often aware of the eyes of Things from Other Times and Other Places. Like nosy neighbours they peered over the back of our compound, leering as we hung out our laundry, snickering as we ran to the latrine with bad stomachs and commenting resentfully on the fun we were having as living beings. We watched them back without looking directly, of course, so we only really saw shadows. It was natural that, over the years, we became acquainted with the strange ways of the Dead and their Friends. Our home was built on their threshold.

The thing that brought a sense of balance was that on the other side, at the front of our house, was the Valley of Beginnings. And that place was Life in all its unexplained variety.

Far away in East Africa there is a valley known as the Great Rift, the place where humans began. But it is little known that the Rift extends into the south, the branches becoming shallow, so that here it fades from the minds of cartographers and the scientists who dig the stone and bone of the Ancients. Our valley was at the very dead end of the Rift, where the land rises into the frozen wastes of the Maluti Range. It was obscure, but we desired nothing more. To those who lived in and around it, our valley was Mosima, the Valley of Beginnings, a place of fertile ground and moderate air, with an endlessly flowing river, and ancient secrets imprinted in its caves throughout the region.

It would not be hard to see how I came to believe that we lived at the perfect point of balance between Death and Life. I assumed that my people had existed in that place forever, a continuous line descended directly from the dinosaurs. Quite suddenly, I was made aware of the truth about that.

Truth, the *real* truth of this world, is a cold, hard thing with no respect for feelings.

This particular truth I learned from Devkumar Uncle, which is ironic considering that he himself was only remotely associated with the telling of truth.

"You got to remember who you are, Girl," he told me once, as I prepared to join some village children I knew. "Don't forget, they are Africans. You are...well...you are not African..."

I must have looked at him with confusion scrawled across my broad face. I was small in those days, and Devkumar was still a living person.

"Well, what the hell you think all this time, Child? Look, they are backward as donkeys."

I gaped.

"To them, we are strange and complicate outsiders."

"Outsiders?"

He looked at me with real exasperation.

"Okay, look. Every somebody the same really – African, Indians – but we came here from another place, see. We are not from here."

"From where then?"

"Well...India. Sort of...okay, from lots of place. Like India rubber, see. Bounce around the world. India, South Africa, America. All those places. Maybe no home really...just a ball that keep bouncing..."

We were what the people call *Lekhula*. Coolies. Indians. Here simply because of the College of Applied Science where my mother and Dr. Patel taught. That was the real truth. I began to know truth by the touch of it, the cold edges of it, edges that were oblivious to the feelings of a child. And of course some part of me knew I was different from the people of the valley. They are people who called themselves Basotho. 'Mè Jane, Flori, and all the others. I knew we were not Basotho. Knew in some part of me that never gave words to the knowledge.

But the further truth was that even the Basotho were outsiders. This land of dried volcanic teats and burned grass rightfully belonged to the *Baroa*, a people known only by what they left behind: caves full of paintings of animals and men, stone implements that stubbed our toes in the grass, certain clicks and clucks in the local dialects. Stories from the time of magic spirits and animals. Stories that were embedded in the rocks of the place as surely as certain dinosaur footprints we knew. There were stranger truths.

According to Glorius Sebane, the truth was that my father was a grasshopper.

We had been sitting in an apricot tree near the schoolhouse. Glorius should have been in the schoolhouse, but it had been easy to coax him into the laden boughs so that we could stuff ourselves with fruit. As we ate we talked. About families and ancestors. About mothers and babies.

About fathers.

I told him I had heard his father was a mine labourer, though I had heard no such thing. But, with surprising confidence, Glorius explained that his father built roads the length and width of Africa and worked with white people. It was when I laughed at him that he made the remark about the grasshopper. I laughed harder. He jumped down from the branch and hopped about the ground. Finally I became annoyed and pounced on him.

"Monkey stories. No one believes monkey talk." I sat on his chest.

"Everyone knows the story but you, Aousi. Ask 'Mè Zara. Ask your mother. She will say your father was a flying insect with thin legs."

I had that uncomfortable truth feeling again. I dared not look it straight in the eye. But my nickname, after all, was *Kokoanyana*. Insect. Somehow this name had flown about on papery wings before I knew my own story.

"WHY DON'T I HAVE A FATHER?" I asked my mother.

Mother, who was not easily startled by questions, shrugged and said, "Who said you don't have a father?" Then she continued her work. When she did not want to talk there was little anyone could do. She was quite able to float out of reach, out of earshot.

"They," I persisted. "Everyone."

"Now," she said, "how could a child not have a father? Does that make sense? A man is required to donate his seed, is that not so?"

"But who?"

"When you are older I will tell you everything." She looked at me. "Anyway, you have Devkumar. He is the father in this house."

Chubby-cheeked, chili-smelling, oily-fingered Devkumar the father of the house! I detected a current of mirth hidden in my mother's calm demeanour. She was laughing at me and everyone else. Devkumar Uncle was Sohrab's father, not mine.

"My real father," I pressed.

"Look," Mother said. "How is it possible for light to pass through a solid object like glass?" She held up a shard of glass and peered through it.

She was a liar. Her lies could be non-answers, planned fabrications of nonsense or omissions of key facts. She thought of it as a joke, but hated to be lied to by others. I had learned, therefore, that her lies were delivered in quiet tones that sometimes crackled with the tension of her amusement. Even so I was often fooled. There was her stare, capable of driving the wedge of a lie into my skull. Or she could change course to tell the truth midway through the story and so throw me off balance.

"Everyone has a name," I said some time later.

"Names are important," Mother nodded agreeably. "Names are history."

At this moment she stared at an empty canvas, about to start something. In one hand she held a writing pen, as though she had been in the midst of making notes, then became distracted by the canvas, or the other way round. She bit her lip.

"So what is my father's name?"

"Who? Oh yes, him. You can call him...Pitso," she said finally. "Better still, make it Pete."

A lie, of course, but I so desperately wanted to hear a name. *Pitso, my father.*

"Tell me a story about you and this Pitso," I asked in an earnest voice.

"A story..." She waved her pen in the air. "There was an evil country... The rulers of that place treated ordinary people very badly. Most endured the treatment silently, but some could not endure. That was your father. He burned with a desire to leave,

a desire so powerful that he sprouted feathers, his arms trans-
forming to wings. He had these wings when I met him. Beautiful,
soft feathers of silver and black, which I pretended not to notice,
of course. Then one day when his wings were strong enough,
they began to quiver. Then they beat the air and he flew away."
  "No."
  "He was never seen again."
  "No, that's not true... Is it?"
  "...and shortly after, you were born."
  "Is it true?"
  Part of me was aware that I was being led along crooked
paths, tricky lies. Another part wanted to explore these paths to
see where they led. Yet another part clung to any scrap of information about my father.
  Something glittered in Mother's eye as she applied small
scrapings of red paint to the canvas. "So much emptiness to fill,"
she said.
  So I waited for this Pitso, this Pete, this father of mine, to
return. I did not mind waiting. I had learned patience from 'Mè
Jane. Patience and how to be still and small.
  "We needn't miss him," my mother assured me.

OTHER FATHERS, the fathers of the village children, eventually
appeared in one form or another. Sometimes, rarely, a father would
arrive with pockets full of loot. More commonly there was tragic
news of a distant mine accident, or a destitute drunk would be seen
wandering from *shabeen* to *shabeen* across the district.
  One day Glorius came running into our compound with the
news that a lorry driven by his father had arrived. We had to see
this with our own eyes. At a skeptical distance we followed him
to his home, a couple of *rondavels* by the edge of a well-tended
garden. There indeed was his father wearing a white shirt with a
pen in the breast pocket. He had a commanding but kind air and

was the foreman of a road-building crew, just as Glorius had claimed. He even had a name: Lebese.

At this point I thought that surely this father of my friend must know of the whereabouts of my own Papa. Were not all fathers linked together in some way? Did not the lost fathers of the world congregate, keeping each other company in the absence of their children? Lebese patted my head and when I asked him my father's name he only looked embarrassed and tried to give me his pen.

My father, whose name was not Pete, remained a mystery.

I imagined him, a grown-man version of me. Big hands, head and feet. He was strong, of course, but shy because of the feathers that hung from his arms. Unlike my mother, he projected only truthfulness. To Mother he was kind and she, in turn, devoted. They would speak in serious tones to each other, with none of the mocking and fighting that went on between her and Devkumar Uncle. They would look into each other's eyes. Once in a while they would hug. Never a quarrel, or a cuff, kick or well-thrown projectile...

"MEN," Mother told me, "are awkward. They can take up your energy. You have to talk to them, take care of them..."

"The way we take care of Kalu and Rajah and Mpho..."

"No, dogs are more capable of looking after themselves..."

Never had I seen her looking after Devkumar Uncle. Most of the time it was Young Flori and Old 'Mè Jane who cooked the meals, cleaned when cleaning was not viewed as an interference, and laboured at laundry when they thought of it (which was seldom since their thoughts were usually occupied with gossip, worries about the children and speculations about the whims of the ancestral spirits).

"What do you say to a man who's with you every minute? It takes time...so much time. All they think of is making babies, making babies, day and night. How is one to think and plan? There's so much else to do..."

The garden, the ant and bee experiments, the light catcher, paintings, lectures and books.

"They are trouble, one hundred percent. What would you do?"

Who knew? But it was not as though my mother did anything important. She had never tilled the fields or stirred a plastic pail of *joala* under the morning sun. Never hung a plastic bag from a bamboo pole inviting the village men to come and sample her brew. Her work was all papers and paints and things made up. 'Mè Jane called it foolery. I concluded that this foolery was the real reason that Pitso (if that was his name) flew off. He would have become discouraged in this made-up, busy-world house of paintings in progress and assorted bird feeder boxes, the leaky ant colony and the broken heat lamp over a reading desk with dozens of unfinished books marked, opened, begun and begun again. Our house was a disaster despite the efforts of 'Mè Jane and Flori. There were times when I think even Mother and Devkumar Uncle became confused by the empty plastic cage at the window, the long-forgotten collection of poisonous plants on the hearth and the shells that spilled from urns on the floor. Our house was just another of my mother's works of art, one in which paints were smashed together in countless layers and flung in dusky chaos upon the canvas.

As for me, I seemed to have been fathered by *Modimo*, or God, or indeed by an insect with long legs.

DEVKUMAR UNCLE had explanations for everything. My mother warned us that he had filled himself with "comical opinions" culled from years of desperate and slow perusal of trashy South African news magazines and popular science journals. He helped my mother by trying to build a Coriolis Force tester, an ant-colony trap and a device meant to measure the magnetic field of the human head. His real job was motor mechanic. He could repair the motor of anything from a wristwatch to a van. From time to time he taught students at the college lessons on How To Repair Motors, and this is how he became an Expert with Explanations.

Devkumar said, "It all began in one place. Single place called Singularity. Gravity in that place so big everything dead-dead. It was different than anything we might imagine in our thoughts or even in our dreams..."

He reminded me of *ghee*, for there was a perpetual film of oil on his hands and hair. He was solid and thick, much shorter than my mother and darker than she, which she told us was due to his southern blood. *Dravidian man*, she called him. He maintained he was the descendent of Tamil kings.

"...no chemistry or physics in that singular place, just candy bars..."

"*Butle*, Nagarajah, you'll confuse the child..."

"She knows about physics, isn't it Kuku?"

"But tell me about my father. That's what I want to know..."

"No matter about father. Where you came from was big, bloody confusion, billions of years ago. Out came..." Here he scrambled for an open magazine that lay under the heat lamp, and quoted ponderously from it, "'swirling mass of gas and dust.' See? That where you came from. Everything just like an auto engine after all. And we here are just a little nut in the exhaust port."

"And you claim to understand how this engine works?" smirked my mother.

"Me? Oh, well. You know me and machine. Sort of like brothers together." He put the magazine aside. A drop of sweat ran along the tip of his nose. "Oh, they will tell you some stupid ideas, Child. Patel got his Hindu mumbo-gumbo and the Basotho got their witch and monkey show. But you got to think like object-if, right Zara? That's what science is all about.

Object-if. If one thing, then the other thing. One-two, cause-effect. Rest is just curry and rice..."

My mother was shaking her head. "Your explanations would be funny if it were not for the presence of impressionable minds around you. Why don't you sit in on some classes at the college so you will at least sound credible on the basic facts of life..." She turned to me. "Don't listen to him. He knows car workings and machines and some things about music and that is all."

"You say? You think university degree only thing that makes someone smart-brain? You think you know better than Someone-me. You? Smarty-woman, big-titted..." Devkumar Uncle's hair bristled up as his blood rose and he charged her with his hands raised, only to stop short when she looked up at him with a bored expression.

"You are better off with 'Mè Jane," Mother told me.

'Mè Jane came and took me outside to the porch.

'Mè Jane was from a village in the mountains, but as far as we were concerned she was a member of our family, with us as far back as our memories reached, cleaning and feeding us, soothing our troubled dreams in the night. Her wizened face was my constant companion, her stumpy arms my refuge. She wore her blanket bunched up around her shoulders so that there was no gap between it and a faded woollen watch cap upon her head.

Now she brought her own answers to my questions. She knew the particulars of every birth in the valley. It was her duty to know such things.

"I will tell you the story...," she said in her cracked voice. "But listen. Do you see the dogs, Rajah and Mpho? You see, the dogs cannot speak, so people think they are stupid. But look! Dogs never lie! They know only truth!" She placed her hands on my head. "So if they say you are simple, do not worry. You have a pure heart like that of the dog, Mpho. This animal heart means you will always know truth..."

"Tell me the truth, then."

"I cannot but tell the truth. I am like you, with the pure heart of an animal."

"Tell..."

"Yes. You see, that night you came it was strange. Our ancestors were in our ears, whispering things, so we knew something was afoot. Then we saw another moon coming to do battle with our own moon. This I saw with my own eyes. We waited to see what would come. We wondered whether our homes and cattle and crops would be lost. No one knew. Aousi, this valley is a hallowed place. Protected. Sacred. *Modimo,* or maybe some other protector, watches over this place. Perhaps one of *Modimo's* ancestors, one of those people who come from the ground.

"Early that morning I was awake. Darkness lay thick about. People were restless, searching for signs of naked witches or the *thokolosi* with his big and troublesome deal waving in the wind. But what came was different. It was a rushing of air and a clatter of mouths. In the dark we saw nothing. Someone screamed that the spirits of the murdered *Baroa* people were wreaking revenge at last. The sun came on, long fingers of light that push away the fear. We ventured toward the eating sounds. At the edge of the valley we found that a mat covered the veldt all around. This mat moved. It was the little thing, *tsie,* the locust, in such numbers as people had never seen. Only the very eldest of the region remembered that during the time of Moshoeshoe the Magnificent, on the eve of a great battle, the locusts came to our country this way. Now *tsie* had come again, yet not one lay inside the rim of our valley. All of the fields outside were beset by the moving brown mat. Even the highway crawled along. Even the trees writhed. Then, after some time, they rose as one, blocking the morning sun for one hour as they shifted from this place. Only when they were gone did we hear the cry of a new baby in our midst. The women went to see, and it was you, *Kokoanyana,* the Child of the Locusts, as your mother called you.

"This is why we took you among us and I myself came to look after your needs. Aousi, everyone loved you when you were born. You are the daughter of kind things who spared our homes, our valley, taking instead a few drops of dew from the hills and veldts around, then moving on to the farms of the rich Boers across the river."

"My mother was made pregnant by an insect?"

Old 'Mè Jane laughed. "Aousi, what do I know of such things?"

Zara

Photo: two ladies, one old and stumpy, the other younger and so endowed with flesh that her body is like a vessel overfilled with ripe vegetables, some of them spilling out, impossible to keep every round and soft piece contained. These ladies squat in the garden picking beans and talking. In the photo you cannot hear what they say, of course. But I know...

"She came out of the night...out of nothing..."

"Eh, her footsteps were hidden by the ululations of the winter winds..."

"Walked like a spirit, she did, through the darkness of shadows..."

"No dogs barked..."

"Eh, they knew!"

"It was the Headman, Ntate Moorosi, who opened his door. Long ago that was."

"Well, maybe she stayed at the college awhile before we saw her...so long ago now."

"I remember, there was a ghost with her."

"No..."

"Perhaps it was her shadow..."

"Yes, there were some strange things."

"Strange things now! But Aousi, you are a tortoise. Aousi, this remembering is an apricot too high for you. You stretch your neck higher and higher but...no fruit in your mouth. Listen, there was really a someone staying with Patel. Really, Aousi Jane, all talk of ghosts aside."

"It was very, very long ago..."

The two of them, 'Mè Jane and 'Mè Rantoa, squatting in the garden picking beans. Picking and whispering secrets.

WHEN SOHRAB was a baby, long ago, before Devkumar Uncle vanished and before Bushman arrived, my mother was easier. She had her dark moods of concentration then, and there were times when I found her weeping for reasons we did not understand. But her darkness was dispelled by Devkumar Uncle and his music and questions and pranks. In a way that no one else could, he distracted her from her dark moods and brought her into the present. In those days she sometimes cooked or told a story or danced with little Sohrab in her arms the way a mother should.

I knew Mother was no ordinary woman, even without 'Mè Jane and Flori to explain it to me. I only had to compare her to the other women of the villages. Instead of a blanket or wide-brimmed hat or sumptuous evening gown, she dressed in worn, spattered blue jeans, tennis shoes, and a rough, mannish shirt. Her long hair was swept into a loose knot.

In her times of concentration or woe, a small wet spot darkened the area between her shoulder blades. I felt certain that her heart leaked through her skin at that spot and I wanted it to stop. A mother with a leaking heart would surely leave the family exposed and vulnerable to all sorts of evil eyes. When I was small I wanted her to cover that faulty and damp spot with a jacket or blanket. When she refused my offers, I placed my hand on the place, then licked my fingers to taste the salty flavour of vulnerability.

She usually flinched to have me touch her so. Only much later did I understand that in her moods she disliked being near anyone, even her children.

I worried for myself and for little Sohrab at those times, thinking I was to blame for her moods. She looked at me side-long, sizing me up, trying to reconcile herself to this large-limbed simpleton she had brought into the world. It was as though my mother's tall grace and beauty had been the subject of some cruel genetic joke.

"Will we send her to school, Madam?" 'Mè Jane asked once as I stood nearby.

"To what purpose?" my mother murmured.

But then Devkumar Uncle jumped in. "What the hell you thinking, Zara? All these kids got to go school. *Got to.* Science and numbers. Just like you. How you know you wasn't just like her when you small, henh?"

My mother shrugged.

SOMETIMES, despite Devkumar, Mother's mood would deepen and persist, like a cloud of dust that stuck in our house, refusing to blow away. Then Devkumar Uncle took it upon himself to manage the household. He revelled in these hours when he was lord and master. It was his chance to freely instruct us in his vision of the world and show us the simple games he remembered from his childhood, games with sticks and marbles and boats he carved himself. He would explain his version of the Rules of Life, rules about truth and honesty and modesty and selflessness that we saw through. It seemed to us that neither Devkumar Uncle nor anyone else in our family followed these Rules of Life.

The rules that my mother followed had nothing to do with honesty and everything to do with secrecy. She lied for pleasure and she lied in desperation. She lied equally when her mood was light and charming and when she was deep in her sorrow.

"Your mother has many considerations," 'Mè Jane told me cryptically and I was left to sort that out.

The rules that Devkumar really followed were the Rules of the Wild, according to 'Mè Jane. These rules were played out in peculiar chase-and-catch games involving 'Mè Flori. They took place in the shed or back room or garden and there was a kind of sloppy secrecy since they took place behind Mother's back and were meant be out sight of the children and 'Mè Jane. We saw too much, of course. The chase had no clear objective and Flori did not always try to escape Devkumar's grasping fingers. When he did catch her, the whole messy game involved a good deal of panting and sweating.

'Mè Jane could not explain what this was about. She would only say that it was hard to keep a sense of religion and decency when the Rule of the House was the Rule of the Wild. At this point she might also mention the Problem of Men, which was often identified as Flori's problem, sometimes as Mother's problem, and usually as a problem in general. This, we ascertained, was something like the Problem of Mice, which was usually followed the next year by the Problem of Snakes.

I remember clearly the day Flori came to our house. She wore a worn print frock that fit her loosely, but could not hide the graceful lines beneath it. With her came a new scent and sound that made us want to laugh and play crazy games. When Flori was around, the improbable and the unplanned were close behind, along with her contingent of admirers. These admirers were simple villagers and men from the town, farmers, drivers and mere boys, prisoners and police. Handsome and ugly, stupid, drunken or learned, they were one and all chased off by 'Mè Jane's raised *panga*, the one she used for chopping the long grass and whipping off the heads of the ringhals snakes that ventured too near our house.

There was nothing that 'Mè Jane could do about Devkumar Uncle. Flori only laughed uproariously when 'Mè Jane scolded her for letting Devkumar touch her.

IF SHE KNEW about the crazy games Devkumar played with Flori, Mother paid no attention. It had no effect on her challenging and mocking attitude. My mother could be cruel, prodding him with her words until he fought back in his ineffective and clownish way. Then, once he was wound up, the string pulled and he was spun out on the floor, she would stand back as if to say, *see, see what a clown you really are.*

He was only at peace, unchallenged and wholly respected when he put a flute to his mouth. Then, late in the evening or as the sun rose, Devkumar transformed into a magician capable of banishing darkness and creating a world full of bright hope. In the depths of his music he became a person of beauty, able to silence the world.

When he played my mother was calm. Only then it seemed that in some way she might be fond of Devkumar.

Bushman Born

Now comes to hand a photo from the only vacation we ever had. We were told it was a vacation but it was not. For a long time after, I was confused as to what "vacation" actually meant. In the photo you see a trio of nattily dressed riders, herringbone jackets with animal skins caped over them. Pressed trousers and two-toned shoes. Their ponies are proud and tough and you see kindness in their eyes, even in the photo. In the background is a high sloping ridge and everything has the clear edges only seen in the high mountains. The year would be around 1976.

THIS ALL BEGAN during a time when strange winds blew across the plateau. *Djinns* were abroad, licking the earth, filling their bellies with dust and news, only to spew it elsewhere.

Some creatures died. Others impatiently awaited birth.

One of these was my brother, Bushman. Like the other Unborn, he possessed the power to bring about his own existence. He commanded the wind. He commanded *djinns* and other spirits. When we sniffed the air, we shivered; when we blew our noses, bits of bad news came out. My mother faltered as she spoke to her class. Devkumar Uncle wiggled his hips and smelled money and distant places.

Then Mother came to 'Mè Jane and told her to prepare for travel. 'Mè Jane and I looked at each other, then we searched for the trick in the dark places of Mother's eyes.

"And where will we go, Madam?" asked 'Mè Jane politely.

But my mother chose not to answer. "This girl," she said, pointing at my feet, "has no shoes." It was quite possible that she had not noticed my bare feet before. "Kamala, child of dust..."

And that was all she told us. We were left to our own devices.

WE DISCOVERED that we would travel by car and that this car would accommodate five, which made us think. Five passengers meant that Flori, Dr. Patel, Susie the goat, Rajah, Mpho and Kalu the dogs were not included. I suggested to Devkumar Uncle that a bus might be better, especially since Dr. Patel was so large.

He said to Mother, "See how mix up that girl has got. Don't know where family end and farmyard begin. Thinks family got everything in it including water pump and spare tyre. Thinks we go on trip we got to bring animals and uncles galore..." I could not tell whether he was laughing or angry.

'Mè Jane did as she was told and prepared a small sack for Sohrab and me. But we observed that Devkumar packed all of his flutes.

On the veranda, careful not to glance at the mirror-bright face of the Lightning Cliff, we sat on the bench and tried mightily to sort out the truth. After a long time 'Mè Jane nodded and sighed.

"There is trickery afoot, Aousi."

"What must we do, 'Mè?"

"Ai, nothing. Perhaps we will not return from this trip, but it is not in our hands."

Perhaps there were mice nearby, sniffing the air, because soon word went out across the villages of the valley that we were moving away and would not return. People arrived with gifts: a blanket, a straw hat, a horn from a charmed buck, a mohair hide.

I watched uneasily from my place on the veranda until 'Mè Jane went to her home to collect her own travelling things. Then I retreated to the quiet and safety of the shed but found that even that place was astir. As I crept among the sculptures of animals and humans, through oily workbenches and the guts of motors, I heard secret voices. Behind the shed, in a nook well-hidden from the house, Devkumar Uncle and Flori played their game. In their play he whispered secrets into her neck while his hands searched her dress for something. His hands searched her taut breasts, travelled to her waist to explore the terrain around her hips and bottom. Then the hands went inside, one in the top and the other up the hem so that it looked as though they meant to meet. For her part, Flori pretended she was trapped, panting like a caught puppy.

I made no sound. It was a familiar and comforting game that I loved to watch. Some days everywhere I turned I saw Devkumar Uncle. We might find him coupling with my mother in the heat and mess of a summer morning and that afternoon see him chasing a young woman who lived by the riverbank. 'Mè Jane's explanation for this behaviour was that he was a cousin of Ntate Lekhlaba's big-balled he-dog. We saw him talking to that dog when he thought no one watched.

We saw these things. We saw and did not need to put the sights into words.

Now Flori heard her name called and pushed him away. Devkumar Uncle swore, the game ended and I was left with my uncertainty. How could we leave this place where every old face and each doorway was like a friend? What existed beyond the edges of the valley? I dug a nest for myself in a pile of rags and slept.

They might never have found me if it had not been for Dr. Patel. On the edges of sleep I heard my name called as the afternoon wore on. Devkumar Uncle stomped through the shed once, then my mother came through, but became distracted by an old piece of work that distressed her. Only Dr. Patel, with his quiet ways, was able to notice my hiding place.

Without looking directly at me, he said: "Nothing, not even reason, can save a person from their *kharm*." He placed a packet upon the wooden bench inside the doorway. It was wrapped in newspaper, tied carefully with a blue ribbon. I did not know then that this packet contained the first glimpses of answers to my deepest questions.

Dr. Patel's eyes were huge, dim lights. At night 'Mè Jane had seen him in his garden, laying stones in circles under the moon.

After he was gone, I tucked the packet in my shirt and went out to meet my *kharm*.

WE WAITED until nightfall to depart. Sohrab lay between 'Mè Jane and I in the back seat of the car, asleep amid the tumult. The engine was started and we rolled down the hill to the road with the dogs running barking alongside until they could no longer keep pace. Then we rushed onward into a tunnel of dark silence.

The car shuddered along dark roads. Every few kilometres a distant lonely light from a gas lamp or torch reminded us that there were living, breathing beings in the night. We were vigilant, though, of the gruesomeness of the Underworld. I did not fail to notice the naked woman who rose from a *donga*, live snakes writhing in her hair, and the headless torso that floated over a field. Caught fleetingly in the car lights, giant crocodiles of times long past melted into the bitumen.

"Did you see?" I whispered.

"Eh, Aousi. I saw all," 'Mè Jane assured me.

WE PUT OUT HEADS DOWN, feigned sleep and waited for Mother and Devkumar Uncle to begin talking, hoping to uncover our destiny. If they talked, they would quarrel, and we had learned well that when my Mother was in battle truths became loosened and fell like stray gems for us to collect, examine and trade back and forth for days on end.

Behind us the Killing Cliff became a distant, vague face in the dark.

Some time later I awoke to the sound of Devkumar Uncle's voice.

"Such fuss they make..."

"What child would want to be taken from her home in the night?" said Mother. "They can't be expected to understand these things. Even I don't see the reason for night travel. So many years have passed...you overestimate your importance..."

"Safer at night. Better to overestimate than bad-estimate."

"I wonder. You seem to think we've left this place for good. You brought your flutes. Everyone saw. The children noticed."

"So? Flute is flute. Means nothing but music."

"Everyone knows how you think..."

"Hokay, maybe we come back. Who knows? Maybe we go find a better place. Maybe we do like ants. Get sweep away, but just come back some other way. Anyway, where we live does not matter, isn't it?"

"It might matter to some..."

"You know Zara, you change your thinking over the years. Really, you change a lot."

We rumbled along a rough road in silence for a time. There had ceased to be any light or other sign of human life. We travelled in a night world of barren lands and ugly spirits. 'Mè Jane's face was in shadow and, unable to see whether she slept or not, I dozed again, but jerked awake each time I heard a voice.

"Trust Devkumar," Devkumar Uncle said. "Devkumar know when to go and when to stay. You will thank me for this. We will go to place where there is real civilized people. Place where children can get educated good and proper."

"This valley has been the centre of their world, this countryside their universe. It's what they know."

"Eh, when is the centre of anything located in the hindquarter? This is the bum-end of the universe, that is all. You think I look good with pen behind the ear like this, or in the pocket, like this?"

My mother laughed quietly. "Idiot," she said.

The outline of Devkumar's face reflected in the windshield. His fingers jerked from one thing to another, touching his teeth, the controls of the car. With every movement I saw a million thoughts darting through his head like fish in an overcrowded pond. Ideas swam into his throat. He worked over words, jokes, expressions and discarded or revised, all to impress my mother. He was always in a state of mystification at being permitted into her circle of intimacy. He was out of his depth with her, so strained to entertain her, knowing that his place was uncertain. Perhaps this was why he sought some relief in the easy company of Flori and the other women. My mother was difficult – everyone knew that.

"You know, Zara, there's good way to fix car and bad way to fix car. Only trouble is, bad way don't work."

"Oh?"

"What I mean is, everyone got to take chance. Take chance to make chance is what I say. If we did not go away, then no chance for us. This way anything can happen. We could even make money!"

"When did that become a priority?"

"Everything change. Kids to care for. Even you change."

"Money is nothing to me. You know that."

"Everything change," repeated Devkumar. "Take chance to make chance."

"What exactly did your message say, Nagarajah? You haven't told me everything, have you?"

"Just a message from old associates, is all. Sort of an invitation for us...from the Republic side."

"Who friends?"

"*Old* friends."

"Do I know them?"

"You never had the pleasure," said Devkumar Uncle. His face worked back and forth in the glass – pride, anger and something else. It was like watching an infant pass gas.

"Was it a comrade, Nagarajah?"

I felt his shudder then. The whole car shuddered with him. "What you talking, woman?"

"I need to know. This family has made too many sacrifices for the great cause already."

"Nothing, Zara. We go and get job, stay away awhile. You know..."

"Ah, they are offering money, is it?"

"Nothing like that, Zara. All that behind us..."

My mother suddenly turned and peered into the back seat. "Do you think he is telling the truth, 'Mè Jane?"

'Mè Jane started as though she had been sleeping. "Yes, Madam."

"You must not call me 'Madam.' You are much older and wiser than I. Perhaps I should call you 'Madam.'"

"Yes Madam...no Madam."

As though unnerved, the car began to weave and rattle.

"Watch how you drive. It would be a pity to die in a road accident now."

"Yes, Mastah, please drive the *koloi* with calm hands," threw in 'Mè Jane.

"Calm. I am calm. Does Devkumar get excited?"

"'Mè Jane cannot leave her place indefinitely," said Mother. "She has her people to consider."

"Yes, it is true, Madam..."

"That is no problem. We can send her back any time. *Holokile-okay*, 'Mè?"

"No, Mastah," muttered 'Mè Jane.

"You know, Zara, in my home they always say family most important of all things. My people say family first, life second. Then money third...or is it money second...something like that..."

"At least you had a home..."

"You call this a home? This tailpipe of Africa place? Village dog-and-monkey show. Basotho Hat: Basotho Bum? Freeze-your-ass-winters...soldiers-bash-your-door-place. You want to stay in such a home?"

"You are fixated on the backsides of everything. I suppose that is no surprise to anyone..."

"Don't try make me mad, Zara. I'm not a man that should get mad..."

My mother guffawed. "Idiot."

DEVKUMAR UNCLE had found this old yellow Mercedes car in a field. It smelled of spiders and smoke and automobile catastrophes. It looked as though it had been stolen, then abandoned for its past associations, which was just the kind of thing Devkumar loved. He worked on the engine quietly for five days, filing and replacing parts. When the engine started it billowed blue smoke, but Devkumar was happy. He claimed that this was engine music and praised the German people for their wonderful efficiency, even though they were not-so-smart at war. But the back of the car was never right. Burdened with our family and our doubts, the car dragged along at a peculiar and reluctant angle. We scraped over rocks as we went from the road onto a dark track. We felt ourselves pushed into our seats as the headlights pointed upward at the mountain tops.

Sohrab awoke and began to wail because he was hungry and wanted to go home.

"Can't stop," puffed Devkumar Uncle.

Mother said, "Make him be quiet."

From the day of his birth they had not been sympathetic toward Sohrab. They acted as though the responsibility for parenting lay elsewhere, which meant that the task of managing him was left to 'Mè Jane and, sometimes, to me.

I whispered a story in his ear. I sang a song. My reward was a high-pitched scream and several wild swings in my direction. The banana and milk 'Mè Jane produced were thrown on the floor. We tried to pacify him in the darkness with the car pitching like an unhappy donkey. In his rage, Sohrab pulled off his pants and urinated against the door so that it sprayed Devkumar Uncle.

Sometimes we really hated having to look after Sohrab.

Devkumar Uncle cursed, saying he was wet and pissy. My mother thought it was funny and then tried to cover her amusement by saying, "This is the worst road I have ever seen."

Devkumar's eyes bulged with anger. "Road!" he growled, "This is no goddamn road! This thing is not even a path for goats! Where the hell we are? Where the hell?" As he said this the car shuddered and gave up. He slammed the steering wheel and proclaimed that we were lost and only God would find us here at the bum-end of the universe. "We are doom," he yelled as he wiped urine from his ear. "We are doom to die on this arse of a mountain..." My mother then told Devkumar Uncle to shut up because he was alarming everyone, which was not true since we were used to Devkumar Uncle.

I needed badly to sleep after driving all night. But sleep was impossible with Devkumar Uncle leaping out of his seat and performing a chicken dance around the car, elbows waving and neck bobbing, kicking at the sides of the car, then cursing at his injured toes. He looked puny against the mountain shadows.

The stars were still clear, but the rim of the world had begun to brighten. We wondered what sorts of spirits lurked in the mountain dawn.

My mother had not stopped laughing since Sohrab had made his pee. She laughed hysterically now, choking, doubled over. Seeing Devkumar Uncle in the lights of the car made it worse.

"Look at you, you damn, damn Hindustani, you are all unzipped. You're losing altitude and about to crash." She climbed out, slipped on the steep incline, screamed like a crazed woman. Devkumar Uncle went after her, swearing, swatting at her with his hands, and she scrambled away with a yelping laugh. Round the car they chased, cat and dog.

"*Modimo*," sighed 'Mè Jane, "They have lost their minds."

We climbed out with miserable little Sohrab in tow. The air was cold. The country of Lesotho was spread out before us, but we could see only a fathomless pit. In the pauses in the shouting and laughter we heard water and found a thin stream cut into the stone. Sohrab plunged his face into the stream and drank, then immediately collapsed asleep into 'Mè Jane's arms. We seemed to hang by our toes, waiting, wondering, as the earth dipped toward a distant sun.

THAT WAS HOW they found us. 'Mè Jane and Sohrab and I in a daze, awaiting the mountain dawn. Mother and Devkumar Uncle still in a maniacal chase around the car.

No one can say exactly how Bushman's messengers located us, although we later speculated that they were attracted by Devkumar's loud voice. They appeared suddenly, five mountain Basotho riders who loomed over the ridge, fur capes curved over their backs. The leader raised his knobkerrie over us and we expected the wrath of the devil. They were muscular and clean as pistols these men, their jackets stretched taut on their shoulders, polished shoes of two-toned leather in their stirrups.

"Which one of you can bring forth a child?" the leader called. His words hung in the mountain air for a long moment. He must have meant to ask whether there were women among us. I said nothing but pointed my finger at 'Mè Jane. The men looked past 'Mè Jane to my mother, little knowing her aversion for the blood and mess of matters human. Her understanding of life was frozen in paintings and writings, theorized in lectures. They could not know how she stumbled and gagged over the suffering of others. Yet for some reason she among us was nominated. So, as the dawn came on, we hiked in silence up a jagged pass. The five emerged into open sunlight that gleamed on their shaven heads. On one side was a chasm, on the other, broken and verdant terraces fell away to the land known as Transkei. We followed them along a narrow path at the crest of a ridge.

At the highest point, set into a rock recess, was a solitary *rondavel*. It was like no *rondavel* we had ever laid eyes upon. Each stone in the wall had been chosen for its distinctive colour – some were of the seashore, some from the red sandstone of the lowlands, still others were the black basalt and silver granite of the mountains. Upon the thatch and wood roof a thick shaft of bamboo was set. The bamboo was carved into a mask with rows of holes of many sizes. When the wind blew through the holes the thing groaned: a wind flute. Around the entrance to the hut *assagais* were set into the ground. Upon each spear point hung the leather of a face. I pointed to each one saying, "Cow, horse, donkey, dog and man..." Even my mother stared.

The riders beckoned us onward. Mother and Devkumar Uncle and 'Mè Jane hesitated here, but I have always run in and out of the open doors of *rondavels* without fear.

In the *rondavel* a woman lay alone on a mat in the middle of a floor of stone. When she saw me she offered her hand and said, "*Kena*, Aousi." Her voice was parched. 'Mè Jane and Mother shuffled in behind me, but now it was I who was chosen. She closed her fiery hand around mine. I saw that she was old. Around her neck she wore a necklace made from hundreds of teeth.

"This baby does not wish to leave his nest," she whispered.

"You must be strict," I said.

"You are young to be a mother," she replied.

It was noon before her opening was big enough for the head of the baby. We brought water, lit a fire to boil rags and a knife. We waited. We argued about when the old woman should push and when she should pull. A large hand reached out, then withdrew. Finally, hours later, a creature the colour of clay was out and cleaned and its rope cut. It was wizened like the mother and calm. The mother took a look at her baby, then closed her eyes peacefully as though to sleep. A short time later 'Mè Jane said matter-of-factly that the mother had gone to join her ancestors.

The horsemen were gone. We stoked the fire and waited, knowing that they would not return to a birth house for many days. The dead woman lay in our midst. No one spoke.

Sohrab slept in a corner as though drugged. I was ravenous. 'Mè Jane looked away with a dry mouth when I told her I needed food. I searched through the hut. Rather than food, I found that the clay pots stacked along the walls contained foul liquids. Wasp nests and clumps of sharp-odoured plants hung from the beams.

"She was a witch," whispered 'Mè Jane.

Devkumar Uncle heard this and told 'Mè Jane not to talk rubbish.

Mother told everyone to shut up and let her think. She then announced that she was going to search the hills for a relative, but Devkumar Uncle would have none of this. *We could not leave the body untended...we had to get on with our own journey.* As their quarrel gathered force I found a musty blanket and, with the wind groaning in the bamboo mask, I fell asleep in 'Mè Jane's lap.

IN MY DREAMS I visited the ancestral dead, dragged along by the departing spirit of the newly dead. The Ancestors would not speak to me but would only groan their dissatisfactions. They reached out with long fingers, wishing me to join them. I fled and forced myself toward wakefulness.

A sustained and chilling note came from the flute mask. Sohrab was tugging gently on my fingers. My mother sat rocking on her haunches with the swaddled baby in her arms. The fire was cold and Devkumar Uncle was curled in a ball by my side, watching me.

"They are not coming," said my mother. "No one is coming."

"What will we do with the baby? We have no idea who this dead mama is," said Devkumar.

"*Mathuela*," said 'Mè Jane.

"...a curer of minds," added my mother.

"How is it she so old with child? Nobody could do that."

"Maybe no one told her the rules. Maybe she never read your magazines..."

"We got to do something with the body..."

"We could make a pyre..."

"Nah, would not burn good. Not here. Maybe cairn..."

"What is a cairn?" I asked.

"Pile of rocks. Pile rocks on top her."

"But she's a witch. She'll waken when we are gone. Maybe when the moon is small. We must leave her where she is."

They looked at me but said nothing.

"If we bury her she will never be able to come back."

Sohrab poked at the baby until it squawked. We gathered around to look at it closely. It was a thoughtful creature, moulded from the clay of the lowlands. It knew something was wrong yet it did not complain or look alarmed. It glared fiercely in our direction with unfocused, slate grey eyes.

Perhaps they were tired of the quarrelling, or perhaps they really believed that the old woman was a witch. We took the baby and left the mother where she had died in her house, surrounded by her magic.

It was cold and bleak on the ridge. The wind had come around from the south and set the mask to singing like a hollow, tortured dog. It sang out behind us as we went away, and the baby in my mother's arms wailed.

Blowhole

This photo is of the land they call Transkei. It shows a beach and palm trees. In the foreground, my mother with a baby the colour of clay. In the background, a vertical column of water, with spray blown off in a plume. This was where Devkumar Uncle vanished.

Now there are those who believe that Devkumar's death was an accident, a freak and, perhaps, bad luck. But we quested for the truth. The quest led us into strange places. Such sights we beheld unknowing, without comprehension and without our own story. They are sights that no photo could capture, etched into the memory of a child...

An old man on a wooden pallet borne aloft by flame while nearby a line of girls parades with baskets of dead black birds. The birds stir, raise their wings and fly as the man joins his ancestors. We run in pursuit of these birds but lose sight of them and become lost ourselves. Then, we come to a place inhabited by toothless people with coins for eyes.

These were the truths of our place. This is where our quests led.

WE DESCENDED from the mountains along bare, seamless rock, the very backbone of the world. The air was thick on this side of the mountains, laden with steam and the sweat of the poor. The colours were no longer red and ochre but heavy green.

"Transkei," Devkumar Uncle told us. "Place where people really got chance to live nice…" He pointed to some farm plots clinging to the slopes of hills, but we saw the stones in the fields and picked out the dilapidated humps of straw and mud that were identifiable as dwellings only by the children and women who sat blinking in their dim openings.

As we went on the air became unbearably hot, and the smell of burning metal filled our noses. After a while we saw tendrils of blue smoke trailing behind our car.

"Wheel bearings," said Devkumar Uncle. "We got to stop soon."

But we did not stop. A high-pitched whine, like an incessant mosquito, came from under the car. We stopped our ears with our hands.

"Port St. John," said Mother.

"We never make it," stated Devkumar. "Nothing there anyway. This is not time for vacation-chakar."

"We need to sort things out, don't you think? It is a quiet, out-of-the-way place. Besides, they will see the ocean and all."

"Sort what things? We get stuck on road, then vultures come peck our eyes. That's only thing get sort."

We saw my mother brush her lips against the head of the new creature. Tenderly.

Somewhere they bought goat milk and a leather gourd and teat which she held in its mouth. We saw. Oh, we saw and we did not need to say. My mother was suddenly stilled, upon her face a look of absorption and contentment. This new clay-coloured thing, this creature of the witch, had seized her soul.

PORT ST. JOHN," repeated my mother. We knew by her tone that she would not be swayed.

"What we do with that Thing, woman? What we can do if we cross border? They never let us out..."

"What border are you worried about?"

"What if we got to take plane?"

"What plane?" Mother snapped.

"I said, '*What if* we got to,' not '*We got to...*'"

"Are we to fly in an aeroplane, Madam?" 'Mè Jane asked quietly. Although her voice was calm, we knew the thought of flying terrified her as much as it did me.

"Of course not," said Mother flatly. 'Mè Jane and I looked at each other and said nothing.

The car limped onward, slowing, engine panting, smoke pouring from the broken rear end. Although the argument continued, Devkumar Uncle aimed the car down the steep incline toward the Wild Coast and Port St. John.

A lush scent cut through the air and sometime after dark we heard the sea. It crashed into the land somewhere near the beehive hut in which we were to spend the night. 'Mè Jane pulled me by one hand, Sohrab by the other. 'Mè Jane's stubby fingers touched my eyelids. "You have not seen the Big Water, Aousi. It is as big as the sky. Many things live in the water without themselves becoming lost or drowned..."

"Tell us about these things."

"Yes. Some are not fish. Some are special things with a dangerous language for human ears. They say if you understand this language, then you are one of Them. And if you are one of Them, then you will go into the water and never return."

In sleep I heard the language of the water creatures. Their voices hissed at me from the sea, words transported on the breezes. *Koko*, they whispered, then other voices, of Devkumar Uncle and Mother, interfered so that the language was wrecked by the usual nonsense.

"...what it means when woman refuse..."

"...fool..."

"...could kill a man...this means the end for me..."

"...you are deranged..."

"...nothing DE-range about Devkumar. All my wires and gauges arrange fine..."

MORNING LIGHT filtered through the thatch over our heads. Beside me lay Sohrab with his mouth agape in his slumber. 'Mè Jane was outside; my mother shifted about through her luggage with the baby-creature under one arm. Devkumar sat cross-legged and dejected.

"You think I derange, 'Mè Jane?" he called. "This woman want to keep strange baby she found on a mountain. But she say it is me who derange. You think she right, 'Mè?"

"Yes Mastah, no," came the reply from outside.

"If I derange, it is you who make me, Zara. I could get worse too. Piston head of this engine could crack completely!"

"Why don't you do what you are good at and fix the car?"

"Don't feel to fix car. You think that is all I am – car repair and baby maker man," he sniffed. He held a flute in his hands, warming the holes. With a wink in my direction he began to play, running up the scale, then pouring forth a stream of notes in one exhalation. The song was one we had heard before, but it was different and new each time he played it. This was Devkumar's magic. This was Devkumar the Flute. We loved and trusted this Devkumar more than Devkumar the Motor, and much more than Devkumar the Wandering Hand.

When he stopped playing, the quarrel resumed along new lines. My mother would not acknowledge Devkumar the Flute. She preferred the simpler task of focusing on the other noxious, troublesome Devkumars she knew. Now a girl was mentioned, someone's clothing, the new baby. My mother alternately mocked him and told him to shut up.

I took myself outside.

"Stay nearby, Aousi," 'Mè Jane told me. "Remember what I told you. Water creatures." She turned her attention back to setting the fire.

I envied a family of monkeys foraging in the big-leafed undergrowth. A newborn clung to the mother's chest as the father watched over them from a branch. Some of the younger monkeys played a game of venturing close to where I stood, then leaping for cover. I finally joined in, pursuing one shrieking monkey down a sandy path to the beach.

This beach was glitter and water noise. Lumpy water stretching away endless, just as 'Mè Jane had described it. For a while I was pleased to be alone in the light and noise. After the car and the quarrels the empty space made me dizzy.

I had learned nothing that had led me to understand adults or the truth of the world. Before me was laid a puzzle of motives and phrases I did not understand. What was the link between this new baby and Devkumar's mission? What was it that my mother refused?

I was wearing the overalls I wore every day. They had twenty-one pockets. Whenever I asked her, 'Mè Jane sewed on another one. The pockets contained pebbles, interesting pieces of wood, the dried body of a spider, a discarded pen. I filled two pockets with white beach sand. From the pocket over my heart I took out the ribboned, flat package given to me by Dr. Patel. It seemed important, and not ready to be opened. As I tucked it away, I realized I was being watched.

There was a girl, tall and straight, with skin was as glossy as the waves. In one hand she carried a basket, in the other a wooden spade. Her eyes were like fish eyes or maybe whale eyes.

"What have you got, Child? Show to Celia."

I displayed Dr. Patel's packet.

"A gift! Are you from Cape Town? Jo'burg? Which city?"

"No city and no place," I replied flatly. I imagined this reply to be worthy of my mother. "I have no father," I added for no reason.

"Oh, a simple orphan. Every somebody is from somewhere, Simple Orphan. Do I not speak English well? I learned in Port Elizabeth. In school."

Her smile was beautiful. She took my hand and we walked together while she sang songs in her language. I asked her what the songs meant.

"It means we are poor," she said happily. "Come, we will bathe, Small Orphan." She removed her dress and folded it neatly. "Why are you afraid? It is only water. Made by God."

I IGNORED EVERYTHING 'Mè Jane had told me and swam with the girl and wandered far from our family camp. The girl was carefree, even though she told me she had no parents and lived with her older sister. We picked mangoes and ate them in the sand while we waited for her friend, someone called George. When he came I followed them along a path to the top of a bluff over the water. There was a stone cross and an engraved plaque telling the story of a white youth who had died diving from that place.

"She has no father," said the girl.

"Oh," said George. Then he added easily, "You know, I can be your father."

"And I your mother. We will make a family."

I immediately agreed.

At the base of the bluff a shelf jutted out towards the sea. The waves had undercut the rock and had formed a round orifice the size of a single long stride. Waves swept in underneath the slab and were trapped. Every so often one sent a charge of water exploding from it. They called this the Blowhole.

I planned everything with my new mother and father. They would go home, collect what they needed and meet me at the

Blowhole at first dark. Then, the three of us would run away together and live in a place called Freetown. "Freetown is the only free place in Africa," George informed me. "Everyone in that place is rich."

They filled their baskets with seaweed and went home. Alone, I lay in the sand. For a few hours the world was a grand place, full of excitement and danger and fun. But then slowly, with each moment I remained alone, my old life seeped back. The others would search for me. Or perhaps not, which was as much a worry. I was impatient for the arrival of evening and my escape.

It was late in the afternoon and the sea rumbled and roared without pause. I spotted the figure of Devkumar Uncle wandering this way and that like a lost dog. His hands were jammed into his pockets. He flopped down in the midst of the glaring sun to scoop handfuls of sand into piles. I went near and began building a sand house.

"Where have you been, *Bhutini?*"

"Nowhere."

He sighed. "Nowhere? You know, no matter what I do, every damn thing difficult in this life. Did you know that?"

"Why difficult?"

"Who knows why. Only *sadhus* know. Things happen that you cannot stop. You think you make decision and that is going to be life. Hanh, hanh. Now listen to me. I am talking like my head is cracked...just like old Patel."

"Dr. Patel is not cracked."

"You know, Baby-girl, Devkumar Uncle may not be smart as your ma or Patel-Sahib, but I know what I believe. Or maybe I believe what I know. Something like that. Anyway, my people, we are honest and clean. You never see someone from my village cheat."

"When will we leave this place, Uncle?"

"You like it here? I saw you made new friends."

I froze. He had seen my new parents.

"You know," he went on. "You and me, Kuku, we are the same. We are not quick, but we go where we want, do what we want, isn't it? What is Devkumar doing hiding down here by the sea? Hell, there are bigger things to see and do. You will understand one day."

"What kind of things?"

"Well, sometimes a person has chance to make right of some wrongs, maybe go back and get self-respect back again. When you get those chance, then you got to do. Otherwise you are not living. Maybe you are just a bug or one of those disease germs. Then there is money, of course. You wouldn't like it if Devkumar Uncle had no money to give you..."

"When did you ever give me money?"

"I said, 'if.' That's future. Maybe I planning to give you money. Can't do it hiding away at the College of Applied Sadhus." With his foot he absently prodded my sand house until the walls collapsed. "Now your ma want to go back home. All because of that new baby she found. You don't want to go home, do you?"

"I like it here," I said obligingly.

"Good girl. Your ma says Devkumar is a fool. A moron...what the hell exactly is a moron anyway?"

"More of something?" I suggested. In the distance I heard the rumble of the Blowhole.

"That baby going to mess everything. I can feel it. He is some bad lucky for us. Got your ma all messed already. You know why we came away from our home? No? I'm going to tell you." He caught an ant and dropped it into the trap made by an ant lion. As the ant scrambled up the side of the pit, the ant lion shot grains of sand at it, knocking it down again. "It's those soldiers..."

"What soldiers?"

"You can't always see them. They been near our place though, checking over that land they want to make into the National Agriculture place..."

The Blowhole thundered.

"Funny weather," said Devkumar Uncle. "By the way, you ever see your ma with another uncle?"

This was a question he asked me from time to time. It was difficult to answer. If I answered "no," he would not believe it. If I answered "yes," his eyes would bulge with rage and he would press for details. I pretended not to hear.

"Don't matter. I know what no answer means. I get no answer from all kind of people. When man asks woman question and no answer come back, I know what it means. What the hell...what the hell. She always got some plan. She is one big thinker-planner, your ma." He fell into silence for a while and I took the opportunity to build up the sides of my house again and release the ant. Huge swells were forming in the bay.

"When was last time you went to school? You got to promise me you go to school. Learn science and all..."

"Why?"

"Why? *Because*, that's why. That's what children got to do. Go to school, grow up, get married, have kids, go to real university like your ma, not some puppy-poo place like Patel-college..."

My sand house was ready for occupation. I thought of my new friends, my new father, my new family and I living within its walls.

"...sometimes a man can even lose hope...," he was saying.

I stood and brushed sand from my overalls. "You have to see this place I found," I said. "It's a blowhole, made by the water. We can make a wish."

"What?"

"A wish..." I took his hand and led him carefully around the sand house so it would remain there for eternity, defying the ocean and time.

It was not easy pulling Devkumar Uncle along. He was a reluctant dog who did not understand. But he came up the path to the bluff. I pointed silently to the plaque. I tried to explain what had happened, but it was no use. None of it would take shape in my mouth. Devkumar glanced at the plaque, then went on to the edge of the cliff. He surveyed the rock slab with its mysterious navel, and then took another path to the thick vine that snaked downward.

"Water blowhole," I called.

"Water blowhole," he echoed as he went down.

He went to the bottom, crossed the slab and peered straight down the hole as if it were another motor to fix. Then he went to the edge of the slab, where it hung out over the sea.

He was calling back to me, saying something scientific, but his voice was overcome by the crash of waves on the rocks. He had changed, as he so often did. One moment he was a lost dog, the next an angry rooster and the next a man full of questions and sense. Now he beat his breast and shouted at the waves. He tore open his shirt. I saw swells climbing one upon the other in the bay. A wave towered up and Devkumar Uncle disappeared, just as the Water of God spoke with its thunderous voice and shot foam skyward through the blowhole.

When the spray cleared he was still there, defying the ocean. I heard him swearing for the soaking he had gotten. His shirt was plastered wet against his torso and his hair was flung up, black and stiff. Fragments of phrases were tossed at me on the wind.

"...goddamn...crazy thing..." He shook his fist at the sea and paced back and forth on the slick rock.

Out in the bay the water was changing from blue to grey and green as clouds moved in and freshets of cool air whipped spray up the bluff. Against this Devkumar poured out his frustration and confusion, looking pathetically small and weak against the ocean's expanse. The ocean cared nothing for him. The waves cared nothing for him.

I retreated into the lee of a warm rock and searched through my pockets. The dried claw of a lizard came into my hand and several beautiful shells. A wooden knife. A yellow feather. Dr.

Patel's ribbon-tied packet. The outside of the packet was wet and the newspaper dissolved in my fingers. But, inside, a sheet of plastic kept the contents dry.

In the packet were two photographs of my mother. In one, her hair was thick and unrestrained, clothes floating out on the wind. She wore a drunken, ecstatic expression and might have been laughing or yelling at the photographer, fabricating some lie. Beside her, in the same wild mood, was a large young man. He had a beautifully shaped mouth and long forelock.

In the second photo, my mother and the man were at a formal occasion. A number of others were with them, some looking at the camera, others not. Despite the presence of this group, the couple were in a vortex of quiet. There were dark secrets in their eyes.

I did not dare to think that this stranger was my father. For a long time I studied every corner of the images from that flat and distant world. I longed to find my way in, to explore and find the hidden truths. I fell asleep.

WHEN I AWOKE it was late in the afternoon. 'Mè Jane was shaking me gently with one hand, gripping Sohrab with the other.

"Why did you stay away so long, Aousi Koko," she scolded. "You have given me a turn. I searched everywhere but the ocean itself."

Behind her, dark storm heads had advanced over an embattled sea. The rock point below was submerged by the waves. Green water spewed from the blowhole. There were no thunderous reports, only a hollow, steady roar. I wondered why Devkumar Uncle had gone back without me. Then we looked up and saw rain like stones flying overhead. It came on fast, the drops pelting the jungle leaves. We ran like the crazed.

MOTHER WAITED AT THE CAMP. The car was packed and she sat in the driver's seat, the motor hissing and belching.

"We're going home," she announced. But she did not set the car in motion. We sat dripping, waiting for an explanation. She said nothing.

"And what of Mastah Devkumar, Madam?" 'Mè Jane asked after a time.

"He will not be returning with us," she answered calmly. But she was false. Her knuckles were white where she gripped the wheel. "He had an accident. Only now the fishermen were here. They saw him in the water where the current is strong. He went into the sea. *Under* the sea. They saw him sink in deep water, struggle to come out, but he was swept down and down…" She relaxed now that this was said. She took the baby up. He seemed to sleep as though the world suited him.

"We can't just leave…," I protested.

"I'm afraid nothing can be done…"

But I was thinking of my new friends. Rain stones were hitting the car; the windows were a watery blur. I pictured them waiting on the beach, boxes and bags arranged beside them, their smiles fading under the deluge.

"But Madam," said 'Mè Jane. "Why do we leave Mastah's things?" She pointed to Devkumar's valise, visible in the doorway of the beehive.

"You don't know? One must never take away the belongings of a drowned person. An old belief but it is customary…"

She put the car in gear and we left that place. As we drove a sickness came to my stomach. Mother's story might be true. I alone knew how Devkumar Uncle would have been knocked from his perch by the waves, swept into the boiling water below the slab.

Through the storm our car retraced our way at quarter speed, limping homeward. I wanted to cry, believing I would never see Devkumar Uncle again. It was strange that only a few hours before I had thought him unimportant, a nuisance, yet how I missed him now. I worried that terrible things would happen to us without him. Already my mother was invaded by a silence that disturbed us. We watched her every movement as she pressed on. It was she who had made Devkumar Uncle angry and careless. We watched her with a resentment that burned and made our eyes throb.

We made it home, the broken car forced along by Mother's will. 'Mè Jane touched my hand and pointed at a silken case that lay on the floor of the car. It had come undone, revealing Devkumar Uncle's flutes.

a time *of drought*

Therianthrope

This is a photograph of an eye. That eye is red and dry and dust has collected in the corners and on the eyelashes. The skin around the eye is wrinkled because this is an eye that has not had a drink or a wash. This is a photograph of drought.

WE ARRIVED HOME on the first day of a drought that lasted for years. Each afternoon clouds swelled and lightning leapt onto the Lightning Cliff, yet only sand and coal dust shook loose from the sky. Winds blew with such ferocity that the soil was carved from the earth like meat from a bone. The soil found its way into our throats, compelling us to close our mouths for hours at a time. We watched our land become a skeleton. Our country became an expanse of red dust, red sky in which people lurched with tongues protruding and starved, bony cattle sniffed at stones, dreaming of water and green fodder, and hollow-bellied curs scoured the ditches.

Two herd boys were struck by a flurry of dry lightning as they crossed the plateau. The smoking remains were buried in water-soaked earth to ensure their comfort in the Dead Place.

Within our home, our place, we endured more than a drought of rain. We endured a drought of life of the kind Devkumar Uncle had made possible. Ours was a drought of fecundity and male folly, a drought of faulty schemes, pawing hands, fighting, comic rage and laughter.

FOR A LONG TIME neither 'Mè Jane nor I would speak of the true and improbable things we had witnessed. Mother told us, even as we came away from that stormy ocean, that to speak of Devkumar Uncle was to invite bad luck. When Flori asked, we answered in dry coughs and averted eyes. When pressed we said, no, nothing had happened. Nothing. Our trip was a non-event, something to be forgotten. Our lives were deserts with only a few scraps of fate blowing along in the wind.

Of course, it was impossible to hide the new baby and Devkumar Uncle's absence. Flori, left to her imagination, became convinced that the new baby was Devkumar Uncle. Her logic, which had an odd and truthful resonance, was that a sorcerer had transformed him. This story caught on and spread throughout the valley. After a time, some villagers came by and addressed the baby in low tones, discreetly showing him bits of machinery or seeking advice on overhauling auto engines.

We watched all of this from the deep shadow of the veranda, our thoughts following the same twisted tracks in the dust. Finally 'Mè Jane said to me, "Aousi, you were the last one to speak to the blood-mother of this infant. It means you know more about him than anyone. Tell them it is not Mastah Devkumar."

"They will not believe that."

"Aousi, because you understand this infant, you must watch over it and see that nothing happens."

"That's my mother's job," I said fiercely.

"Yes, well. Your mother is busy with her work..."

"I don't love it."

"You will learn."

"It is the baby of a *mathuela*. It might have powers..."

"It almost certainly has powers," said 'Mè Jane smoothly. "Listen. I know one thing about these witches. They are careful about who they speak to. In time that old *mathuela* will return for the child. In the dark, or when the sun is so terribly bright it is difficult to see. They are never careless, but the young can catch them out with sharp eyes. When she sees that you look out for the child, she will be grateful. Witches repay debts of gratitude. When she is grateful, you must ask for something in return. Something big."

"I do not like *mathuela* – witches or their puppies," I muttered, but I was not wholly truthful. In fact, I had been impressed by the strength of that mountain *mathuela*. She seemed powerful but kind.

"And there is something else. You did that famous thing...you prevented Devkumar Uncle from covering the witch with heavy stones. She will be doubly thankful."

"When will she come?"

"In her time...in her time..."

I peered into the creases and folds of 'Mè Jane's face and felt abandoned. I was not prepared for these tasks. My skin was breaking out in a rash.

But 'Mè Jane and I were two hearts bound together by truth and secrecy. We knew that which few knew, of life and death. So I went to the baby and observed him closely in the way that 'Mè Jane kept watch over Sohrab.

From the beginning we noticed the smell. It was not the sweet perfume of a regular baby, but a dense odour that clung to the air. In time we recognised the musk of wild creatures: boars, *boks* and predatory cats. It misted our brains and disturbed our sleep. We dreamed in new ways, our heads filled with wild creatures that trampled through steamy grasslands. We remembered things we had never known: *boks* with horns longer than their bodies and cats with teeth that dragged on the ground.

"Baby-witch things," said 'Mè Jane matter of factly. "Nothing to worry about."

My life filled with the baby witch. We sat on the veranda and watched him grow by the day, by the minute. Soon his skin became the colour of the clay and rock around us. His hair was dark but firelit in the sun. His eyes became slits, his features flattened.

"Is he human?" I asked.

"He is from the Beginning," 'Mè Jane whispered. From the ancient time of the cave dwellers, the painters of stick animals, and the speakers of clicks. "*Primitives*," she said with a frown. "They are not quite human. A people God forgot to finish. Then, you know, us Moderns came to push them into hidden caves. They knew not how to fight, Aousi, but they had many magics. Some may still be found here about in the hills..."

Baroa. Bushmen.

In time this was how the new baby was known – Bushman. Only Mother called him Amreek. Flori, of course, called him Ntate Devkumar.

Bushman was a tough, watchful thing who never cried. Hungry or wet he would stare at us, and penetrate our skin with his stink. Flori tried to purge him, performing elaborate cleansing procedures with soaps and oils. But I knew better how to deal with him. I brought him and Sohrab into the garden where they were rained on by dust and wind. The dogs found Bushman attractive, sniffing and licking him thoroughly, but he did not complain. He blinked his eyes at the dust-shrouded sun as though he were enjoying the best of pleasures.

If I were to be faithful to the truth, I would have to say that the witch-baby loved no one. Mother and Flori were held in a spell and imagined that because they were needed they were loved. But 'Mè Jane and I saw through this trick. We saw the way he controlled the air. We saw that he thought not in pictures, like a human, but in smells, like a dog.

Oh, yes, we saw. We saw and understood.

We saw him walk through the house before he could walk. In the night he awoke and went to the window, peered into the compound and beyond, into the stars. He went to my mother's side and cast spells over her sleeping face. We heard the snake-skin whisper of his feet on the tiles and saw him in the half-light of the moon and stars, in the deep of sleepless nights. He spoke to our dog Kalu, whispering in an animal language that made Kalu whimper and shake. And in the midst of a wild night in which the clouds spilled fire on the Killing Cliff, we heard him alone on the veranda calling to a tall grey bird that flew in the storm and would not land.

"Eh, Aousi," 'Mè Jane nodded her stumpy head. "He is *Baroa*."

My mother, after a long time, caught wind of the Bushman name. She captured me and asked for an explanation.

"He comes from the Beginning," I offered.

"Beginning of what? What beginning?"

"Beginning of everything."

She did not want to understand. But the truth is something that cannot be denied. Her head tilted and her eyes wandered. "He is only a baby," she said vaguely.

"It is where he gets his powers..."

"What?"

"We have seen his magic. At night," I maintained.

"What is this about powers? You have been listening to the local nonsense. Anyway what is magic really? Nothing is more magical than birth and life. Of course he's magical. He is new life, a new beginning, just as you say. A chicken from an egg. As magical as a planet that changes the direction of its rotation, or an ant who mourns the death of her queen..."

"But what kind of person will he be? How do we know that in the end this baby will turn out fine? Maybe he will run to the mountains and steal the faces from creatures."

"No one knows," said my mother. "If he does, then he will have our best wishes. In the meantime, we do our best..."

MY MOTHER DID NOT grieve the death of Devkumar Uncle, and neither did we. But we were not allowed to forget him either. It was as though he had known all along that he would leave us behind in the world. I sometimes thought he left reminders of himself that were made to appear at those moments when our memories of him weakened. Not that I could ever forget him really, but we knew how badly Mother wanted to erase his memory. It would have taken days of concentrated effort to sterilize our house of him. She did not try. Once in a while an article of his clothing appeared with the laundry. Once I found a bristly work sock in my pocket, the bottom worn thin, the upper portion stained with oil. Then there were motor parts, unrusted after days, then months, then years, scattered through the sheds among Mother's discarded sculptures or perched on cement blocks in the long grass of the compound. Three years after he vanished, a truck driver came by to retrieve a fully repaired generator. He left money as though Devkumar were still among us.

I came across Devkumar's shaving razor and soap, which caused me to lay awake for nights afterward, feeling that I had seen a spirit. The razor looked as though it had been used recently, the edge speckled with black whiskers.

"Maybe he is still alive," I suggested once.

Mother scowled. 'Mè Jane pursed her lips.

Devkumar Uncle was known, and even admired, in the valley for the help he had given with cars, machines and practical advice. Elders came forward with messages of respect and were suspicious of my mother for not receiving them with great ceremony.

Then that period in which we were supposed to grieve passed.

Mother pretended he had never existed. But without rough games to remind her that she was no more than a thing of flesh, without squabbles to remind her of the mundane concerns of raising a family, her focus thinned and scattered over vast horizons. She could no longer finish a project. Her attention wandered from idea to idea. And her beam of motherly love gradually flickered and was extinguished in favour of endless new investigations. She undertook ambitious experiments; but the results, recorded in large black laboratory books, resembled no known science.

She created things we could barely look at. Clay creatures with the bodies of animals and the heads of women. Creatures beyond our imaginations and dreams.

I noticed a sculpture the size of a newborn baby, with the skin of an antelope and the torso of a human.

"What is it?" I asked.

"*Therianthrope*," she mumbled without looking my way. Her eyes were red and circled. "The Basotho call it a trance-buck."

"Devil-things," 'Mè Jane muttered.

I followed 'Mè Jane to the veranda. She sat on the bench rocking on her haunches and gazing out over the valley.

"What is a trance-buck?"

"It can be a man whose nose bleeds as he enters the spirit world. In the old time trance-bucks brought dreams and took them away, at night or during the day, either one."

Even then I was not a good sleeper. As the boys slept I watched them dream. Sohrab dreamed of balancing a ball on his foot. But Bushman's head produced the stubs of horns. His little legs stirred with electricity. In the moonlight he sprang up and disappeared over the veldt, cutting the earth with sharp hooves, fleeing invisible stalkers in the cool night air.

"At night he flies," I told 'Mè Jane.

"Is it?" she answered.

I WATCHED my mother's hands at her workbench. They were very long hands, fine and strong. Their movement reminded us of water. When she was at peace, her hands were a still pool, but when her mood was stormy, they flowed like a torrent over brush, paint, clay, her own face. I searched my hands for signs of this magic water power, but my hands were clumsy and dry, the hands of drought. I wanted the power to create a trance-buck who could bring me dreams of Devkumar Uncle in his under-the-sea home. I wanted a trance-buck who would make my mother laugh or cry or become angry with us. I needed a trance-buck to transport me to my real father, so I could watch him in his life or death.

Mother's trance-buck came out of the cracked, smoky oven in the compound. It looked mauled, like so many of her works, the horned head caved in and slumped to one side. She looked at it, perplexed, then placed it in the shed among her other flawed works.

For years we pretended the shed was a hospital for deformed creatures. With the help of special night nurses, the cracked skin, broken heads and legs and melted torsos healed.

I lay awake dreaming of the whispers and soft footsteps of the nurses. Not long after Devkumar Uncle died I heard soldiers and saw the glint of gunmetal in the moonlight. Those soldiers took the nurses away, leaving the patients to suffer in silence.

The Head

ere is our first-day-of-school photo. We are dressed in the school uniform, about to take our first walk to our new school. Even Bushman is dressed, although it is obvious that the clothes are foreign upon his wild skin. Our new school is not in this picture, but that picture would have been dark and strange...

IN THE YEARS AFTER Devkumar Uncle's death, I remembered his last words of advice and went to school with the two boys. But school days were brief.

For a long time my mother refused to have us in school. I assumed I was not fit for school because of my ungainliness, my stupidity and my general unworthiness. Dr. Patel, as principal of the college, had questioned her on this, even though my mother rarely listened to anything he had to say to her. She said to Dr. Patel, "School will kill them," and he accepted this obscure statement. 'Mè Jane had raised a grumbling objection from time to time, since everyone knew she believed in school.

Once in a while someone sat with Sohrab and me with the aim of tutoring us in reading and writing and sums but, in truth, we did not feel deprived, since our old school by the main road was a mucky little place with broken windows and a single, unutilized latrine. Those few children who attended this school read and wrote as poorly as we did. Then Sohrab and I became too big.

We spent the days wandering the paths and fields of the valley discovering important things that we kept secret. On the opposite side of the valley we saw men in suits arrive from the city to direct the construction of a fence around the lands of the new National Agriculture Corporation. The National Agric, as everyone came to know it, was supposed to demonstrate new farming methods, but instead it took land away from ordinary farmers. After a while a few crops were planted and an airstrip was cleared and several low buildings erected. Guards were hired to keep farmers out of the fenced lands. These bored guards, in their crumpled brown uniforms, were seen moving throughout the district after a time, looking for something more to do. They were known as the National Agric Police but people knew there was more. Those men consorted with Evils from somewhere else, and we were afraid from the beginning.

IN OUR CURIOSITY we ventured near. Perhaps if we had not been curious nothing would have happened. As it was the spirits of those places had a chance to see us, sniff our blood and think.

One day we followed the new National Agric Farm fence from the sloping sides of the valley up to the flat plateau where a crop of maize was ready to harvest. The fence was made of steel mesh and it was high and topped with razor wire. We came around to a gate, saw two of the National Agric Police, and moved quickly past, following an old path up the hillside. If it had not been for the policemen, Sohrab would have run into the compound just for the thrill. Instead, wearing a bored expression, he ran a stick of wood along the steel mesh, making a broken and plangent noise. Behind him came Bushman at a respectful distance, doing exactly as Sohrab did. Bushman was capable of following us for great distances. He wore a toy drum that 'Mè Jane called his *situpu* or healing drum around his neck. Once in a while he stopped to collect something he found on the ground and shove it into a rough leather sack.

At the top of the hillside we came to the large area of burned grass and a sign that read "Order of the Mission of Jesus Christ," the site of a new school.

Over the next months we watched them build this new school. Rumours went around that dignitaries of the Order of the Mission of Jesus Christ Church and the National Agric Corporation would open the school. Excitement spread through the valley. Students lined up to register. It was said that the school would be staffed only by the best headmaster and teachers. There would be a library filled with books.

Eventually my mother caught wind of this and decided that all three children would be registered at the Order of the Mission of Jesus Christ School. She told 'Mè Jane to see that we were not forced to pray to the God of Jesus Christ.

"The God of the missionaries is everywhere, Madam. I have seen."

"You have seen God," cracked Mother.

"Yes, Madam," said 'Mè Jane seriously. "There is no avoiding that God. If you do not let the children pray, they may become confused. Especially the girl, Madam. But you know, Madam, that God is not really bad...," she added quietly.

My mother dismissed this with a wave of her hand. "Make sure that they do not come home as little Christians, please," she said under her breath.

With that we embarked on schooling.

ON THE FIRST DAY OF SCHOOL I awoke early and lay in a swath of blankets, wishing I could hide. The future was spread before me in the light of this dawn. I saw myself as a very large 'Mè Jane, searching out the true and the concealed from beneath hooded eyes. I saw myself bent with age, lost, wandering a vast road. I was not clever and everyone knew it. In the pit of my stomach, I was certain that school would be a disaster.

I climbed from my bed. 'Mè Jane was sweeping the bare clay of the compound with a bundle of grass. We roused the boys in the chill air and dressed Bushman in the khaki uniform of the primaries. Sohrab wore a white shirt with grey flannel trousers, while I donned a black tunic that threatened to spread into a windborne kite. On that first day Mother saw us off with a doubtful, troubled look. We watched her wave, then she went back inside. In my mind I followed her to her desk, followed the strain of her eye as she looked upon her work. I knew that she retreated into chaos. It was the same chaos from which we had sprung, and it was this chaos we carried with us to school. We may as well have been raised on the wild, open veldt.

As we marched down the path we heard the urgent whistling of a strange bird. This was Glorius, Sohrab's pal, calling Sohrab away to freedom. Then we saw in dismay that Glorius too was shackled in school clothes and was being led, like the other lambs, to the Mission of Jesus Christ School. We laughed, though, to see his brown ankles sticking out of his trousers as he and Sohrab ran ahead with heads together, planning escape. 'Mè Jane and 'Mè Anastacia, Glorius' aunt, struggled to keep up but soon fell behind.

It was by accident that Bushman and I turned from the path that first morning. We lost sight of Sohrab and Glorius and I decided we should shortcut through the bottom trails. Bushman had his head down, searching out insects; then he raised his eyes to a flock of birds. I pulled him along as well as I could.

The air at the bottom of the valley was cool and contained a breath of moisture from the stream. We passed through an abandoned village and into thick, dry brush and a eucalyptus grove. Then Bushman ran ahead to stand motionless, peering into the branches. I ran after him but stopped short. Above, in a tangle of branches, a detached head was strung by thick cords of hair. It swayed slightly with the breeze, then revolved slowly until it faced us. The eyes opened and it stared at us.

"She cannot get us," I choked, but our legs were frozen by that stare. Our skin inched along our flesh. Our lives were small and distant events. Rags of light danced over the mouth as it tried to speak. Then the wind shifted and we heard the hiss of its tongue.

"Look," whispered Bushman, and I saw scorpions marching on the tree trunk, moving toward us. We broke and ran for the path, then kept running until we were out of breath. I tried to think this through sensibly. My mother would tell me, no, real heads cannot live without their bodies, but I knew, in my heart, that it was the mama of Bushman, the *mathuela* from the mountain pass.

Devkumar Uncle would say, let us climb this tree and see better, perhaps ask the head questions.

'Mè Jane would pray. She would think about sorcerers and in time she would find out who the head was and what it wanted.

"She had a good look at both of us," I said as we ran.

"Yes," said Bushman, and he smiled as though nothing could be better.

In our panic we fled along unknown paths. For the first time, I became lost in the valley. The sun ballooned into an eye that examined our progress. The rustle of branches sounded like women gossiping.

"Where we go now?" asked Bushman with a smile.

"School," I said. "It will be nice, like Dr. Patel's house."

I lost my direction again and again, my senses scattered in the dappled light. From time to time I looked over my shoulder. I saw living things burgeoning from dark fissures. Bushman squatted and shat amid the living, crawling stuff. It was difficult to breathe, the air overcrowded with growth, excrement and death. With each breath, our bellies filled until we became weighted down with syrupy vitality; it dragged us into the fissures, into the dank underlayer of earth where Things were not alive.

Somehow we found our way to the riverbank and escaped that place. We saw light and leaves blazing with green fire. We followed the tracks of a large animal whose claws had pierced the clay, until we came to the base of a great tree. In the tree was a monkey, but the monkey turned out to be a man painted white who climbed down to splash in a pool in the river, washing the paint away to reveal iridescence. Then that too washed away. Nearby a band of naked girls paraded by on their return from Initiation. They burst into song; the song was taken up by the man in the pool and by a crowd of women who panned for gold in midstream. The bottom of their pans captured the white and iridescent paint. Babies squalled like insects. The song of a bird transformed into a human voice.

On the other side of the river we climbed the ridge to the National Agric Farm, and followed the fence to the dusty hill where the Mission of Jesus Christ School awaited.

THE SCHOOL BUILDINGS were zinc-roofed and painted white and red. Each doorway had a white cross painted above it. In each room Jesus Christ bled where he hung from crossed sticks. In the midst of the schoolyard the students were assembled in rows, according to size, with teachers patrolling between them, and everyone listened to a speech by Headmaster Tubay. He was a tiny man with sparse rings of silver hair and small, bloodshot eyes. Behind him, in the distance, the fenced expanse of the National Agric Corporation spread vast and deserted, the buildings and fences glittering despite the thick dust.

"Let us pray," intoned Father Tubay, and the students bent their heads. Some closed their eyes, others searched the ground muttering, "Our father whose art is in heaven, Hello would be his name. Our kingdom come, it will be dumb..." We thought this a strange prayer and had no idea what it could mean. Bushman looked at me and smiled dreamily, a creature of bliss.

Then the students dispersed to classrooms. Bushman disappeared and I fell in with some girls my age. We had been late by almost an hour and had missed the introductions and our classroom assignments. I drifted along in the yard with the other girls until I saw Sohrab and Glorius, with Bushman trailing behind them. I noticed that Bushman's pouch hung open, spilling dirt and live insects onto the school ground. He was the only student with a drum dangling from his neck.

"What is this pouch and drum?" an older boy asked.

Bushman opened the pouch and let a tiny bird tumble out onto the earth. It called weakly for its mother. Other students gathered.

Perhaps they had heard of Bushman, or perhaps they recognised his *Baroa* blood. Perhaps they sniffed his pungent musk.

"He is like dirt," I heard a girl say. "And he smells."

More students came. The orderly first-day procession of the students to their new classrooms was giving way to the chaos we had brought with us from our house. Sohrab and Glorius plunged into the crowd. There were shouts. By the time I shouldered my way in, Sohrab was beating another boy in the dirt, Bushman was dancing a jig and screaming with glee and the students were yelling encouragement.

A teacher came. She pulled Sohrab off and marched him and his opponent away. Another teacher, a fat woman with a narrow-brimmed hat set at a sporty angle, sniffed the air around Bushman. She told him to remove his drum and pouch.

"This is not a play place," she said. "And these vernacular customs are not permitted." She seized the drum and pulled.

Bushman dug in his heels. She tried to untie his pouch. He fell to the earth and bit her leg. He did not bite hard, but his lips were back from his teeth and his long eyes were inclined across his face, prompting the teacher to scream. "Chinese! Chinese boy! Let go of me, Chinese!"

A man lifted Bushman and bore him away. I followed, of course. He was taken to the office of Headmaster Tubay. Sohrab and a few others waited outside on a bench. Sohrab did not look at us. He looked neither sullen nor rebellious but like a boy indifferent to his fate. He pulled a coin from his pocket and studied it. When Bushman came near him to have a look, Sohrab put the coin away.

"What will happen, Saba?" I asked him.

He shrugged. "Are you afraid of a little old man?"

"I run and bring 'Mè Jane," suggested Bushman. I made him sit still on the bench.

"No one here will hurt you," said Sohrab airily. "He would not allow it." He pointed to Jesus Christ bleeding on his sticks.

Headmaster Tubay came and looked at each child who waited in the shade of his office porch and shook his head.

"New school, new students. Even on the first historic day of this institution. Even on this great and remarkable day, there are troublemakers. Human nature, human nature. Everyone but the fighters must go to their classes. If I see you here again tomorrow, there will be punishment of the kind you will appreciate." He clapped his hands and all but the fighters scrambled away unscathed. Only the four of us remained.

Headmaster Tubay looked at me with a friendly grin. "And why is a girl left with the fighters?"

"Yes, Ntate."

"You must not use vernacular here on the school premises. As I said during assembly."

"Yes, Ntate."

"*Yes Headmastah, yes Seh,* not *yes Ntate.* And who is this?"

"Bushman Amreek," I answered for Bushman. "Seh."

"Does he have a tongue?"

"Yes Seh, but he is small."

"And you?" He turned to Sohrab, and Sohrab pulled his coin out and examined it minutely.

"He is Sohrab, Ntate. They are my brothers."

"You. Get to Mrs. Rantoa's class," he told Bushman.

Bushman skipped away a short distance clutching his drum, only to stand uncertainly by a wall, since he had no idea who or where Mrs. Rantoa might be. But I could not help him now.

Headmaster brought us into his office where we sat on another bench. He took up a bamboo cane and tapped it absently on the desk in front of us.

"Do you know what this is for?"

"Yes, Ntate. For walking. For an old person..."

"Do you think I am so old I need a cane?"

"Yes, Ntate."

Sweat beaded on Tubay's brow despite the cool air, and I knew the conversation was not going well. He seemed exhausted from a lifetime of student assemblies. "Perhaps," he said, "you are as intelligent as your mother. Or perhaps not. This cane is for caning. Caning of girls we do not like to do. But, if called upon, we will not hesitate. Do not be late again. Do not, do not, do not..." He waved me out of the room.

I went round the side of the office and waited. Without further preamble Sohrab and the other boy were caned. The cane made a cracking sound on their hands. Five times each, and that only because it was the first day.

Sohrab did not glance my way when he came out. There were no tears in his eyes, only an angry red tinge.

In my class I read through a textbook, then sat through the droning of the teacher's voice as dust and clouds drifted in a stagnant red sky. It was impossible to follow the pattern of classroom activities. At any time a lesson might be interrupted by songs or prayers to the God of Jesus Christ. Sometimes the bell boy ran among the classes tolling his handbell, and the lessons would abruptly end. Sometimes the students assembled in the school-yard to pray and listen to Headmaster speak of God and learning and the National Agric Project.

We were told that if we missed school for reasons other than illness we would be punished. "By police," Headmaster said.

Someone giggled. But we saw the brown uniforms of the National Agric Police at the school.

THE MORNING that 'Mè Jane and Flori gave up trying to walk us to school, we showed Sohrab and Glorius the Head. Sohrab threw stones at it. I had to drag the boys away. After that, Sohrab and Glorius were late every morning. From my place at the back of the classroom I saw them sneaking across the schoolyard hours after the bell had rung. They were wet and dirty and sometimes shoeless. The whites of their eyes gleamed from encounters with the Head. Once they were caught watching girls bathing in the river. Another time they were chased from the National Agric Farm.

I tried to concentrate on 'Mè Pitso and her lessons about Shaka Zulu, Vasco DaGama and other men. But the Head intruded on my thoughts. Every day she was there. I tried to keep Bushman away from that glade, but he followed Sohrab whenever he could. I gave in and visited the Head every morning with the others.

We found her moaning and humming to the music of the wind through the leaves. Her hair became wispy as the days went on. It floated about her in a halo. We grew less afraid. The face revealed different moods, swinging this way and that, the eyes finding us where we hid in the bush. Tears would some-times fill the eyes.

"See," I told Bushman. "It is a mother. She looks everywhere for her child. She can only watch and wait because she cannot speak."

My fear shrank as I understood. Under her tree, Sohrab and Glorius constructed an altar of wood and stone during the mornings that they were supposed to be in school. I would drag Bushman away, but still we were late. By tea I would see the two older boys stealing across the playing field, their hair flecked with dirt and bits of wood.

I dreamed of the *mathuela*. I pictured her in the darkness, swinging alone beneath the moon. In the night I imagined that she was afraid of the powers greater than she.

After a time we were sent again to the office of the headmaster. Bushman still refused to surrender his drum and sack and had decided not to speak to any teacher. We had by then been five weeks in the Order of the Mission of Jesus Christ School and we had learned nothing.

We sat in a row in the shadow of the headmaster's office. Students on their way to class waved at us or mocked us. A boy from my class whom everyone called Machine walked back and forth singing, "A full taste you will enjoy, a full taste you will enjoy," until Headmaster appeared in the doorway.

Headmaster Tubay pulled a note from his pocket and read it aloud.

"'Dear Headmaster,'" he read, "'Please cane these boys. They are late twenty-five times. They are late purposely to vex Headmaster and to disrespect. Maybe they respect cane. These boys are nothing but disrespect and insolent.' Signed yours sincerely, Mr. Kaba."

"'Nothing but disrespect!' Not really English, but the point is there. Late too many days. Why?"

He read similar notes concerning Bushman and, finally, me.

"Why, why, why?"

"Yes, Headmastah," we said in unison.

"Do you like cane?"

"No, Seh."

Bushman was caned first. He took ten on his rump and was released. I took ten on the hand, which made water jump to my eyes. Outside, Bushman and I awaited Sohrab and Glorius. But Headmaster made a mistake by having them in his office together. We heard a cry and a scuffle. The cane cracked five times, then Sohrab and Glorius burst from the door and sprinted from the school ground as though the God of Jesus Christ were after them.

We glimpsed Headmaster Tubay in a lump on the floor, blinking in surprise. His cane was broken beside him. Then we ran and hid in our classes for the rest of that day.

Sohrab and Glorius took refuge at the altar of the Head. For several days they stayed there under her protection. She fed them her buzzing sound and her flaying eyes. She locked them in her heart and taught them things that they would rather not know. Then they shaved their heads like initiated tribesmen of the highland and grew hollow-eyed from staring at a moon that made night shadows come alive in the glade.

Eventually 'Mè Jane realized that something was wrong and made me tell what had happened. She said, "*Modimo,*" and her face clamped into her thinking-to-herself look.

We waited for something bad to happen. Our skin itched with anticipation as we cocked our ears for the utterings of mice, or warnings of reprisal.

After some days the boys ventured out of their hiding place. They wandered in the glade and further, into the college and home, as hungry as vultures. They ate all the food in our house, so that 'Mè Jane had to make a trip to market before Market Trip Day. They hung around the students and villagers cadging handouts of anything edible. When these sources were depleted they wandered the fields stealing vegetables. They captured small animals and birds that came in their way. They were forced farther and farther afield in their hunger, like two young and insatiable lions. We saw the hints of young manhood in them, in their brooding silences and long strides, but it might have been the influence of the Head. She made them bold and urged them to venture near the National Agric fence.

That was how they were caught. That was how Sohrab first met Thabo Majara.

The National Agric Police who caught them knew of the broken cane of the headmaster. They did not say as much. But we knew they knew. We had seen these men lounging in Tubay's office, laughing with him on the way to Caltex's Roadhouse. They were red-eyed and lazy-limbed, those police. The tallest and boniest of them carried a roughly fashioned knife which he used for killing goats. That was Thabo Majara. He brought the boys inside the National Agric Farm.

They were inside the fence for an hour, in one of the shiny new buildings of National Agric Corp. Later they found their way to the head and the altar with clothes ripped and brains scrambled. They threw down the altar and broke it apart. The pieces they threw at the Head, trying to knock her from her place. But the *mathuela* had the last word – she cast the trance of silence upon them and made them forget everything.

When he came home, Sohrab said nothing about the Head or the National Agric Police. His appetite was cured and he was no longer friends with Glorius Sebane.

'Mè Jane only shook her head sorrowfully.

We never went near the Mission of Jesus Christ School again.

Cobra (How Life Began)

No one had the courage to take photos of live snakes, but if they had, the picture would have been of the mother cobra with her eyes flashing, counting her eggs, then counting them again...

IN THOSE DAYS, the sun was particularly cruel and stalked us even where we waited in the shadows. At midday, winds tossed chaff and dust and trash into the air. By four o'clock a cloud would appear, spout fire, cause the winds to reverse and send one or two futile drops to be swallowed in the dust. By the river, the thin margin of green shrank with each passing month. Snakes ventured down from the cliffs in search of food.

One day we found two cobras, one black and one gold, stretched across the path leading down to the college. Unlike normal snakes that fled when we stamped our feet, these cobras ignored us as though they were the master and mistress of our compound. We were afraid and dared not interfere. They became bolder, sunning themselves in the early morning at the compound gate, tangling themselves in snake love where all could see.

"Do not look," 'Mè Jane warned us. She eyed Bushman who, like the goat-herding boys, bore a stout stick. "These *nohadi* were sent by someone. We can only watch our feet."

But we looked. We saw the he-snake hunt a rat and present it to the she-snake. We saw the couple rear up and spread their hoods to catch the breezes of the evening. We watched the glitter of their eyes and saw the strange intelligence within. We saw them mate. New snake life was about to begin.

After this Sohrab searched the grounds around the compound, probing with a stick in the dried tussocks and among rocks. When we asked him what he was doing, he told us it was nothing. When we followed him, he said we should mind our business. After we thought it through, we realized he searched for the cobra eggs so we followed along, wary of annoying the he and she cobra.

Sohrab turned boulders with a steel bar. When he found other snakes – and there were more than we had ever seen – Bushman and he pounced with stones and sticks and left the remains for Kalu and Mpho to finish. Sohrab wore a pair of leather boots that had belonged to Devkumar Uncle. We noticed that the boots fit quite well.

THIS IS A PICTURE of the brothers Sohrab and Bushman. They are both pretty to look at, with the bright sun in their eyes making them squint. Unconsciously Bushman is mimicking the casual and careless slouch affected by Sohrab, which makes me think, when I look back on it, that Bushman might have seen himself as a smaller version of Sohrab: taciturn, brooding and youthfully arrogant, unaware of the differences between them.

At this, 'Mè Jane shook her head and looked grave. "These boys, they have no father to guide them in the ways of men. Troublesome boys, they will be. This is the way of boys without fathers…always the way." I suppose it was 'Mè Jane's heart that told her things that others missed.

In due course, Sohrab's chopped hair grew back to the soft black fur that matched that of Kalu, our dog. That Kalu stuck to Sohrab's heel, took the place of Glorius Sebane as Sohrab's companion. The two rose at noon to vanish, silent and mysterious and preoccupied.

'Mè Jane appealed to Mother to pay attention. "Sohrab must be turned back, Madam, before it is too late."

My mother squinted at 'Mè Jane through her reading glasses. "Too late for what?"

"Trouble, Madam."

"What kind of trouble?"

"Bad seed trouble, Madam. Bad seed trouble."

Mother did not see what she meant, and 'Mè Jane would not elaborate. Instead, 'Mè Jane and I consulted a herbalist.

In the valley there were several different kinds of herbalists. Some advocated cannibalism while others prescribed certain plants for medicinal purposes. Some claimed special *mutis* for common ailments. Some classified diseases as Christian, Islamic or *local* conditions and had huts that were also shrines.

We discovered that 'Mè Jane's ancient and traditional herbalist had recently died in the mountains. She was told that the practice had been handed down to one Ntate Hlalete, grand-nephew of the old man.

To find this Hlalete, we were directed to an old storage hut behind Caltex Roadhouse. The place reeked of beer and urine. In the candlelit interior, plastic dolls lined a low shelf behind a teenaged youth. He had orange hair, pink eyes and several fingernails which had been tended to unusual curling lengths. He asked to be paid before we told him our problem, but changed his mind when 'Mè Jane muttered dangerously under her breath. 'Mè Jane told the boy she had not seen him before and asked if he was from the Republic. He declined to answer, but instead began to sing loudly a traditional song. He sang with such distraction and strength that 'Mè Jane said, "Uh-HUNH," when he was done. Apparently satisfied, she described Sohrab to the herbalist.

"Ah," said Ntate Hlalete, "It is good you chose to come here. I learned special *muti* from my uncle."

The solution, he told us, was to transform Sohrab into a girl. "It is the only way to divert him from the path of manhood."

He prescribed a mixture of red and green leaves to be given with his food at certain times. More important was the dust of another *muti* that was to be sprinkled on Sohrab's man parts every night that the moon could be seen, and another to be applied every night that the moon could not be seen. "You will see. He will grow titties," said the herbalist. "Nothing else will work. When his man parts fall off, you must collect and bring to me..."

The treatment went badly from the start. Sohrab often returned home only after we were asleep. When we offered him food, he refused it. I had trouble waking myself to carry out the nighttime part. When the opportunity finally arrived, I forgot some of the instructions. The leaves seemed to have lost their colour and when I sprinkled the dust, some went onto Sohrab's belly and chest, some onto his face and none onto his privates. I tried for five days when the moon was bright but got the *mutis* confused. At last I gave up.

Sohrab's man parts did not fall off, nor did he transform into a girl. Instead his eyes took on a pale glow and his stare was difficult to match. His shoulders thickened and his back became straight and flexible as a jetted flame. His feet became quick, his legs powerful. On the football pitch he easily guided the ball around his opponents, and his strides were longer than anyone in a sprint. He became known for his special football magic and was praise-named "Touch." Soon this new name, Touch, was on the lips of girls in the valley and villages around. He was handsome and fleet, this Touch.

We watched all of this uncomfortably, wishing we had not meddled. 'Mè Jane once again tried to bring matters to the attention of my mother.

"He is simply a growing boy," my mother said. "Boys are that way..." She turned back to a patch of canvas onto which she painted a figure too tiny to be seen by ordinary eyes.

It became terribly hot. Waves of heat pressed on the earth. We could not move, yet we boiled in our own sweat. Birds fell from the sky. Dogs tried to dig their way into the cooler reaches of the Other Place.

The heat found its way into my blood and surged through my temples. It found its way to my insides and caused me to expand. I grew, and then I grew too much. If I turned my ears inward, I heard the creak and groan as my seams burst and were reformed. My muscles stretched my clothing, then the clothing gave way. I was all shoulders and muscles and thighs. Humps of muscle for bearing heavy loads and fighting enemies.

"What did you do with Sohrab's medicine," 'Mè Jane asked casually, looking at me.

I shrugged and said, "Sohrab's medicine, 'Mè?" but I could not meet her gaze.

We found the cobra eggs clustered in a patch of leafy weeds near our house. Bushman immediately ran to report this to 'Mè Jane, but Sohrab snagged him by the ear. "Deadly great secret," he said, twisting.

Bushman croaked, "Deadly great secret," and went limp.

We collected half the eggs and hid them in a warm spot by the Lightning Cliff. The other eggs we watched from a safe distance. Each day Sohrab inspected the eggs before stuffing his hands in his pockets and wandering away. Bushman would follow him, often returning with his face streaked with dirt and his ears red from being twisted. He told us that Sohrab often went to the place of the head and that he had built a fort of cardboard and scraps of wood there.

We saw how the cobras brooded over the eggs that remained in their nest, counting them, thinking, calculating. They were resentful, but they did not know whom to punish. Those eggs grew, fed by the spirit of the mother. Our stolen eggs grew too, but fed by some other spirit that troubled our dreams. I would have asked 'Mè Jane or Dr. Patel about this, but Sohrab said, "Deadly great secret." He did not risk pulling my ear.

At night the cobras hunted together, leaving long grooves in the dust. They captured night creatures, paralysing their immaterial bodies with their breath.

SOMETIMES WE SAW Dr. Patel in his garden laying out intricate patterns of stones. We never asked him why he did this. It was night and private. But during the day Dr. Patel took some interest in us. He knew we were up to something. He brought us lab books and pens from the college so we could write about it. "Keep a careful record," he nodded. "A journal provides one with perspective."

I wrote that there were twenty-one eggs, each of them a victim of our wrongdoing. This was the reason that the snakes, if they were born, would be troublesome.

Some eight weeks after the eggs were laid, we noticed the she-cobra looping her length in coils over her brood. She counted them for the hundredth time. We heard her sigh. Then we saw one morning that the eggs were no more. In their place were shreds of collapsed egg skin. As we went about the compound we scanned the ground and saw the curving signatures of tiny snakes. The trails led to the Cliff where they disappeared into the rocks.

But our eggs, the stolen ones, remained unhatched. Sohrab shone a light through one and replaced it without comment. He went to the house and brought a sleeping bag and told us that he would mother the eggs himself.

"The snakes will love me and do my bidding," he said.

That night Bushman slept out there too, a safe distance from Sohrab and the eggs.

"WHY DO THE BOYS SLEEP OUT?" asked 'Mè Jane. "With snakes and things about, it is not safe."

"For no reason," I said. "For fun." Of course lying to 'Mè Jane was futile and I avoided her eyes. She pestered me until I told the deadly great secret about the eggs that had hatched and the ones that had not. It was early in the morning. Someone beat a drum far out on the plateau. I lingered in bed, listening. I ran my hands over my new muscles and wondered what 'Mè Jane would do. She said nothing more to me about the eggs, but went out to the shed and brought back a tough old rhino quirt belonging to Uncle Devkumar. I dressed and came out to find her creeping about the yard with the quirt held high over her head.

"Young snakes are foolish," she muttered. She made tight circles around our house but found not one young snake. Then she set her sights on the Cliff.

The sun was blazing on the rocks by then and the boys had left their sleeping places. In the near distance we heard their voices.

"Mine."

"Stay back."

"I will bring 'Mè Old Jane."

Bushman came running from behind the rocks with the limp-and-hop gait that 'Mè Jane once said was very like a hyena. When he saw us he stopped short.

"Snakes, 'Mè..." he said.

We found Sohrab sitting near the stolen eggs. A single hatchling lay coiled in a dirty bottle.

"Mastah Sohrab," said 'Mè Jane. "What evil sorcery have you planned with these things?"

"Pets, 'Mè. Experiments." He plucked at the lone baby snake with a pair of tongs. It responded by spreading a narrow hood.

With great concentration, Sohrab moved the remaining eggs into a box under the squint of 'Mè Jane. He picked up the box and moved off, ignoring us as we ran behind him flapping our hands. At the gate to the compound 'Mè Jane managed to bar his way.

"Not here," she puffed.

Unhesitant, down-looking, eyes locked on his eggs, he turned and went on, past the shed and on down the path. Perhaps the golden cobras slept at that hour. They let Sohrab pass on with their eggs in his arms. Sohrab went quickly but not running, legs lithe and swift through the morning rock shadows. We heard the distinctive croak of the laboratory door and we knew where Sohrab had gone.

The lab was Mother's domain, and though she did not invite us there, we felt that it belonged to us. When we wished to, we poked freely through the storeroom, through samples of butterflies and leaves and other stranger things. We knew how Sohrab thought. He meant to find a safe and secret nook for his box amid the shelves that were never cleaned and the closets with their years-old, never-inventoried supplies.

"Sohrab, I will tell Madam of your doings," called 'Mè Jane. "I will tell Ntate Dr. Patel. You will meet resistance, young Sohrab. You will encounter big problems..."

Sohrab came out of the lab after a few minutes, with his hands stuffed far down in his pockets. He was no longer in a hurry. He smiled at 'Mè Jane. "Say nothing, 'Mè. The eggs are my children. If you say something, Sohrab will not love you, 'Mè. Say nothing of this great secret, eh?"

We noticed how he sounded like Devkumar Uncle when he said this. His talk was smooth, his voice undulating like a long, scaly muscle. He winked at us and walked away.

"How did Life begin, 'Mè? How did snakes begin?"

"In the River Caledon. Down in the place where the river is born. You can see this any morning, for it is each morning that Life begins. Every day. It begins in the murky places in the weeds and mud under the water. The mud becomes squirming things that have no memory. Then come the fish and those other things that fish can eat. These things form by God. In the night they die and the spirit creatures roam about. That is why we must sleep then. That way we do not encounter trouble..."

Early in the morning, we took Bushman to the place where the river begins and found weedy, muddy pools, despite the drought all around. Bushman stripped off and leapt in and out of the water, his penis jiggling like a worm. We searched the waters for stones that caught the morning light.

In the mud we saw clay-coloured fish rise sleepily into the water, then swim away, touched by the power of Life.

I felt myself expanding, growing, unstoppable under the influence of the misdirected *muti*.

The Encampment

This is another of Sohrab: a close-up. By this time, he is lean and his skin and eyes are smooth and glowing, and it is obvious that he has the constitution of a warrior. His look of stupid superiority is made worse by his level, handsome face and his black mane of hair. Here is a youth to whom the ancestors have given beauty and grace, and said *go out into the crooked, unhandsome place of South Africa so that we can watch and laugh at what happens...*

WE SOMETIMES FORGOT that Sohrab was Devkumar Uncle's son. But as he grew he became more like Devkumar, and we were reminded how Devkumar Uncle had been a dog who sniffed for pleasure and love amid the tin cans and wrappers and trash of the dongas and lanes. We forgot how he was rough and playful one minute and a gentle musician the next.

Sohrab took to pacing over the ground of the valley, wetting the places dogs wet, looking for something in the dells and shacks near the road. And when he was not satisfied with what he saw, he went further, onto the main road and past that into the encampment. And he went beyond.

When Sohrab came home, he was as dark and moody as Mother. He could be as easily a playmate or a tyrant. There were times when we saw him show Bushman a secret bird call, and then there were other times when Bushman's ears were red from being pulled and he ran into the shed to hide his tears.

We consulted Ntate Hlalete again, although we were dubious of him. Hlalete had moved away from Caltex Roadhouse and cut his fingernails. A sign by his *rondavel* read "Special Clinic." He wore shoes. 'Mè Jane made me go along to explain how I had faithfully followed his directions. She made me tell him how Sohrab had not responded to the treatment the way he should. All the while, Ntate Hlalete stared at me, admiring the muscle and height. He stared in amazement at each shift and ripple of my shoulders and arms. If he saw through my lies, he seemed pleased with them.

The herbalist told us to send him a chicken and give him time to think about things. "You ever visit doctory hospital?" he asked as we prepared to leave.

We shook our heads as though we did not believe in such things.

"Those white coats they wear," he said knowingly. "Nothing can touch those white coats. It is strong *muti.*"

When I heard the word *muti*, I felt my bones bulging forth, bent on expansion.

MY MOTHER NOTICED my changing dimensions. Even Dr. Patel noticed.

"Look how you look," Dr. Patel said, looking at me up and down. "So...mature!"

"It's the heat," I said uncomfortably.

"Yes, the heat..."

He came to our house bearing letters from the Post Office. He handed my mother an airmail letter with stamps across the top. We both watched as she stuffed it unread into her shirt pocket. My mother had never liked post from afar. I sometimes found the letters ripped to pieces and burning in the fire, too late to be rescued and nosed through.

At that time, Dr. Patel seemed to find many reasons for being at our house. He engaged my mother in dark conversations that no one understood, even when we could hear. We were not welcome at these conversations.

"What is it that he wants?" I asked 'Mè Jane.

"That usual thing that men want," she answered. " It is the Problem of Men..."

"What thing, 'Mè?"

She looked at me sharply. "Some day you will understand..."

But I already understood more than she knew. The cobras, the eggs, the dogs and all the other creatures had made me understand. Now I was aware of my female parts twitching, pondering the last step toward womanhood. They had been thinking that way for some years. I was well past that Age of Change but I waited, hesitant to release my blood, like a person holding her breath. The more I waited, the more choked was my heart. If I was not a whole woman, then I could not have the heart of a whole woman either.

So 'Mè Jane waited, looked at my size and wondered what had become of Sohrab's *muti*.

Woman or girl, I was not free like Sohrab to scour the region, curious for love. Men looked at me, then looked at me again. Sometimes the boldest of the boys looked at me with a glance that conveyed the Rule of the Wild that the dogs and horses, goats and cobras and mice seemed to obey. But more often they saw that I was a towering person who waited, stuck, choking on childhood, anxious for womanhood to begin, my heart sealed tight from the emotions of women.

"She should prepare herself," commented Dr. Patel. "For college, I mean. She needs bigger places, the way she is growing."

He would know about being big. Dr. Patel was a massive winged creature, shoulders folded, but capable of spreading to great width. He stooped under their very weight and had to move carefully to fit through doorways. If I was huge, then here was a model of hugeness.

Dr. Patel was always courteous around my mother and rarely gave advice without being asked.

"That is my responsibility," she said after a moment. We had the feeling that she too was waiting for me.

"I wonder. Perhaps you should not presume. It would be quite wrong to be solely responsible. Unless you wish to pretend," said Dr. Patel.

"Am I a person who pretends?"

"Sometimes, yes."

"Then perhaps we both pretend..."

They looked at me and I at them. Secrets and lies. At least I could see that Dr. Patel was having no success getting the thing that men wanted.

Now he said, "And what of Sohrab. I see him coming, going, late at night. Do you know where he goes?"

"Of course not..."

"You are not concerned about him, then."

"No." My mother was now daubing paint along the bottom of her canvas. Her brow was creased in concentration and I knew she was not thinking of Dr. Patel or Sohrab. She was somewhere else, her words cleverly made to sound real.

"He goes to the encampment," I said suddenly.

They both stared at me as though I had committed some outrage by speaking. I feigned nonchalance by leaning back in my chair. The chair collapsed, leaving me sprawling on the floor.

"If you do not move," said my mother drily, "nothing more will happen. So, tell me. What does your brother do at night in the encampment? Shop in the Spar? Play soccer?"

I sometimes hated my mother, and when I hated her the breath seemed to go out of me. I needed to be in the open air. I left those two to themselves.

Who didn't know what Sohrab was about? I had seen enough with my own eyes, drawn on by some vague pull of my undelivered ripening. (Sohrab's yearning, Sohrab's lust, I told myself, but I knew it should be mine too.) I had wandered near where he sniffed at the dwellings of certain women, then near the tavern where he hung outside but would not enter. I saw how he followed the prostitutes as though he were a hungry cat.

And what I did not see myself, I discovered from Bushman who was, as ever, drawn to Sohrab, awed by his elder brother, even though he loved to mimic and mock Sohrab's misadventures. Now he went with him to the encampment when Sohrab allowed him, and he came back and told me things, and would have told 'Mè Jane too if I had not threatened to feed him to the cobras if he did. Sometimes he had to remain outside of the range of Sohrab's throwing arm. Other times Sohrab was glad to have a companion, even a strangely perfumed, dancing Bushman that caused women to laugh hysterically or run away in panic. Sohrab had taken to bathing and donning clean clothes, the effect of which Bushman inevitably ruined.

They paraded into the encampment, this strange couple, Sohrab with clean shirt and trousers that hung down his behind. They were Devkumar's trousers and, although they were of the correct length, they bunched around Sohrab's thin waist. He tried to fill them by wearing his playing shorts beneath. He wore soccer boots or Devkumar's old workboots and cultivated a moustache, but it was downy soft yet, like the underfeathers of a young bird stuck beneath his nose.

He hunted through the encampment, through the Spar store, Seanamorena, Dhamba's and the Post Office. Then he circled through Angie's Bar, where they refused to serve him drinks and where drinks were not what he wanted anyway. If it was light enough, he would strip off his pants and join in a football match at the steel-fenced, concretized-clay pitch they called the Football Ground.

But he was not entirely satisfied by the physical thrill and strain of baffling defenders and humiliating the goalkeeper. He thought of women all the time. When he cradled the ball on his foot, he thought of skin, and when he fell against the hard, denuded ground he thought of ecstasy instead of pain.

Sometimes he would meet a young woman and he would follow her until she looked back at him with a laugh. "Touch, Touch, be my husband, Touch," she might say. Sometimes the girls mocked him and ran away. And sometimes a girl did not run and he would follow her to some secluded place where he would touch her, all the time conscious that he was watched by the little laughing orange boy.

He was not satisfied with the encampment. Beyond our small world, there was much more of the thing he sought, but did not well understand.

The two boys flagged a ride one day from the son of an Indian trader. He was only a couple of years older than Sohrab, yet he drove a new BMW car and said he was going past the town to the border post.

"You going to border post too?" he asked casually, as if it were no big matter to cross into the Republic and back again. "I'm for Ficksburg today. Maybe down to Durban next week. And you?"

"Just to Ficksburg," Sohrab said quietly.

At the border post the two were not able to fill in the day-pass applications. The trader's son had to complete the forms and tell the border guard that they were his assistants.

And what of that first day in the *dorp* and the township? What would Mother or 'Mè Jane say if they knew the boys were malingering in another country? What would they say if they knew that Sohrab sniffed hatefully at that country, even on the first day. The signs for WITS and EUROPEANS and COLOURED were ugly. There were no signs for bum Indians or sons of mountain witches. No signs for girl-hunters.

THE PLACES WITHOUT SIGNS were worse. Everyone expected him to know the rules. During the day the farmers came and went with their fat-limbed children. Some had Africans who waited for them in the backs of trucks or in trucks that followed the family car, or stood about in the baking Free State heat while the farmers did their business.

"In this town you must be careful who you talk to and how," the trader's son warned and Sohrab merely glared, knowing that what the boy said was true, but not liking it and not liking the boy because he said it. "They are Boers, you know," added the boy unnecessarily.

"And what is a Boer, anyway?" Sohrab asked.

"Where did you say your people are from?" asked the boy.

"America," answered Sohrab. Then he and Bushman left the trader's son without thanking him.

They came to a shop in which a pretty white-skinned girl stood in the window. She was seventeen or so and had large blonde curls. Her eyes met his and stuck there for a moment despite her every effort. He walked by, then told Bushman to go to the corner and wait without saying or doing anything, or else the Boer police would come and beat him. Then he went back into the store – it was a clothing store for women – and stood among the dresses and pictures of women in knickers and finally, after a long time, the girl came and asked him what he wanted. Sohrab affected a strange accent he had heard in the encampment. "Looking for a gift," he said.

"Where are you from?" asked the girl.

"America," answered Sohrab. "California."

"Ah," said the girl and she blushed and did not notice Sohrab's workboots and the trousers bagged around the thin hips because of the playing shorts worn beneath. She did not notice the clean shirt, or the darkness of his skin either, only the catlike amber of his eyes. "America. How exciting."

She showed him a magazine. It featured photos of actresses and actors walking and waving. It had photos of America. There was a picture of a woman in a bikini walking on a beach, waving at the camera. "Is this where you are from, really?" she gushed.

"Really," said Sohrab and then he leaned over and kissed the girl on the lips, which surprised them both.

Sohrab quickly left the shop, to find that Bushman had deserted his corner and begun walking home in a straight line, singing gaily.

Sohrab returned to the shop three times but never had the nerve to ask the matronly attendant what had become of the girl. On the last occasion there were two guards at the shop doorway. He knew the guards were there to prevent him from entering. They wore the saggy, single-buttoned brown uniform of the National Agric Police.

As for me, I drifted further and further from the shores of womanhood and the rich torrent of emotion and warmth that was part of that distant land. For me there were no kisses or fondling, no soft lips or breathless touches, forbidden or not. There was no feeling of any kind. I was different, my heart closed, on my own journey, the purpose of which was hidden.

Thabo

There was never a photo of Thabo, nor should there have been since he was both evil and ugly. And though his mind and his spirit were dull, he had a burning appetite for our Flori.

Of course Flori can be found in many photos. She had a bright smile that warmed the hearts of women and a figure that warmed the private regions of men. Her face was alive with a kind of mischief that people seemed to want to capture so they could study it later.

In this particular photo, Flori sports a woolen beret and her whole lithesome self is engaged in an act of mirth, her shoulders shaking and her slim hips gyrating.

FROM THE BEGINNING, we suspected that Thabo Majara was not human. He was too tall and narrow and the bones of his shoulders protruded at strange angles. The bones of his head were knobby and misshapen beneath the scant wool of his hair.

So we had hints about what Thabo Majara actually was, and we had a good idea where he would end, even before his throat was cut and his blood soaked the sandy banks of the river. "He is from a nasty place and going to a worse one," 'Mè Jane muttered. She meant *hell*. Now hell was a place both blank and dull. In hell, life and thought were impossible. In hell even the hardiest of spirits withered and weakened. It was worse than the Place of the Dead. Said 'Mè Jane, "It is a place so bad I do not like to say the name."

We could see the hell in Thabo's eyes. When he was drunk it flickered there, red and dangerous, the starved look of an animal from hell.

This Thabo began his life in a stony cluster of huts on a hill near Thaba Phatsoa. It might have been a pleasant place for a boy to grow. A shallow lake, the only one in all the region, nestled between the hills. But Thabo Majara could not swim in the lake, knowing he would sink in the water, dragged to the bottom by his own bones. In the village he was known well as a boy with no sense. Often he suffered beatings at the hands of his uncle or his father for losing goats, breaking bowls, thieving food for his own belly. He became nervous and one day shat in the house. When his father discovered the smelly heap in his usual eating spot, he beat the boy so fiercely young Thabo's brain became unstuck from its moorings.

After that, when Thabo moved his head the brain rolled about making a terrible clatter. It drove him to distraction. He ate grass, roots, feathers, anything to muffle the sound. Nothing helped. They say it was this noise that drove him to capture insects, mice, lizards, dogs, cats. With his brain loose, his skull bones leaden and jutting, he disembowelled, dismembered and decapitated each living thing he caught, staring with his blank red-tinged eyes at the writhing flesh.

Once in a while his brain would find its way into its proper position and he would become still, listening, waiting, stupefied by the sudden silence.

His father and uncle disappeared one day, crossing the border into the Republic in search of money and women. They did not return. Thabo walked out to the roadway in the dusty light and saw below him the glittering lake and beyond that, the black ribbon of bitumen that led to the encampment. He knew nothing of the town except for crowds of strangers whose sheer numbers were a fascination and a danger, and that the uniforms of the policemen down there were held in place by a row of fascinating silver buttons.

Perhaps this was all a loose brain could contain.

He followed the bitumen into the town, thinking to wear one of those uniforms with the silver buttons. He was sixteen. After a few years he was taken on, not by the proper police but by the National Agric Corporation. The crumpled brown uniform had a single silver button which he polished unconsciously while he shuffled, with limbs lank and shoulders stooped, in the places policemen stay: brothels, taverns and sometimes the National Agric Farm. His trouser legs dangled high on his ankles, his neck bobbed in the bulk of the tunic and the bones of his head shifted restlessly as his brain rolled about, untethered and noisy.

The first time he came to our compound 'Mè Jane chased him away, her shovel looking more potent than the "K" gun that Thabo dragged in the dirt. He had tried to explain something to her, but he was not a man of words. Words confused him, as though he could not hear the sounds that his mouth formed because of the noises already in his head. Or perhaps his brain was too jumpy to cling to a sentence over the time it took to say it from beginning to end. No one knew. He said, "O 'Mè, I look for...for...for..."

For what? We did not know at first.

"What can that lost soldiah want here?" 'Mè Jane asked the house in general.

From somewhere within came the silvery laugh of Flori. Then we knew.

It was easy to see why men came looking for Flori, for she was of taut figure and quick eyes. There was a way her head dipped as she gave a glance that slid from beneath her lids, like a hand slipping along a leg. And she knew how to walk in a way that made men stop. In fact, she had all the womanly things I lacked. My body was a landscape of drought, unable to bloom without rain. Hers was a lush and verdant garden.

"Is this your boy, Aousi," 'Mè Jane demanded of Flori.

"No 'Mè."

"When has this soldiah seen you? In the town? On the street? I will belabour you with a stick, Aousi. *Belabour*, do you hear..."

"'Mè?"

"That one is not nice. Ugly, in fact. Ugly! At least you must leave the ugly ones and the bad ones..."

THABO DID NOT RETURN to our house right away. But we discovered that he was nearby, lurking in the valley, sitting alone in makeshift *shabeens*, the women avoiding his red-tinged stare, the men repelled by the shiny button and the constant racket emanating from his skull.

"Tell him you are unavailable for his *soldiah* nonsense...," muttered 'Mè Jane.

But Flori took this as permission to leave the house. She sneaked away, tossing her work frock into the shed as she went. She would speak to Thabo Majara, poor soul. She liked his bony head as much as she liked any other part of him. Down the path she went with hips a-sway. Down into the parts of the valley where it was still green. Then she came home hours later with pieces of grass woven through her hair.

'Mè Jane was furious, but there was nothing she could do. She belaboured Flori with a stick but Flori only giggled under the blows and skipped away. "'Mè, please 'Mè, you must not kill me..." she called with her silvery laugh.

She snuck away to meet Thabo Majara regularly. In the mornings she had bruises on her face and cuts on her legs.

Majara became bold. He found out when Mother and 'Mè Jane were away from the house, then came clattering along the path in the middle of one afternoon, and on into our house.

When his blank eyes fell upon Bushman, Sohrab and I where we sat huddled around a smoky coal fire, he stopped. Those eyes passed over us one way, then the other, causing our mouths to dry. We could see that the eyes were remembering Sohrab from that day Sohrab and Glorius were captured and taken inside the National Agric Farm. His gaze clung to Sohrab. He stepped forward as though curious to see him better, perhaps to seek forgiveness, or perhaps to touch the soft new hair on Sohrab's head. But he could not maintain this concentration long enough to finish whatever it was he had started. His eyes changed, went on, taking into their emptiness the contraptions and heat lamp and opened books, the prayer flags, the canvas on the easel and my mother's latest experiment – something concerning the power of water to draw itself along glass, except that the water escaped to drip onto the paint-spattered floor.

Flori emerged and jumped as though Thabo Majara were a puff adder. She threw off her dust frock and left the house without a word, Majara clattering some way behind.

After this, Sohrab stayed carefully out of view when Majara was near.

But Bushman took an unhealthy interest in the couple. Flori and Majara's wandering search for privacy was excellent entertainment. He took to following them to where they lay in the long grass or stood coupling in the shade of a rock. He came home choked with excitement, telling me of the way Flori's rump looked with the stalk of the policeman's sex stuck into her, or the way she squealed and laughed and scratched and bit.

"See, first they push, then he hits her, then she hits back," he told me, bursting with laughter. "Push, push, push, that is what they do." He bore down so his eyes went red and the veins bulged in his neck as he thrust with his hips at me grunting, "Push, push..."

I told him that if Thabo Majara caught him he would slice off his little worm before he could run away. Bushman just laughed. "If he pull my trousers, he find snake..." He yanked out his penis and swung it around until I spat at him. He was getting too big for such pranks.

That was how Bushman came to track and hunt out the Pushing Thing. He hunted throughout the valley, poked his head into the rooms of lovers, followed the slick track of their matings.

It would have been better not to have heard about this spying, but Bushman relished explaining everything to me, as though these couplings were the doings of some strange insect species only he had observed. "Even the old people do it, even men do it with goats," he yelped, and I had to listen. It filled my sleep with naked sweaty figures and I awoke many nights sure that the *thokolosi* was prodding me with his stiff pecker. We became preoccupied by Push. We suspected everyone of doing it, planning to do it, or remembering the last time they did it. I took to secretly watching the ways of Flori, her svelte grace, her leonine readiness. I saw what men saw: her ripeness, her openness and her heat. I became fascinated with the men who watched her. I saw their coiled cobras and stones hanging in sacks. I saw the rise of blood and the ideas that flickered across their eyes. I saw it in Sohrab and Glorius Sebane, and even Dr. Patel. Only Thabo Majara's eyes were always empty.

Bushman went where children were not allowed, behind the taverns and by the windows of darkened rooms. In the alley behind the brothel and in the dells and holes of fornicators. More than anything he loved to follow Flori and Thabo Majara, for they bore with them the pungency of danger and violence, the dizzy scent of steam and sweat and the juices of sex. And there was more, sometimes before and sometimes after the coupling, when they went at each other with tooth bared and fist clenched. There were robust blows exchanged and even the glint of Thabo Majara's knife. Sometimes we saw her bruises and cuts the next day. Sometimes she groaned with pain as she moved around the house.

"Fight, then push, then fight," chanted Bushman.

But Flori knew she was being watched by small eyes. Rather than chase her pursuer off and risk being ridiculed, she played another game, a game of chase and hide. She took to meeting Thabo Majara at places far from the house, running to catch a ride at the road, casting a laughing glance behind her. Bushman was forced to find resources. Sometimes he searched the house for money, wordlessly, his cheeks flushed with excitement, as he scrabbled about the floor of Devkumar Uncle's shed for the few tarnished *lisente* pieces there. Sometimes he begged rides on trucks or on the carts of farmers. Then he would wander at the edge of the district, tracking with his nose until he found traces of them. Semen in a clump of grass. A hastily cast-aside pair of knickers, still damp and warm. And blood. Like the spoor of a wounded prey-animal, there was always blood. The smell, the residues of lovers, filled the holes in his head like dirty tar.

Flori knew all of this and more. She knew that it was not only Bushman who spied out her coupling.

During this period – it may have lasted a year – we saw little of Sohrab and presumed that he had his own business in the encampment or across the border. He was secretive, and came and went without his Bushman shadow.

THAT LAST TIME Flori and Majara met was during school vacation and the college was almost empty. Nearby the watchman, Ntate Lekhlaba, could be heard muttering and spitting as he stalked some unfortunate cat near the trash pit. The wind swirled upward, filled with dead grass. Bushman loitered nearby in the shadows.

We knew that she had become tired of him. Her bruises had become fewer, while Thabo now walked with a limp, and when he opened his mouth there were gaps in his teeth and his lips were cut.

Flori was impatient to be left alone. She walked with him part way along the drive to the road then came back. We could hear her voice drifting toward us on the heated, upwelling air. "*Phoetsak, phoetsak*, why you don't have some other wife..." and then she called him some names we had not thought of. Small boy, one-eye, fat nose. She walked fast under the eaves of the classrooms to the end of the campus, Thabo trailing awkwardly. Then they suddenly vanished into a doorway.

THE WIND BLEW Flori's hem up and she swept it back. Only Bushman saw the glint of Thabo's homemade knife and heard a strange rasp in his breath.

"Stop killing me, Ntate," Flori said. "These winds are my ancestors. They will remember every time you kill me..."

Thabo stopped, and his head rattled noisily as though a marble were searching for the bottom of some battered bowl. He tried to see the wind and found he could not. He looked forlornly at Flori, opened his mouth and said only, "Oh?"

There was no saying how it was that they came to be in the laboratory. That the door was not locked was not unusual, since my mother used the classroom and the library and the lab as places to escape the chaos of our house when she needed to. Perhaps they had discovered every unlocked room and every shadowy place in the region. Or perhaps there was some magic that hung about that place that drew them in.

He shoved her ahead of him into the laboratory and she fought back. She bit and scratched. She got her arms around his bony neck and almost broke it. But he cut her on the leg, on the thigh, then he ripped her dress from bust to hem and caught the knife tip in the wooden bench between her legs. She broke from him with a shriek, fled into the storeroom as he worked the blade loose. She crawled under a table and seized a bottle and broke it.

Bushman heard all. He danced outside in the dust, for this was the best push-game he had seen. It made him want to sing. Then Flori came out of the laboratory at a run, her dress ripped, her leg bloody. She ran up the path and into the house.

Thabo Majara emerged from the laboratory a while later clutching the body of a large golden cobra. With the limp snake hanging from his hand, he went away along the road from the college and on toward his home. He staggered, but his head was quieter than it had been in years. Now and again he stopped to hear the unfamiliar quiet.

As he came to the clinic of the herbalist Hlalete, he slung the dead snake over his shoulder. A new sign had been erected in front of the clinic and the clinic had been painted all white. The sign said, DR. HLALETE (KIEV).

Majara staggered into the white interior. "Listen," he said to Hlalete. "Listen to my head..."

Hlalete listened. "Hm," he said. He looked at the snake on Majara's shoulder and invited him into an anteroom. Hlalete wore a T-shirt and white clinician's coat, topped by a woman's red bouffant wig tilted to one side like a jaunty bowler hat. His pockets jangled with metallic medical instruments alongside bones. Around his neck he wore a stethoscope.

Hlalete looked at the snakebite on Majara's leg. He cleaned it and patched on a *muti* of herbs and mud. Then he filled a syringe with fluid, which he injected into both legs. There were a number of customers waiting outside, so he went out, returning now and again to look in on Majara.

After a while Majara addressed the snake. He told it that he loved it and that he knew it had acted correctly. As he talked his eyes became round, his breathing shallow. Yet his voice was clear, his words precise. He spoke as he had never spoken before, of

matters that had always eluded him. He spoke of his future and
of the past, of his hopes and regrets. He told the snake he
wanted above all to leave this place and go abroad in the dying
day. There were many tasks to be completed, things that he had
left neglected. He had wronged people because of his noisy
brain. Now he wished to make amends. All of this in a continuous river of eloquence from a body ridden with cobra poison.
His brain had swollen to fill the inside of his head perfectly.

Now his legs and head became hot, his muscles spongy. He
stood. His words became a whisper. Quietly he bathed his head
in a pan of water and, tossing his companion on his shoulder
once more, slipped away from Hlalete's clinic.

As he walked along, falling sometimes, but hardly noticing,
he became aware of Bushman. He turned to face Bushman but
saw only a shadow. "Are you the spirit of snake?" he asked.

Bushman said nothing.

"Spirit of snake, the poison has blinded me."

Bushman came close. He walked in front of Thabo Majara,
circled him, then took his hand and led him along the road into
the darkening valley. They stopped every few metres so that
Majara could rest. They listened to the whisper of other things
slithering in the air.

Bushman led Thabo Majara into the blackness of the grove
where the head lived and sat him on the ground. Majara waited,
his eyes no longer distinguishing light from darkness, the sounds
around him diminishing, his breath slowing.

Afterwards, Bushman came home. He said nothing of this
night until a long time later.

In the morning Thabo Majara was found by the bank of the
river with his throat cut.

deadkumar

The Money Game
1986

The police never told us that Sohrab was charged with the murder of Thabo Majara. There was no official letter. That was not how they worked. They wanted us to come to them, to their web and their nest, where the rules of the world were different and policemen were respectable and other people were laughable and stupid and sometimes annoying enough to beat. But we were restrained from going forth to the Police Fortress, even though in our hearts we yearned to find Sohrab and rescue him. There we would at least see with our own eyes, know that he had not already been killed and dumped behind the dam. But my mother told us that if we were caught near that place it would bring more trouble. She held us back with the look in her eye and her silence. That silence spread like an infection, among us, so that for a long time no one talked or made a sound.

In all other ways, Mother was at a loss. She said little, though we sometimes saw her confer in secret tones with Dr. Patel in the corner of the compound. They brooded over new lies, two cobras counting their eggs. Even with Sohrab captured and his life in mortal danger, she shunned the truth.

In the silence we imposed on ourselves, our dreams were cold and dark. We dreamed of Sohrab with eyes faded and body

III

hanging. 'Mè Jane burned dead grass and let the smoke entangle our hair. She made us eat *moroho*.

Eventually mice must have found a way up the path from the valley. They found places to leave their droppings in our house. We heard rumours that certain of Thabo Majara's internal organs had been stolen before he died. That Sohrab was beaten, had fought and was bloodied but alive...

Then a strange thing happened. These rumours, left behind by wandering rodents, went beyond our community and travelled all the way to the Dead Place. That was how dead Devkumar Uncle heard. That was how he appeared among us.

In a way, we were prepared to receive him. So much had happened. We were now forced to open our minds. We listened for the strange noises of spirits and lesser beings. We listened to everything.

THERE WAS SPECULATION about the Devkumar Thing:

That Devkumar had come back for Flori (we heard this from Flori herself); that Devkumar was really a vengeful spirit who had taken over Devkumar Uncle's corpse; that if we ate too much we would attract many, many Devkumars and that they had so proliferated in the Other Place that they had run out of food and women.

Speculation about Thabo Majara:

That he had been seen talking to a white man in a uniform. This caused many people to wonder about South Africans, and we thought of Defence Force Police; that Thabo Majara was himself a South African and was actually a white man in disguise.

No one laughed at these stories. 'Mè Jane waggled her head from side to side and said it was all entirely possible, since we now knew that the Dead could return any time they chose, even during daylight.

Everywhere we looked we were reminded of the queerness of life and death. We heard the fish-flopping footsteps of Dead Devkumar Uncle in the shadows of the classrooms. It was hard not to raise our eyes and look upon a thing from the Afterworld that wandered among us as though nothing could be more normal. It was an inescapable presence, a bad smell that hung about the compound, poking about in the vacated flat opposite our house. We noticed that only we understood what it was.

Typical of the Dead, it preferred the dark.

IT SOON BECAME EVIDENT that Mother would not have a dead man back, even if the person it came from had once shared her bed. She was not the lonely type and had always been uncomfortable around the messes left behind by others.

"Why is he back? What does he want?" she finally asked.

"Sohrab is his son," Dr. Patel reminded her.

"How can he stay? There is no place for him here." Her voice was quiet and intent. It was this voice that one had to beware of. The ears of the dogs Mpho and Kalu perked up when she spoke that way. So did ours. So did Dr. Patel's. "What would you have me do?"

Dr. Patel cleared his throat and said with some effort, "Welcome him home, of course."

The worst was yet to come. One day Dr. Patel and the Devkumar Thing nosed through the long-abandoned flat at the end of our compound. The next day Dead Devkumar and Ntate Lekhlaba were in there cleaning the place in preparation for a new occupant.

My mother said, "You welcome a coward? A man driven by fear?"

"Fear drives all of us," shrugged Dr. Patel. "Heroes and cowards..."

"How could you?"

"He needs a place...everyone needs a place..."

"But why *this* flat?"

"It is the only one."

"And have you not noticed that our colleagues have all run away? There are no teachers left here but you and I."

"Officially the flats are still occupied. You know, Zara, I do not understand you. He needs *discretion*. You know this very well. You must not let it bother you at this time."

"Well, it bothers me at this time."

"Zara, this is the man whose son you bore," whispered Patel.

"That was nothing...you are right. You do not understand me. You never have."

Patel cringed, unprepared, as usual, for direct frontal assault. Without intending to, he had crossed the border from Mother's ambivalence into her resentment. This resentment was a rocky country and windy. He tried mightily to find a way back but was quite lost. One day he brought her a cheap set of paints, another day an old book of poetry from his shelf. Mother noticed none of it. She was preoccupied with the fate of Sohrab. She was outraged at having to share her grieving with Sohrab's dead pa.

"Old Patel might want push," Bushman commented as he scratched his crotch.

I slapped the side of his head but he only giggled and slapped back.

THE DEAD DEVKUMAR moved things into the flat. The place was small – one room and a bathroom. The floor was littered with mouse turds and the shredded paper and the threads that mice use to build nests. Dead Devkumar stumbled through the remnants of furniture that someone had broken up for firewood, ducked its head to avoid the bats that flapped down from the ceiling. Sighed at the broken windows and doors. The Dead Thing was as quiet and solemn as a Dead can be.

But in other ways it was not what we expected of a Dead. All those years Devkumar was gone, we had pictured him dissolved into dark bubbles and an eternal sludge at the bottom of the sea. We had wanted to remember Devkumar Uncle the way he had been. But all we could see was his eyes drowned in seawater, the last breath sliding from his mouth, his flesh limp, his flesh decayed and sodden. Fingers curled, clutching for his lost flutes. It was a shock to see this dead remnant of him walking about, and, stranger still, clambering into the papery car that had brought it. The Thing oddly seemed to believe that this fragile and decrepit-looking auto would bear it along in the Living World. We were amazed to see that car go out and come back, until we realized that it was from the Dead Place and so ran on some other principle.

That car went out and returned with salvaged machines. Broken radios that belonged to villagers. A tape recorder that could be held in the palm of one hand. An oven that used no heat. A television that functioned for a day, then reverted to a flickering fog. We suspected that these things came from the Dead, or at least from across the border in the Orange Free State.

The dead Devkumar tinkered listlessly for a time amid the wreckage of the flat. Then it seemed to collect itself and methodically began to restore the place. It cleaned out the mess, erected a new wall, repaired the plumbing pipes and electrical wires. As the flat improved, Dead Devkumar began to resemble the living man it once had been. One day the car failed to start and the Thing performed a furious car-kicking dance, leaving pockmarks along the thin metal.

We watched all this from where we sat in the shade of the roof. We were as still as lizards, hoping the flow of our lives would slow to a trickle. But our concentration had been ruined by the Thing.

"Mastah Devkumar, he looks almost alive..." 'Mè Jane uttered with a dry cough.

WE HAD BEEN CAREFUL to keep our distance up until this point. We had stayed upwind as much as possible and, when it was not possible, we had held our noses for fear of whiffing the rankness of the Dead. But our curiosity was gradually overcoming our fear. We let ourselves move closer, to hear and see how a Dead seemed to live without breathing and eating. Finally one day 'Mè Jane muttered that Mastah must be famished and she prepared rice and savoury curried chicken and apricot pie. We brought these to his door, our noses twitching and our eyes wide.

"Mastah Devkumar," called 'Mè Jane. "We have brought you victuals."

Then we looked upon the dead man at close range for the first time.

A short, narrow-chested man like the live Devkumar Uncle must overcome his lack of physical stature with boldness, even though there is nothing that can overcome well-oiled pink lips that slide continually over protruding front teeth. Photographs of Devkumar Uncle showed a man hiding his mouth with his hand, a glass, or a handkerchief. In some photos his lips were curiously apelike and mischievous. In no photo was his face revealed in its entirety. I understood other reasons for this later, but at the time I thought that he must always have thought back to his childhood when a photo was a rare and important record that might last, yellowed and entombed in glass, for generations. In real life his teeth gave him the aggressive, greedy look of a rat.

Of course, the Thing lacked the boldness of the live Devkumar Uncle. The hair of the Thing was grey and thinning at the top, the face creased. It sat at the table with the pieces of a revolver arrayed upon a clean cloth. It beckoned to us to come forward. It inspected us.

"How come you took so long to visit, hanh?"

We held the plates of food before us.

The flat did not smell like the sea. It was clean and fresh, the floor waxed and polished to a gleam, the windows spotless, the walls newly painted. The few chairs and the low table had been stripped of paint to reveal the brightsome grain of pine wood. The refrigerator in a corner hummed. Through a doorway, the many machines he had collected stood on a workbench awaiting repair. Below the bench was a travelling bag.

The late Devkumar Uncle ate our offerings with dedication, then sat back and sighed. "I know why you never came before," it said, holding up a finger. "Devkumar goes. Devkumar comes back. No one ever tells you what he is doing. Where is he gone? As far as you know, Devkumar might have gone hell and back."

'Mè Jane and I shuffled our feet uneasily in the supreme effort it took not to look at each other or say something obvious. We took heart from the fact that it took extraordinary nerve to listen to a dead man speak of its travels to hell.

But because it seemed to await some word of reply, I stammered, "Was it nice?"

"I'll tell you all that later when you big," it said, then its eyes widened and it added, "which might be soon by the look of things..." The dead man reached across and pinched my cheek as though I were a little girl. I failed to suppress a shudder. "And beside, we got more important matter to think about..."

"Mastah Sohrab," sighed 'Mè Jane.

"Money," corrected Dead Devkumar Uncle.

"Money?"

"Hanh. Money. Whole world made up of money, did you know that, Child? It is money make us rich and money make us poor, money make us prisoner and money make us free. That is what I found out all this time I was gone. Money, money, money..."

"And what of the young mastah?" sputtered 'Mè Jane. She found this money talk alarming.

"Money make Sohrab free. All we do is put money in right keyhole and door open. Magic." It said this with such conviction that I almost clapped my hands.

"Yes, Mastah Devkumar, yes," said 'Mè Jane happily. "Let us just do it."

"Course, you got to have enough of the damn thing..."

"You don't have any money, do you..."

"Nah, Child. Had money, lost money..."

"Maybe Mastah D. knows someone with money...," suggested 'Mè Jane hopefully.

I looked at her carefully, wondering if she remembered what quarter such help might come from.

The dead remains of Devkumar Uncle shook its head slowly. "I fought against money. Money is my enemy, not my friend."

"Or how to get money...," she persisted, her voice dropping half a tone.

It squinted at the floor and shrugged. "Money got no sense of value. It just follow along according to game of rich and poor. It's a big game, nothing more," it said. "All we need is to know the rules, start playing, then – freedom for Sohrab. All we need is to know rules."

"And to win...," I added helpfully.

It frowned.

At this point our noses were tweaked by the smell of the sea. We were reminded to look for barnacles on Devkumar Uncle's skin.

"Good game of money is not too hard to play," it was saying, eyeballs bulging. "Just like stick and ball. But everybody, sooner or later, they got to play, even that monkey kid you found..."

We took the empty dishes and retreated. When we were well away from the door, we released our held breath.

WE WONDERED what money game Dead Devkumar Uncle could possibly play to win freedom for Sohrab. The fact that he had none of the stuff did not give us confidence in his abilities.

"Maybe Madam has money," hummed 'Mè Jane.

"Yes. Locked away in a box somewhere."

"Or perhaps she has some but does not know she has it... Madam is forgetful."

"Maybe she knows how to play Money Game really well."

"Or maybe Mastah Patel..."

We struggled up the path from the river. Our well had gone dry. We had gone from piped water to rainwater to well water. Now we made the trip to the river each day carrying plastic pails and cans. Deep down, we suspected that our dreams of playing with money were ridiculous, but somehow we took some solace in our stupid hopes.

We heaved the water into our storage barrel. A mouse jumped out of the spout and Bushman shot out of the shadows after it. He caught it in his hands and sat on the step nearby muttering and trying to see through the cracks between his fingers.

"Deadkumar cannot help trapped mouse," he said.

We stopped talking and looked at him.

After some time 'Mè Jane remarked. "He is *Dev*kumar not *Dead*kumar."

"Deadkumar," said Bushman. "Only some of him not really dead. The push parts – they not dead..."

With a shrug, 'Mè Jane went inside to prepare the evening meal.

"What do you mean?" I hissed.

"Not all of Deadkumar is quite dead," said Bushman. He opened his hands slowly, but the mouse had forgotten how to run. It sat frozen in his palm, only its nose atwitter.

COAL SMOKE wreathed the buildings. Women called out in tired voices as they brought their water home. Nearby, free mice rustled in the dead grass, dodging cobras and collecting seeds.

These free mice smelled our caught mouse and became still and watchful. In the distance the car of dead Devkumar Uncle grunted along the lane to the road. Bushman beckoned me to follow him down the path to the college. There we waited in a bush until darkness and the return of the Devkumar Dead Thing and the car from hell. After some hours we saw the car scrabbling along the rocks like some sea creature trapped on dry land. It lurched to a stop in the dried brush.

We could not see who was in the car at first, but after a time we heard two women and Deadkumar talking quietly. Then they climbed out and were silent. We thought we could see the glow of the Afterworld on those people. Small lights flickered in the place where real people have eyes. We detected the faint sweet odour of rotten flesh. Then they turned away and walked back up the road through the normal sounds and smells of the campus.

"...more of the Dead."

But Bushman said, "Or maybe from Jo'burg..."

"And do they...do the Push thing?"

"Well...," he said. "No."

Deadkumar stood by the car in the gloom. It was the still time of day when the Dead slip over the rim of the Living World to create problems for those asleep. When the women were well out of sight and Bushman and I were beginning to itch, Deadkumar went round and opened the boot of the car. He shifted something in there, stood over it silently. Finally the boot was closed and the Thing shuffled away on broken-backed shoes.

We crept to the car and opened the boot. I stood back expecting some evil thing, a *thokolosi* or worse. But there was nothing save for a spare tyre covered neatly with a clean blanket. In my heart I knew that this empty compartment, or even the overly neat spare, were the secrets of the place Deadkumar Uncle had come from. But we were afraid to know more. Bushman shuddered and closed the boot. His mouse climbed out of his hand and stood waiting by his foot. Then we went our way under a moon that looked like a bowl of maize spilled on someone's dirt floor.

Our Friends

We had never seen my mother ill.

We thought it strange though, how Mother reacted. First she was silent, then she gave up on Sohrab and did not like to hear his name. She became weak and pale and ill. The less she heard about him, the more ill she became. Of course, it seemed to us that she had a bad reaction to the stench of rotting seaweed and the futile flopping sound of a fish out of water. Sohrab's father walking dead among us made her head ache. She began to shrink and fade and her shoulders sagged.

Then, just as Deadkumar settled into the flat at the end of the compound, my mother began to move out. At first she stayed away for a few hours at a time in the college library, saying she needed to think. Each day she shifted more of her things there. Books, an easel, paints and charcoals and pencils. Not that she was using any of these things. She sat at a large study table amid bookshelves that supported wisps and scraps of paper and large, sluggish silverfish. In the midst of this dust and abandonment, she thought empty thoughts that were not properly of this place.

Dr. Patel made Ntate Lekhlaba forsake his morning cat hunt in order to stoke the fire and charge the kerosene lanterns in the library. Our part was to ferry trays down the path. This was not difficult since my mother ate almost nothing. She drank tea, so 'Mè Jane made us strengthen it with red roots and condensed milk and honey until Mother complained.

"Madam needs special strong tea," announced 'Mè Jane.

"I am not a Madam anything. And since when do I need strong tea? This root tea is for the old folks that wander the villages."

"It is for the ill, Madam," 'Mè Jane said respectfully but definitely so that my mother had to hear it.

"I?" she scoffed, but we could see in her eyes that she was sick, and, now that 'Mè Jane said it, she knew she was sick.

She had us make up a bed in the midst of the abandonment and despair of the library. After that, my mother never really went home again.

AS JULY CAME ON, a bitter wind blew down from the icefields of the highlands. On these nights Bushman slept with the dogs and I curled myself into 'Mè Jane's bed as I had since childhood, although lately she had begun to mutter about it. My feet hung out the end of her short pallet. I could not get comfortable thinking about my mother freezing alone and empty-minded beneath her *rizahi*. On some nights I went down in the dark to sit miserably by her for a few moments. I would return, driven back to warmth.

Everyone began to worry about my mother. Dr. Patel found he needed to order about Ntate Lekhlaba more than usual and came shuffling about the library several times a day to see that things were looked after. Mother did not seem to mind.

And there was that Deadkumar. It dared not invade Mother's sanctuary at first, but we saw it peering in at her doorway and windows. It made its strange, otherwordly sounds as it crept about the countryside, circling the encampment but not daring the police by going in. We assumed that it searched for a money game to play. Other times it appeared with the Jo'burg women in its car, or met them by the road. Bushman and I caught a good look at those ladies once or twice. They were strangely alive, two of them sinuous and svelte as cats, their long limbs slicing smoothly through the air, the muscles on their haunches rippling through their scant skirts. I had to admire the ease with which they wore their high-heeled shoes. The third woman was younger and had not learned these graces. But she seemed made of some special live rubber material, her breasts and bottom springing in unpredictable directions whenever she shifted her weight. We had never seen a woman who had that much bounce.

Bushman was fascinated by this young rubber woman. He stopped making jokes about pushing, became solemn and respectful and clutched his crotch with both hands. It became his business to follow her, and he eventually let on that she came and went freely from the police fortress.

I lay cold in bed thinking. How was it that Deadkumar consorted with police agents? I tossed this way and that and finally 'Mè Jane sat up and said, "Tell me what is your trouble, Child." I told her everything. About the neatly placed spare tyre and the women and the police fortress.

When she heard this, 'Mè Jane lit a lantern and went out to the latrine. She came back and piled her day blanket atop the other blankets and turned the other way. By her breathing I knew she lay awake, sharing my confusion.

The next day when we brought my mother her tea we found her weeping by a window. I put my arms around her while 'Mè Jane muttered and fussed with a broom. Mother was cool, her tears icy.

Dr. Patel came. He was useless in this storm of grief. He fretted and squirmed while my mother said nothing and wept as though she were alone.

"Tea, tea," 'Mè Jane hissed at me. I poured tea and placed the cup in Mother's hand. As I looked upon her, I suddenly saw that she was as weak as an infant. I stepped back, startled by my vision.

"We should not have come here. It was a mistake," said Mother. She seemed not to address anyone. We looked at one another.

"Everyone makes mistakes," Patel offered. He moved aimlessly about near the window, squinting now and again at Mother as though she were some brilliant light.

"Now Sohrab is gone. He was just a child..." she wept.

'Mè Jane straightened up. "Madam. Is Mastah Abuti Sohrab gone to the Ancestors?"

Mother wept at the floor. "His life was all ahead of him."

I sagged and might have fallen had not 'Mè Jane come and held me up. "Who has brought this news?" she finally asked.

Mother shook her head and wept with new vigour.

"Go," said Patel. "Go and bring Nagarajah."

I went out of there, somehow making my numb legs work the path to Deadkumar's flat.

Deadkumar said, "Crying? Only time I saw that woman cry was when she got her hand jam in water pump. Then she cry like cat and dog both." He pushed his feet into his broken shoes and stumped behind me down the path. "That woman your ma. All kinds of things happen in her life so far. She never cry. Then that pump bite her right in the soft part between her thumb and finger and she wail like baby for a whole day. Hoo! I thought she never stop! She must have saved that crying up for years and then it all come down at once."

As we came to the door of the library I told him about Sohrab.

Deadkumar stopped and said, "You sure she said this?" Then he scratched his head and stood for a moment scanning the dull sky. His eyes were red from years of salt water. His eyes must have stung. "Anyway, don't worry about anything."

And, for some unaccountable reason, it seemed as though everything would come out right. I even had the most fleeting and absurd sensation of joy.

We went on through the door into the dark and cold of Mother's place. She was not pleased to see Deadkumar Uncle. She went to the coal bucket and selected a handful of coals, which she placed in a neat row on the window ledge next to her.

"Zara, what is this big news I hear about Sohrab?"

"It's too late for talk," she said flatly. "No one did anything and now it's too late."

"Now what do you mean by that, Zara-woman?"

"What do you think it means, you stupid little man?"

"But how the hell you know anything about Sohrab? I never saw you leave this place. You never went down to the town to check on that boy..."

"He's dead. I know it."

"When you went to town, Girl?"

Mother said nothing now.

"Maybe you heard something from someone...?"

Then she began weeping afresh. "I saw what they did to him. They tied his hands and feet. Grown men set upon him..."

"But how do you know all of these things, Madam?" asked 'Mè Jane.

But Mother would only shake her head and sob and fiddle with coals on the window ledge.

"She had the dream of death," said 'Mè Jane finally, her voice low.

Deadkumar Uncle winked at me and said something like, "Ho, ah-hah, ho, ha..."

There was no use trying to explain a death dream. They are as real as everyday life.

Dr. Patel said, "We must not delay any more. We must go see for ourselves. We must go to the police fortress."

"They will beat us away, Mastah," said 'Mè Jane. "They will beat us away like flies."

"No, we must go. What do you think, Nagarajah?"

Deadkumar Uncle had wandered away with hands out-stretched towards the fire. As the fire heated up, his smell, sharp and briny, wafted about the room. It was easy to forget that Deadkumar Uncle was a member of the Dead. "You asking me what I think, Patel? You really want the opinion of a useless thing like me?"

"Please, Sir, now is not the time for that...," said Patel.

"Okay. I will tell all of you something. I did not come back here for zero-nothing. You know I cannot go in the police fortress any better than you can. But I have got my eyes down there watching for me."

"Who?" asked Patel.

"People."

"Who people?" demanded Mother.

"Brothers, sisters. People I trust."

'Mè Jane suddenly plucked at my sleeve and said it was time to fetch fresh tea.

I pretended not to hear. I felt the presence of an important truth here. It was a shy creature, lurking in the shadow. There were phrases, tones, a certain look in the eyes of the adults. Perhaps this was the truth that had always fetched up beyond my reach, just out of earshot. I suddenly felt that I had always played along, unconscious, perhaps fearful of what I would know. Now things were different.

In this single day I had sniffed the mortality of my brother Sohrab, and yet also glimpsed a strange realm of joy.

'Mè Jane was still tugging at my sleeve, but I stood large and immovable. The three, Mother, Patel and Dead Devkumar, looked at us sidelong.

"Go with 'Mè Jane and prepare tea, Girl," said Mother heavily. "Go on."

I almost obeyed. But my feet were planted, refusing to listen. I looked at my feet in wonderment at being forced to follow their will. Then my voice spoke as if it too had a will of its own. "I know your secrets," my voice said. "You think I don't understand, but I do. I do."

Mother was startled at first, but she carefully composed herself and flushed with life for the first time that day. Even Deadkumar looked alive, saying, "What secrets you talking about, Honey." It was the old, smooth voice, the one we had so often heard him use on Flori, Mother and other women.

"About the thing in the boot of your car..." I said carefully. Part of me wanted to tell them that I knew everything about the Place where Deadkumar had come from, about the pushing that had been going on all through the district and about all the people who had done it. About how Deadkumar and Flori were once quite good at it and how Sohrab had been doing it more than most adults and how Dr. Patel, despite his grey hair, sometimes longed for it so much he did it by himself. But my voice had a will of its own. It sounded cool and adult. My voice held back and used the tactics of liars, concealing more than it revealed.

The smell of seagull poop and slippery stones and dead fish and half-rotted weeds steamed off of Deadkumar. He fixed his eyes on my feet, blankly staring at their autonomous nature. Mother studied a lump of coal thoughtfully.

Dr. Patel said, "Well, she is your daughter, Zara. Your responsibility. Perhaps she would like to tell everyone about the boot of Mr. Nagarajah's car."

Dead Devkumar continued to stare at my feet and they began to sweat and to wonder if they had made a mistake. "Never mind that," he said when it became apparent that I was not saying more. "Important thing is we get that boy back. Look at your ma. She needs calm. She got a lot of strain on her lately. You just leave everything to Devkumar, Zara. Devkumar will manage."

Mother hefted a piece of coal, estimated its weight and hardness, then she wound up her arm and hurled it at Deadkumar. It bounced off his belly. "Stop," she hissed. "I have no patience for dishonesty."

I would have laughed if my mother had not looked so awful. Black lines spiralled around her eyes.

"I think she wants you to tell us about this boot-of-car matter," suggested Dr. Patel. "You better tell us, Nagarajah. What is going on?"

Deadkumar sucked on his teeth, then seemed to change his mind about something important. He shrugged, lifted his palms in appeal. "Devkumar never say anything but truth. I tell high truth, low truth, all different kinds. Different story, different people, right Patel-Sahib? This-a-way, that-a-way, right? You know what happens when an animal is hurt. You better not trust it, because that thing will get mad. It could attack, even bite when you don't expect. Animal in pain is not reliable, you know? I am one of those animal. I got pain, you know that? I bust my heart to come back. I give up things, take biggest risk of my life to come back. What I find? Place of pain. Not just because Sohrab detain. But you people! Pain from everybody in this place, my home. That crying woman right there. That Zara. She kill me every day. Kill the life right out of me..."

Mother picked up a piece of coal and glared at it in a kind of fury. She wanted to throw again, to shut his mouth, but she could not. She needed Deadkumar. We all did. "I'm sorry," she muttered.

Deadkumar held up his hands with palms up, accepting this small apology as though it were great bounty.

"Now, Nagarajah, please. How is it you are so certain that Sohrab is alive? And what is this about the boot of your car?" said Patel.

"Hokay, that. See, I got girlfriends working in the police fortress. The police chaps like them, everybody likes them. They like me. They watch out for Sohrab for me, and I do favour for them. Nothing big, just small favour – keep spare tyre in boot of car is all..."

"They watch out for Sohrab."

"I get news every day..."

"And the tyre, what about this tyre."

"Nothing much. Spare tyre..."

"And inside is only air, is it?"

"And another thing or two..."

"What?"

"Grenades," said Deadkumar quietly. "Some plastics maybe...gifts for Our Friends."

New York and Safari

"Our Friends?" said Dr. Patel. "What business do we have with Our Friends?"

The wind rattled through the loose roof panels of the library. But inside we were hushed and the world was hushed, awaiting the truth.

"No business," answered Deadkumar quietly, "but even so."

"You have this tyre on the premises?" asked my mother.

Deadkumar nodded and grinned impishly.

"Get rid of it," said Dr. Patel. "Do you know the kind of trouble this can bring?"

"Trouble already been brought," said Deadkumar flatly. "No point we pretend. You thought your secrets well-hid? You are wrong as dog on highway about that..."

"Well hidden before you...," murmured Mother.

"No, Zara-darling. You may not like your Devkumar anymore. But Devkumar would never put you in danger. See, I came behind trouble, not trouble behind me. Look, Sohrab, he is sitting in Police Fortress. No accident, hanh? He may be a mischievous boy and even a *tsotsi*, but he is not a murderer of grown policemen. You and everyone know that."

Mother waved this off, not wishing to hear it, "If there is trouble then we will leave..."

"How is that?" said Deadkumar. "Can we leave Sohrab behind in detention?"

"He is dead," said my mother. "That boy is dead."

Deadkumar waved his hand as though he knew things Mother did not. "You people forget everything you ever learned. Or maybe you never learned everything you need. I can't get rid of tyre. They need me to keep it."

"You have put everyone in danger," said Dr. Patel. "You must get rid of it at once."

"Okay, I get rid. Then what. Then people find out. Then no more brothers and sisters. No more anyone watching over Sohrab. No more news about him. Maybe Sohrab in worse danger than ever."

"The tyre must go," insisted Dr. Patel.

Deadkumar shrugged. "If you say. You know I always listen to you high-caste folks. Hey, you tell me to deliver tyre, then who the hell I am to say 'no, Patel, that is wrong.' I am nobody. I am nothing. You educated people...all that stuff in your brains – you know better than a Nothing. You are the goddamn principal of goddamn college. And me? *Car and Driver*. Now retired."

My mother suddenly seized a book and pitched it with all her might at Deadkumar's head. It spread ungainly wings in midair and alighted on Deadkumar's shoulder. Deadkumar did not move.

"Why can't you visit your son yourself instead of making dangerous deals with strangers? How can you know anything without seeing him yourself?"

"Present myself at Police Fortress?" Deadkumar asked ironically. "Oh, that would be a good laugh. Then you would be rid of me for good."

Mother bit her knuckles. In this silence, a voice told me to keep my mouth shut and my questions inside. But my mouth was independent, in league with my feet. My mouth refused to listen to reason. I heard my voice say, "Grenades? Grenades for what?"

All three adults turned to me. They had forgotten me and now they stared, unsure of which path the next lie should follow.

I stared back and said nothing more. There was nothing more I needed to say. I would not offer them a way out. I blocked all the paths their lies frantically explored. Then my mother stammered, "She knows nothing. All this time..."

Deadkumar said, "How this girl is grown. Look how big and mature and all."

Then they were all quiet again, checking for new ways around me. I offered nothing.

"There is nothing to tell," assayed Dr. Patel.

Deadkumar snorted. "Nothing? Nothing? How long can you say nothing to this child? She is our child, not some stranger. She only ask about grenades, Patel-sahib. That's family business, no?"

"Shut up, Kumar," my mother warned.

Deadkumar Uncle stepped away from the other two. "Grenades, Girl. Explosive kind. Those things are for blow things up," he laughed. "It is what happens when there is war."

"War?"

"War. Soldiers."

"Blow things up?"

"People too. Blow them to pieces..."

"Enough, Nagarajah," hissed my mother.

But Deadkumar Uncle had not had enough. He moved closer to me, his eyes wide. "Sometimes they blow up Post Office. Sometimes army truck. And sometimes," he said quietly, "sometimes the other side do the blowing up..."

Understanding, the much awaited revelation, trickled through my brain a grain of sand at a time and the voice said, *ah...ah...ah...*as each grain fell.

"You see, the truth," Deadkumar Uncle went on, "is that your mama was part of that war. Even Patel, even me. All underground, though. All secret." He laughed loudly. "See, all this time you and Sohrab brought up by secret army...revolutionaries against the state and all that..."

Dr. Patel and Mother did not join in the laughter. In fact, Mother had grown quite pale again. She looked at Deadkumar Uncle as though she were very tired of trying to hold down a badly behaved rooster. Her tears had dried.

"He's joking," she said, but her voice lacked conviction. "Of course we are nothing of the sort. We were students. Dreamy youth not much older than you are."

"Shit-makers and fighters," giggled Deadkumar Uncle.

"Your mother and I ceased such activities long before you were born, actually," said Dr. Patel.

Deadkumar Uncle bared his teeth at Dr. Patel and grinned. "Me too," he winked. "Actually."

Around that time I wondered if someone could be part dead, part alive. Or dead sometimes, alive at others.

Deadkumar drove away the next day with his little car with its spare tyre. He drove carefully, crawling along the humped road between the college and the main road. He waved at Dr. Patel, who watched from his front door.

He went along the road through town and on between the baked fields with their corn husks that rattled like dry bones. He drove on around Qoqologsing and down the gentle slope to the Caledon River and the border post. It was busy there. A Hippo was parked on the South African side and a yellow-haired SADF man was pulling on a frightened mule while an old Masotho woman pushed it. There were other white men with guns slung at their shoulders, laughing at their comrade.

Deadkumar turned the car around and came home. By the time he arrived it was dark. He carefully removed the spare tyre and stashed it in the back of the shed. Then he stayed in the shed staring at all the things he had stored there over the years. He must have yearned for real life once more. He must have remembered broken things he had repaired and the fun he had had chasing Flori. He might even have recalled the sensation of having blood rather than sea water moving through his veins.

We could only guess.

We left him standing in the shed, remembering life, and when we returned later we found him in a kind of sleep of the Dead, his eyes rotating around in his head and the arid winds of the Land of Dead blowing from his nose. He had wrapped himself in an old blanket and made a bed of burlap among the pieces of machinery and Mother's discarded sculptures.

Then we too fell asleep in the nests in the dried grass made by the dogs.

WHEN THE DEAD awaken in the night they are unsure of which world they are in. They move in silence, worried lest they disturb other sinister things. They feel their way through the darkness guided by the heat of the Living. Yet they are clumsy.

That was how Uncle Deadkumar moved. It was only his shadow in the starlight that stirred us awake as it passed by. Naturally, we averted our eyes. Naturally, we saw all.

There were strange voices at his house and the lights were on. Shapes loomed against the inside walls. He crept forward to his own window with his dim shadow watching his back and we studied this scene carefully and thought that this was how the *thokolosi* must look when it comes around to bother virgin girls in the villages. Deadkumar and his shadow peered in at the window for a long time, then retreated on stiff legs to the safety of the corner of the shed.

Was it a dream? Had the shadows of the Dead slipped under our sleeping eyelids? We lay still for a time, Bushman and I, not moving a muscle. The strange voices became hushed but the lights remained. Even though we were chilled through to our guts we made ourselves get up and look in the window and see what he had seen.

We saw two men. They sprawled on chairs and slung to their lips bottles of Castle Lager from a case of twelve. They were bad, we could see that. But of the Living or the Dead we could not decide. One was lanky and long and yellow-eyed and wore an ill-fitting pale blue safari suit. The other had the small, perfectly rounded head of a monkey and a bloody t-shirt with a sentence across the chest: "I love New York." It seemed they had been fighting. Between them were the pieces of a broken chair, a broken bottle and a knife. But now they only drank and waited in silence. I love New York slumped over and began to snore. His nose was squashed and bloody.

We went back to our nests but found them too cold, so we sought the safety and warmth of the house and our beds. We sank into a bountiful sleep, unaccountably dreaming the dreams of small children, of animals and sweet foods, of kind voices and mud puddles under rainy skies.

IN THE MORNING 'Mè Jane brought a hard-boiled egg and roti and tea to Deadkumar's house and discovered the two men lying on the floor amid the bottles, the broken chair and the knife. She awakened us by thumping through the house, frantic, muttering and hissing and clicking, like one of those cobra-hunting birds we call the Secretary.

"Ach, this is what happens! If you tell trouble to God, he answer with trouble! First Sohrab and now these irregular men. I know them! Soldiers of the worst, drunken, devilish sort!" She stumped about my room, picking up my things and arranging them according to some order I had never understood. Clothing in a tippy, impractical stack on the table and all else in neat ranks. "Army soldiahs finally come for Mastah Dev... First Sohrab and now this."

At the library Mother still mourned over Sohrab's death, but we had stopped believing her. She sighed when we told her of the men, then she came up to see for herself. She glanced in at the window at the men sprawled on the floor, then went on to the shed.

Deadkumar was still asleep under his blankets, as though he had taken too much *jouala* and slept drunk. Mother stood over him, unable to decide whether to kick him or break something over his head. M`Jane touched her arm, saying, "Respect, Madam. Respect for the Dead."

"Wake up, goddamn it. Wake up, Nagarajah, and tell us what is happening...," Mother hissed. She shifted her feet, suppressing the urge to kick.

"You promised you going to be nice," said Deadkumar from beneath the blanket.

"Answer!"

"Hanh, woman. You going to wake up the whole valley. Those guys is just some old friends, that is all."

"These *thugri* are your friends?"

"Okay, not exactly like friends," sighed Deadkumar. "Some boys I play cards with once or twice."

"Gambling cards..."

"Little bit..."

"They came for their money..."

Deadkumar tried to pull the blanket over his head while Mother said something about testicles and idiots. "And what will you do to get rid of these men? I won't even ask if you have the money you owe."

"Money, I got money. You think Devkumar comes home without pockets in his pants?"

"Then just pay them so they will leave. We have enough troubles without them." Then Mother stopped. She looked at him carefully. "They are your comrades, aren't they..."

We could see how badly he was trapped. He glanced at 'Mè Jane and Bushman and I. "What is that boy doing here?" he said, scowling. Then, "Okay, not my best comrades though. They need money, those boys. What can I do, hanh?"

"Everyone knows where to find you..."

"I told you, Zara. Everybody knows I am here. Everyone knows you are here. Soldiers, South Africans...you know you can't keep anything secret from the S A D F. You just say to yourself, 'okay man, they know we here,' then you go along make your mind up what you going do about it. Because some day they will make up their mind and they will send soldiers again. They got Sohrab in the Police Jail. Next time they come here for someone else. Maybe you, maybe me, maybe Patel-Sahib..."

He jumped up and rubbed his face with both hands. His crumpled shirt had a large oil stain on it. A moth fluttered out of his hair. "What the hell," he said, and stumped out of the shed. "You people quit follow Devkumar about. And get that Bush-kid out of my sight."

Safari and New York were still asleep. "Okay, boys," said Deadkumar as he marched into the flat. "Wake the hell up." He gave New York a nudge with his foot, then shoved him roughly. But New York was as heavy as stone, his skin the blue-black of certain scorpions. He snorted loudly in his sleep.

"Bring me water, Girl," he told me. I took a pot to the barrel and returned to find Deadkumar extracting the bullets from the gun. He set the beer bottles in a neat line and collected the pieces of the broken chair as the men slept on. He held the pot high over them and poured the water on their heads. The men spluttered and staggered out of sleep, cursing in Zulu. Safari stood up, though, ready to fight.

"What the hell you want here?" Deadkumar barked. "You look for some trouble, hanh?"

"Papa Ku. Papa Ku," said Safari in a sandy voice. He looked at the pot in Deadkumar's hand and gave a short laugh. "Hey, Papa Ku, you left Durban without say goodbye!"

Now New York stumbled to his feet. He groped for reflective sunglasses in his shirt, placed them over his red eyes. "Yes, that right. Everyone miss you, Papa Ku," he mumbled. "All your friends say hello, hello, hello, hell-ER."

"Jah, HELL-ER..." enthused Safari. "You know why we came all this way, Ku?"

"Just because you love my face, nah?"

"Ah, Ku, you are laughing," said New York. He looked at me now, looked me up and down, as though planning how best to taste me. I pulled Bushman after me and we went back to our house.

After that, we heard loud voices coming from the flat, then laughter. We smelled eggs being fried. A while later the men went down the path. When they reached the roadway, a car appeared and took them away to the hotel at the encampment.

Deadkumar made a deal with the men. He told them he needed a few days to organize. In turn, they promised him that they had no regard for children or women when they were drinking. "In fact," laughed New York, "God is nothing to me."

Prison

In a photograph of Deadkumar from this period his hand is in front of his face, as if to shield himself from a blinding light. There is no blinding light, however, only the regular light of the World of the Living. The rest is what could be expected of a dead man trying to fake his way among the living: balding head, saggy dark pants on legs that are neither long nor well-shaped, and an ill-fitting and stained shirt over a compact potbelly. This photo does not resemble the real live Devkumar, but nor does any photo, for he is one of those people on whom the science of photography is a wasted effort. Living or dead.

DEADKUMAR UNCLE slumped in the repaired wooden chair before his house. His dead knees were chilled and the sun, though bright, was powerless to warm them. Now and again he shook his head in woe and rubbed his eyes. Problems multiplied at his feet like apricots shaken loose from a burgeoning tree.

"I need one good luck," he moaned.

His eyes were remote, and his thoughts were disjointed ones of complicated and hopeless money schemes. "Money, money," he bubbled as though trying to capture a song he could not quite recall. The college was bankrupt, the rains a distant memory. Prosperity and money were beyond the reach of our place and time.

We came and sat near him to better sense his turmoil. Bushman picked up the money refrain and mimicked Deadkumar's voice. He sang in a warbling voice, "A-money, a-money, can I catch a-money, mon..."

"That boy is going to make me scratch," muttered Deadkumar. "And he smell like a goat."

'Mè Jane and Flori came out on the porch. Flori wore a dress and pumps and 'Mè Jane wore her best blanket. They were ready for town. Now Glorius burst up the path, although no one could remember inviting him.

'Mè Jane looked at Deadkumar and said, "You must gird yourself, Ntate."

"I am gird," he said. He stood and straightened his shabby clothes. His face was covered with an uneven grey stubble. His eyes were undersea stones, dark and cold. 'Mè Jane pulled him into his house, where she made him clean himself and shave and change out of his oily shirt. Then we trooped down the hill to the car.

Including Dr. Patel, we were now seven. The car was meant to accommodate four.

"That stinky Bush-dog can stay behind," growled Deadkumar Uncle. "And Sohrab's friend here and Insect-girl too. They all too big for light car like this..."

My mother turned on her heel and went back to the house. Bushman wandered away barking like a dog and Glorius and I climbed into the back and tried to make ourselves as small as we could. It was not easy. I sat on Glorius's lap, my head against the ceiling. After a minute I could feel a stony thing beneath my bottom that grew and grew as I squirmed on him. "Stop it, stupid," I hissed at him. He grimaced in embarrassment, but the stony thing was not under his control and we both knew that. As we drove I shifted this way and that and Glorius broke into a sweat.

We came into the encampment. Twice we drove by the police fortress before Deadkumar stopped the car far away at the edge of the town. He muttered that he was staying outside. "I go in there, they never let me come out again, I know..."

"And your contacts?" sniffed Dr. Patel as we extricated ourselves from the car.

A heavy cloud of dust blew down upon us as we moved past the bar, Angie's Restaurant, the bank, the Spar store, Seanamorena. As we approached the iron gate, I noticed a tide of sweat advancing along Dr. Patel's shirt.

The sandstone fortress had been built by the British. The front part of it was called the Gun Tower, where some white soldiers had defended themselves against other white soldiers. People feared it, knowing that white ghosts resided there. The sentries kept themselves in a state of drunkenness to overcome their fear. As we approached, these men flared their nostrils at Flori. To me one of them whispered, "*Kena*, Aousi, we want to sweet you." Then they laughed in corrupt voices.

We waited for an hour before a little wooden desk propped against a wall of the Gun Tower. Each leg of the desk stood in a tin can, defence against some predator of paper. At this desk, the desk officer dealt with each matter before him without raising his eyes from his papers. Finally it was our turn.

"We have come to see a prisoner, Sohrab Nagarajah," Dr. Patel told the man.

The officer scrutinized some papers that had nothing to do with Sohrab. "We know nothing about that someone."

"Oh, he is here," said Patel impatiently. He leaned over the desk and we saw a jagged thing in Dr. Patel that we had never noticed. The desk officer shifted in his chair and gave the briefest glance upward, then hopped from his seat and disappeared inside. He returned with an older officer with a moustache and bright badges on his shoulders. The senior man said nothing, but stared at Dr. Patel with narrowed eyes. The desk officer said, "That someone has gone this day to the prison at Maseru."

The senior man followed us to the door, watching Patel closely. Only when we had passed the sentries did we let out our breath. We each thought the same thing: Mother's dream had been right after all.

I looked back at the Gun Tower. Through a barred window, I caught the glimpse of a bright colour, a city gown from Jo'burg.

DEADKUMAR SAID, "Hokay, we go to Maseru..."

"Hunh. Contacts!" snorted Dr. Patel.

Deadkumar shrugged. "Something happen. Something always happen. You know that, Sahib." Then he sank low in his seat.

Safari and New York were swaggering up the road toward the car, broad smiles across their faces. Their hands were bandaged. They peered in the window at Deadkumar, who looked at their hands and then looked away.

"Your son in prison, Papa Ku," said New York. "That is bad. I went in prison once."

"Bad place," said Safari.

"Boring place," said New York. "Boring, then beating. Not everyone is friends. Not like here in the road."

"Yeh, in the road – friends, friends..."

"We friends, Ku?"

Deadkumar rubbed his eyes and muttered, "Shut the hell your mouths."

"That does not sound like friend-y," said New York. He scratched his balls. "You got our thing, Mon? We is tired of wait for you."

"I told you. Thing take time. I meet you later at my place." Deadkumar started the car.

New York reached in and turned it off.

"Then we need something small, Ku. We need food and beer so we wait better. We drink the beer, then we talk more, yah? Take money, go home, fine."

Dr. Patel had had enough. He had pieced together something about these men. He got out of the car. "You think we have all day to sit and listen to your stupid riddles and poor oration."

These were men who understood physical dimension. They peered up at Patel. Safari took off his sunglasses and blinked in the sun. "Poor or-rate-ee?" He scratched his head with his bandaged hand.

"What do you want here?"

"No, nothing," said New York, plucking at his pocket. "Just friends, is all. We meet our friend Ku..." He appealed to Deadkumar for verification.

"Yah, yah," said Deadkumar impatiently. "Boy, my head is ache."

Safari held the door open for Patel unhappily. New York held his hand out to Deadkumar. "Hey, you have some big friend, mon," he said.

They trotted along beside the car for a way, unsure of what else to do. Then we were out of that and onto the main road to Teyateyaneng. In the seat beside me, 'Mè Jane prayed.

THE LITTLE CAR was lost on the open road. It sputtered each time a lorry swept by. We had not gone far when Deadkumar suddenly swore and pulled over. We saw a knot of people gathered near a row of prickly pear and a pack of dogs. All of these dogs seemed to be missing legs, which was what caught Deadkumar's eye. He stopped the car for another reason, though. In the midst of the dogs, urinating on a large rock, was a boy. He walked on fours with his skinny rump waggling in the air so that even though we could see no tail, we felt he had one somewhere on him. Then we saw that this boy was Bushman. As we watched he urinated on a post, imitating uncannily the stiff-legged strut of a road-wise he-dog out to mark his territory. He kicked at the dirt with his hind legs, hung out his tongue and panted. He sniffed another dog's rear end. When he noticed us staring, our mouths agape, he gave us a chesty bark. The other dogs cocked their ears and whined.

'Mè Jane prayed again while we sat and watched our brother. We wondered what we had done to deserve such strange sights. Deadkumar murmured, "Koko, go and get that boy before someone kick him..."

I stepped out of the car and whistled the way I would to Rajah and Mpho. Bushman bounded over and leaped into the car, slobbering over everyone. We cuffed him and sat on him until he stopped playing that game, then we drove away, leaving the people by the road to look upon us with bad eyes because we had ruined their entertainment.

We drove on to Maseru in the reek of dog kaka.

"What were you doing with those dogs?" I asked Bushman after a while.

"Those no dogs," he answered with a quick grin. "Those were some other things..."

'Mè Jane overheard this and crossed herself. Flori giggled and said, "*Modimo!* Abuti Bushman needs bathing!"

At Maseru it was not only Deadkumar Uncle who refused to show himself to the guards. Dr. Patel seemed to have acquired the same fear and asked 'Mè Jane to lead us to Sohrab.

"Just check if he is really there, 'Mè," said Dr. Patel, and they made us walk from the town centre up the steep hill to the prison.

The prison was a high fence, a gate, a sentry and a hard-packed clay yard in which hundreds of men sat, lay and stood. There were dormitories made of cement blocks.

'Mè Jane pressed money into the hand of the sentry. He waved us into the yard.

We wandered and stared at the inmates, not sure of how to look for our brother until 'Mè Jane saw a grey-haired man she knew from her home. This old prisoner was pleased to see 'Mè Jane. He offered her *baap* from the iron pot, then they sat and talked. After a time some young men came and sat with 'Mè Jane and the old man. She greeted each one as though he were her son and they, in turn, treated her with great respect. These young men told us where we might search in the sickroom.

We went to this sickroom. It was a dim place and smelled of urine and sweat and rot. The beds of the inmates were nothing more than blankets laid out on straw mats. In a corner, curled with his face to the wall, we found Sohrab.

'Mè Jane and Flori pulled him over on his back, thinking the worst. But he was conscious, his eyes swollen, blood caked around his nose. He sat up trying to smile.

"I am all right," he said and he let 'Mè Jane bury his face in her old bosom. We went near and touched and patted him, carefully though, knowing he would not tolerate much of that.

'Mè Jane made us fetch water and beckoned Flori and tore the hem of her dress to make dressings. With rough efficiency she set about cleaning blood from Sohrab's wounds and clothing him in clean underwear and a strong, protective work suit she had brought in her bag. She was well along feeding him *pranta*, *gobi* and chicken by the time the guards came and made us leave that place. Then we were suddenly back in our car and wondering whether it was really Sohrab we had seen.

IN THE DARKNESS our car pottered homeward along the bumpy road. Qoqolosing, the great mountain of our home, stood far in the distance, smaller and somehow feebler than I had ever imagined it. It had shrunk, beaten down by the impossible tasks set by this world. We were naked and fragile this far from our place, in a weird black land of looming volcanic spires.

Before us on the road there appeared a single yellow eye, which bore down through the gloom. It might have descended from the sky or from some place beyond our world. The sky lit with sheets of lightning and we that saw that no, the yellow eye belonged to a lorry or bus with one headlamp, careening down a long hill toward us. But it was an unearthly vehicle, hulking on the narrow highway, bent-framed and lopsided, straddled over the road. We saw that it was a Death-thing, a vehicle sent to further our destruction. We drew our breaths and watched it come. "*Modimo*," gasped Flori. "Ntate Dev..."

Then that thing was upon us and swept by in a cloud of burned diesel fuel.

Ngaka of the Dolls

My mother refused to believe that we had seen Sohrab alive. Her death dream hung about the corners of her eyes and she lost weight. Her skin was as cool as the hide of a snake.

I spent more of my time watching over her naps and her sleep. I observed how her face came to resemble the head that long ago had hung in the tree in the valley, and I realized, with a pang, that I knew almost as little about my mother as about the head. Once, in her sleep, she muttered strings of words I could not understand, and for a moment I saw Mother as a foreign creature, meant to bring us into the world then return to her place.

"She grieves and worries for Sohrab," said Flori. "It is a poison eating her away. All because she thinks Sohrab died in prison..." She looked at 'Mè Jane with an afterthought. "He won't, will he, 'Mè?"

"That is the business of the Ancestors and Jesus Christ and *Modimo*," muttered 'Mè Jane.

But 'Mè Jane knew what we did not. I saw hidden things flitting across her brow.

"Tell me what, 'Mè," I said to her, but she would only shake her head and pray louder. She prayed to Jesus and his mother

Mary, and she prayed to gods she did not know so well but had heard about, like Allah and Shiva. Mostly she prayed to her dead relations, appealing to each of them and reminding them of their responsibilities.

I found my mother collapsed at the latrine behind the library. She was absolutely still, her limbs collecting a film of the red dust that fell from the sky.

I carried her back to the library and wiped the dust carefully from her eyes. She looked at me as only a creature might, then she whispered, "Koko..." and she smiled at me.

Some time later, Deadkumar brought Dr. Hlalete. They arrived in the doctory car which was painted to look like a government ambulance. The real ambulance had driven off the road into a deep gorge near Oxbow some years before, so Dr. Hlalete and several others had created new ones with spelling mistakes, red-painted bottles glued on the roof to appear like emergency flashers, and bad drivers.

Hlalete had taken on other airs since we had last seen him. He brought with him a large leather bag that was meant to give us confidence. He opened it to show off an array of gleaming instruments, which he admired for a long moment. Then he closed the bag without touching a thing. "Hm. Take me to the patient," he said.

Mother was so weak she barely resisted Dr. Hlalete's inquiries. As Hlalete's questions turned to her bank account and the state of the college finances, Dr. Patel appeared and picked the doctor up by the shoulders and tossed him out of the room, then he looked at 'Mè Jane. "She needs to go to Maseru for tests."

"Not the Republic, Mastah?" asked 'Mè Jane, but Deadkumar and Patel just glanced at each other.

"I am not going anywhere," said Mother. "And I won't have tests."

Everyone left me and Bushman alone with her.

"We need water," croaked Mother. "We are going to dry into husks and blow away."

"Will you die?" asked Bushman.

"Everybody dies," she answered, "except you perhaps." Mother looked at me. "You should not be hanging about this place. You should be off preparing for university. Preparing for real life."

"That's not important," I said.

"You are big now," she said. "Really big," she added. Then she closed her eyes again and fell asleep.

I watched her sleep. Her body had become childlike, her face pliable and innocent. She was going backward in time, even as I moved ahead. In the small mirror by the bed I studied my face against hers. I had the same firm mouth and wild hair. My breasts were *rondavels* full of maize. I looked like a woman. My eyes were bright and soft.

"Yes, you are big," said Bushman. "Strong too," he added diplomatically.

I cuffed the side of his head.

IN THE EVENING 'Mè Jane and Flori returned to Mother with a doll. It was a hastily made thing, of twigs and grass. They placed it next to my mother. I knew they had gone to the hills and consulted with a *ngaka ea baloetse.*

Mother awoke after a time, dazed by her sleep. She noticed the doll and picked it up and examined it closely.

"Good, Madam Zara," said 'Mè Jane. "She is here to help you."

My mother smiled wanly and drifted into sleep once more.

IN THE MORNING the *ngaka* himself came to our compound. He wore a patchy cape of animal hides. His eyes were yellowish and rheumy behind his thick spectacles and he was drunk, having just taken in a pail of *jouala* made especially for this visit. As he circled the house he shook a bundle of beads and rattles, then he entered quickly and went straight to the doll. Soon we heard the doll speaking in a scratchy, grass-in-throat voice, telling the *ngaka* what ailed my mother. The *ngaka* shook his rattles in every direction, then carried the doll outside into the compound, where we gathered to hear his pronouncements. Not once had he looked at my mother.

"She must not stay here," growled the *ngaka*. He looked at Patel and said, "She must stay there, in his house. At the very top."

"But what is wrong with her, Morena. Tell us how she is sick."

"It is the cancer," he replied.

MY MOTHER was insistent on two things: that we move her to Dr. Patel's place that afternoon and that we investigate her illness no further. We could do nothing but obey her. Even Dr. Patel said nothing.

We were well familiar with the austere plank floors and bone-white walls of Patel's house. It could be a relief to be away from the clutter of our place. The only concessions Dr. Patel made to decoration were a gigantic brass vase on the floor by the front entrance and a black beret, always clean and dust free, which hung from a single hook and which we had never seen Dr. Patel wear. In one room there was a desk and chair and shelves of books of every kind. In another room, a table, a chair and a rough-hewn bench, and two or three unlabelled texts. It was as though two people lived in that house, one an incessant reader, the other a man of quiet uncluttered thoughts. Some days we would find Dr. Patel at the table and some days at the desk.

But the upper floor was unknown to us. There were stories, told by Flori and others, that the house had been used during the war known as the Gun Rebellion that happened between white men. A band of men had been besieged in the upper floor of the house for weeks and had been finally forced to eat one another.

In desperation, the last soldier had eaten himself, hands first, so that the enemy had found the house empty but for blood stains. According to Flori, many people had seen the dead white man in the window on dark nights, waving his handless arms.

So it was with some anxiety that we crept up the stairs with the things my mother needed. We found a short hallway with a door at either end. One door was locked, the other opened into a bare room with a sloping ceiling. No blood, which was a relief. We set up a bed for Mother and another for me. We brought her paints and books to lift her spirits, even though we knew she would not use them.

Later that evening we climbed the path to our house and found Deadkumar Uncle sitting sullenly on a rock. We had seen him poking around in Patel's place earlier but he had not helped us move Mother's things.

"What that big Hindu up to, hanh?" he demanded.

'Mè Jane prodded me to keep walking. We could smell the whisky as we went by. Deadkumar's eyes glowed red in the last sun. "You are a big Hindu also, Ntate Ku," Flori said gently. "You too are a big man..."

"What the hell Zara move there for, anyway?"

"The *ngaka* told us..."

"Aw, monkey-shit..." said Deadkumar. Then he seized Flori by the arm and whispered something in her ear that made her giggle and struggle. Deadkumar's hands seemed to take on some of their old life and rustled into her frock so that Flori had to slap him away.

"What the hell you goats looking at?" he glared at us. "You never seen a man doing man business?"

"Mastah Devkumar, please do not be evil. We have enough worries," 'Mè Jane scolded. She let go of my hand to drive Flori ahead of her up the hill.

With only Bushman and I to watch him, Deadkumar suddenly deflated, his hands dropping dead to his side. "Oh, hai..." he said despondently and sank down on his rock to resume his vigil over

Patel's house. "What the hell they doing down there? She is sick anyway. Devkumar give her better caring than Patel-Sahib. She never give Devkumar a proper chance..."

We sat down on either side of Deadkumar Uncle. The sun was dropping the last distance over the horizon and stars sprang out in the eastern sky. From far out on the road we heard the bray of drunken laughter emanating from Caltex Roadhouse, and from the valley the singing call of the women coming in from their dessicated fields.

"Are you coming alive?" Bushman suddenly asked. "You do not seem drowned in water." He stared closely at Deadkumar's face and sniffed, peered up the dead man's nose. "You do not seem dead. Who are you?"

Deadkumar straightened his shoulders but for once did not lose his temper. "What the hell this boy talking about?" he asked quietly.

"Oh, he means nothing," I explained. "He's just tired, nothing more."

"He is a strange kid and he says strange things... Hey, Koko, you miss your Uncle all that time I was away?"

I stared out over the valley without moving.

"You know, I got something for you. I just needed a good particular moment..."

We followed him back to his flat. He poured himself a glass of whisky and drank it off. He went to his room and brought back a paper bag.

"All that time I was gone I thought of you and Sohrab and your ma. I even miss 'Mè Jane and Flori. Even Patel. Even the dogs. Now listen, both you kids. You got watch out for soldiers these days. You see any soldiers or policemans coming here, you tell Devkumar." He handed me the bag. "You got that?"

In the bag I found an old watch and an army compass and a book of poetry by Kahlil Gibran. I looked over the verse quickly and decided it could not be Deadkumar Uncle who read that.

He was watching me with as much of a warm glow as a Dead can muster. He wagged his head, "Just some things for you, Girl. Keep them. Some day you will know they are important."

Bushman smelled each item and placed them all back in the bag with some reverence.

"Whose stuff is it?"

"Yours, Kuku-girl."

"I mean whose really..."

Deadkumar smiled weakly and wagged his head.

"Are they yours?"

"Hey. A father wants to give his kids something. Sometimes it does not seem much."

"You are not really my father..."

"No, but I did the best I could. I love you just like your father would..."

"She never told me anything about him, you know. Nothing real."

"Him?"

"You know..."

"Oh. Well...maybe she busy...or maybe after a while she forgot about him..." He rubbed his teeth, then suddenly became uncomfortable and went out.

It did not matter much. I had ceased being concerned about my father over the years. I had opened my heart to let him in, but he had chosen not to appear. Dust, lies and other detritus blew in there. My heart closed and I locked it. Now I looked at the few items and listened. My heart remained tight.

"All old things," said Bushman casually. "All old things from long time ago."

I WENT TO MY ROOM and lay on my bed with the bag on my belly. It weighed nothing, but I could feel it nonetheless. We were surrounded by death. My heart was closed.

From where I lay I could reach up behind my head and pull out the packet of photos Patel had given me years before. I looked at my mother and father in the photos. I tried to see myself in them, and to see if they knew or cared about me. For that moment, I wished time would cease its relentless forward march and just wait for me to think things through. Or maybe dream.

But time would not stop. In the kitchen we could hear 'Mè Jane and Flori doing their best to prepare a meal that Mother would like. And, down the hill, my mother's mouth had become parched as Dr. Patel watched over her without understanding her.

"She needs water."

Bushman brought a steel bowl, which we cleaned until it shone. We boiled water and let it cool, then filled the bowl and covered it. I carried it down the hill, through Dr. Patel's lonely house and up the stairs. When I entered the room Mother opened her eyes and took the bowl and thirstily drained it.

"You must stay by your mother," Dr. Patel told me gently. So we three sat together as the light went out of the day and she fell into an even-breathed sleep.

AFTER AN HOUR Dr. Patel lit a lamp. Darkness had deepened across veldt and valley and mountain. "Sometimes it is easy to take water for granted," said Patel quietly. "But when the water is gone, all manner of things go awry. The brain cries for water. The heart grows panicky. Eventually, the blood becomes thick and sticky and ceases to flow. Inevitably death..."

"Death can be driven off," I interjected firmly.

"Is it?"

In the corner of my eye, I caught a glimpse of a white-skinned, handless figure. But it stayed back, cowed by Dr. Patel,

who sat with his great shoulders folded like the wings of a predatory bird. Light seemed to collect in a pool at Patel's feet,
awaiting his command.

"To know death, you need to know life. But perhaps you
already know these things..."

"I know nothing. No one has taught me."

"You know more than you think. You know water, you know
air, yes?"

"Air is thin," I offered. "Too thin to see."

Bushman giggled and lay on the floor.

"Air is a mixture of gases. Well...let's think another way," said
Patel. "Imagine a flame. Now take that flame and split it a million
times into a million and one pieces. Can you see each piece? Of
course you cannot...too small and too dim. That is air. Many
small pieces of light, too small to see. But is it alive?"

I became aware of sparks swirling through the room.

"The fire is soaked up by blood, as the ancient people said.
They would say we breathe the fire. Now the flame is within."

"How did they know?"

Patel removed his shoes and sat cross-legged on the floor. He
placed his hands together and closed his eyes. He breathed in
and his lungs filled in a great swooshing that caused all the
sparks in the room to swirl into him. When he exhaled, the particles were dim, the fire of life quenched.

The lamp ran low and sputtered out.

"*Pranayama*," he told me. "One must learn restraint."

He breathed in through one nostril and out through the
other. Then he breathed through his skin, the pores opening and
closing, the tiny fires flitting like insects.

"If the posture is good, the senses turn inside. *Asana*...the
mind enters the heart, the heart becomes a boat of Brahma, carrying us across the river..."

Hours later I slept against Mother's cool back. In my sleep I
drifted upon a wide river without banks, safe in the Brahma boat.

I OPENED MY EYES to a room flooded with light. Mother sat on the *dhuri* drinking tea.

"So Patel teaches you the Hindu arts." She had been awake all through the previous night. "Between Patel and Kumar one has a full range of choices, yes? At one extreme, yogic arts; at the other, a man seduced by *maya*."

"Maya?"

"The veil over our eyes, Child. The things of this world. Money, wealth, power. Which do you prefer?"

"I prefer no teacher."

"One must have teachers sooner or later..."

"My father should have been the one to teach me..."

Mother looked surprised. The beginning of a lie flitted across her face, then she lost it. She was too weak to invent and evade, yet she would not answer my challenge either. She locked herself in this battle between will and weakness, pain and mendacity, the battle raging in small nervous tics around her eyes and mouth, the battle barely concealed, raging there within her until both sides were spent. Finally she whispered, "If only it would rain." She closed her eyes. "A proper rain that soaks the ground...an all-day, all-month rain that makes the green slime grow over everything. We would sit in the puddles and soak it up..."

"I cannot remember when it last rained that way," I said quietly.

I suddenly saw the lights in Mother's eyes flicker as the fire of life flagged. The sparks she breathed were of another kind, messengers who rode the winds on dark feathered birds from the Death Place. I sniffed the corrupt breaths of these messengers. A sorcerer was at work.

"Let us walk," I said with a shiver, and I pulled her up roughly. "Come, we must."

We walked along the row of dried eucalyptus trees and through grass stubbled and worn to the roots by cattle, across the bare, concretized clay and denuded rock, all of it devoid of water

and dead. Behind my mother a comet tail of evil particles show-
ered the ground. When we stopped we were by the river.

"Why did you bring me here?" she asked, looking at the
riverbed. "It is the place where the soldier died, no?" It was indeed
the place. A small stream of mud in the middle of the channel
was all that remained of the river.

Mother studied the ground, then she sat on a rock. "I'm tired,"
she said, but I could see that she wanted to absorb the place and
think.

In truth, I did not know I was bringing Mother to the place
Thabo Majara was found. Some spirit had turned my feet this
way. I kept my eyes squinted down in order to better glimpse the
foul messengers of a sorcerer. The wind dropped. The air was
empty, all birds and insects knowing to avoid this place. Then,
after what seemed like a very long silence, I heard the dry rustle
of scales and saw the regal head of a gold cobra rising among the
rocks not far from where we sat. The snake regarded us with
equanimity, nodded its head to catch our scent. I sensed the
spirits withdraw to a distance. The snake flicked its tongue to
taste the breeze, then abruptly dropped out of sight. I took
Mother home.

Soldier Mans

"What old Patel got up there in his house, Girl?" I described the house to Deadkumar Uncle and then told him about the boat of Brahma, knowing it would irritate him. We stood on the path overlooking the house. Deadkumar wanted to see my mother, but no one had invited him.

"You know, that Patel is just old *sadhu*, after all. You know, *sadhus* think if they spit into the wind that wind going to stop blowing. Look how Patel plant rocks in his compound instead of maize like everyone else. Now he tell you Brahma-boats? Let me tell you, Child. There is no boats in a dry country like this. River Caledon runs when it rains, then dries down to mud. You know that..."

"They say the river always runs underground."

"Yeah, well, you listen Devkumar. Only way you going to cross river is when you walk across the mud or use bridge. Beside, who the hell knows when the Brahma-boat going to get here and what the damn thing look like. What else he tell you?"

"Secret of Life," I said, because he was staring hard at me with his beady, drowned eyes.

"Secret? Must be some great secret. Big man and big ideas..." he muttered. A ragged fringe of seaweed was growing from

Deadkumar's nose and he wiped it away in annoyance. I knew he had great respect for Patel, even though he did not understand him. "I tell you great secret of life. Great Secret of Life is we all going die, that is all. Everyone and everything, and we got to just play along living like as if everything just okay. Great Secret is we headed for *dead*, Child, from moment we born. Might as well we dead already..."

I did not like this conversation and wanted to leave, which is why Deadkumar tried to find new ways to get my attention.

"Your father was my friend, you know that? Someone else could tell that long time ago but they did not. So busy-busy and all. Now your ma is sick and old Patel, he going off into Siva, yogi, monkey gods and who knows what funny things he tell. Yah, your pa...if he could have been here, he would *definitely* be here. Look after you just fine. But he could not be here so only I am here. Sort of like replacement part. Used part, not factory part either."

He watched me carefully under his eyebrows, but I did not react. My heart closed and locked tight. "Maybe you should take me visit your ma, Child."

We went down. My mother had been reading, but slept now in a small rectangle of sunlight near the window. The rock doves cooed in the eaves. Somewhere a mouse scampered in the rafters.

Deadkumar was happy to fuss around her for a minute or two. Then he pulled the blanket around my mother and took my hand, saying, "There, we let her sleep..."

But we did not leave the house. Deadkumar stopped at the top of the stairs and listened for Patel, and I realized that he had other reasons for wanting to come into the house.

Patel had gone into the town. Deadkumar went along through the house looking for something. He went into each closet in each room, then he went to the locked door opposite my mother's room. It took him only a second to release the lock with his pocketknife.

That room was dusty and bleak and cool. The only furniture was a table and a single chair in the middle of the floor. Upon the table was a battered valise.

Deadkumar sat on the chair, opened the valise.

In it there were some clothes: trousers, a white shirt, shorts and socks. A pair of football boots and a tennis racquet. A medicine kit contained a razor, a toothbrush and a yellowed and cracked bar of soap. A wallet contained a library card, student card and passport. When I saw the photo I knew immediately it was my father. The name on the card was "Hari Lal."

"He used a different name sometimes. At the end..."

My father looked happy in the photograph. His face was relaxed and smiling. It was a strong face, the eyes wide set and clear, his hair long and swept to one side.

I put the things back, closed the case and went out to sit in the last rays of the afternoon sun. Deadkumar left me alone.

The sun tumbled down over the edge of the world and small things flew through the air around my head. I sat very still, my heart locked and still. Hari Lal. Long black hair. My heart was cool and steady. My father was long dead.

Bushman found me and crept nearby, looking at me from various angles. Finally, he sat behind me and put his hand between my shoulder blades so that I felt a small warmth there. Secrets abounded in the twilight, flitting through the sky and ground, mating and multiplying.

And further away in the big world, fathers were dying. Behind, they left secrets and questions. But now my own questions were locked up within my closed and quiet heart. A million girls lost their fathers every day. They went on playing and laughing and sleeping. I wanted to think about this. Yet time would not stand still while I worked through each death, each father, each child. Time rushed impatiently onward. New history accumulated, even as the old was left behind, unexplained.

Now Bushman grabbed my hand and pulled me roughly to my feet.

"Time for sleep."

At the house, 'Mè Jane and Flori had left us stiff porridge and *dal* and beef congealed on the stove, but our appetites were weak. I lay on my bed, while Bushman curled in a ball on a mat to be near me. He did not undress this night, so neither did I. I lay a sheet over him. He threw it off.

WE MUST HAVE SLEPT for a while, or fallen into a trance. It had become cold and the night was astir. I suddenly worried that Mother's blanket had fallen away, her fire gone out, and she was alone in her suffering, too weak to move. I pulled on an old pair of Mother's hiking boots and touched Bushman awake. He followed me half asleep, his head swinging from side to side.

The sky was partly closed over with strange, broken clouds. Between the breaks a lonely star shimmered. Night spirits crept in close to sniff at our necks and small hunted things scurried from the jaws of their predators. Something in the distance screeched in terror, a person or creature or spirit being torn apart by fear, hunters or bad visions. Bushman took my hand.

"Listen, Aousi."

I listened, "A nightmare, perhaps."

But he squeezed my hand hard to tell me there was more. I heard the distant sound of a motor slowing, slowing, drawing nearer. Then the motor was quiet. It had stopped somewhere out on the road.

We continued down the path to Patel's house and I would have crept straight up to Mother's room, but Bushman stopped me again with a pinch to my waist. He was completely awake now, his shining, narrow-slitted eyes bulging like those of a captured mouse, his eyes the only light in this night.

"Soldier mans coming," he hissed. Then he vanished into the house. I heard him a moment later saying, "Soldier mans, Patel, soldier mans," and after only a few seconds, Patel was at the doorway clothed and awake.

"Go and fetch the others," said Patel. "Girl, you must bring your mother. The boy and I will go back to the house," and he went on at a bent run, not hesitating a moment to doubt Bushman's bright, bulging eyes.

I ran silently, took the stairs three at a time, and burst into the dark, close room where Mother slept, her blanket fallen away. She stirred but would not wake. I bundled the blanket around her and lifted her. She was light as a doll, and I thought, she is hollow, her insides have dried and blown away with the other dust and that is why she is ill. In another second I was down the stairs and outside and feeling my way along the wall of the laboratory towards the bushes where Deadkumar hid his car.

Then the soldiers came. They were dark as spirits but their noises betrayed them as flesh and bone. Boots crunched on stone. Someone broke wind. A ray of light from a star reflected on gunmetal. They went by me stealthily but blind. Then they moved up the hill and closed in on our compound.

Two familiar voices came along well behind the others: Safari and New York. They waited near me and one of them lit a cigarette. One of them giggled and said, "Oh, Papa Ku. Oh Papa Ku..."

I did not wait to hear more, but slipped away along the wall holding my breath. When I was well away, I noticed that Mother was awake, looking at me like a strange child with ancient eyes. "Why," she whispered.

"I don't know. I don't know."

I put Mother on the back seat of the car and wrapped the blanket tightly around her. Then I went back, slipping like a thief through the dark, waiting, listening. I heard the sound of a window breaking, then a door. I ran back to Patel's house and dashed up the stairs. I put my shoulder against the locked door and felt the wood splinter as the lock mountings gave away. Then I seized my father's valise and ran, light as a cat, silent as an owl.

Up the hill the lights had come on and there were shouts and I ran and did not stumble or doubt my bearings. When I came to the car the others were there: Patel, Bushman, Deadkumar, 'Mè Jane and Flori. We pushed the car, not out to the road, but down through the bushes into a deep donga that ran along the edge of the hard-packed riverbed, upstream toward the hills. It seemed we pushed the car for miles before Deadkumar deigned to start the motor. Then we kept on upstream, away from civilization and South Africa, back in time into smaller and smaller riverbeds, until the ground became soft and we found a way onto trails and on across fields of stubbled, dead maize to a road. We fled into the night, back-looking into the darkness, and on and away from our home.

Do Not See Me Pass

Our journey took us through passages of night that skirted sleep and health and all that is godly and whole in this world. We travelled with the *thokolosi*, and devils that steal things from the bodies of sleeping youth. We negotiated with the demons that breathe the foul airs of the nether places, pretending we were their equals. And we let ourselves be led into darkness by a dead man with a bloodstained eye and a stench of the rot at the bottom of the sea. We followed the twinkle of his cigarettes, hoping for clues as to our fate. We followed him faithfully through villages, and endless, blank fields of scorpions and snakes, where tall maize had once grown. Nothing else lit our passage. Even the moon had surrendered on this night. Even the stars. Then we were driving upward into the mountains, the way we had so many years before. But this time the car stopped where the road abruptly ended against a stony recess.

Deadkumar switched the motor off and we sat there for some moments watching 'Mè Jane mutter and struggle to climb out. We thought she too had been among the followers. Now we saw otherwise; she knew where we were and seemed to have directed Deadkumar here. We silently unpacked ourselves from the car and followed her up a footpath that looked to us like the cloaked and black path that leads to the World Underneath. Instead we came to a *rondavel*, a lamp, a wizened and welcoming face.

We collapsed and slept.

WHEN I AWOKE I was upon a clean straw mat covered in warm mohair blankets. The air was sharp on my face and I thought of snow. Through the single window sunlight fell in a wide slab upon my family, where they lay in a circle around my mother. 'Mè Jane and Flori lay on either side of her as though she were a dearly treasured newborn.

The room was immaculate despite our chaotic arrival. It was painted in laundering blue and ochre. A small fire burned without smoke, tended by an old woman. She noticed me after a while and brought me a tin cup of hot, sweet tea. Then she took me by the hand and led me out to a small compound formed by a rocky wall and a sturdy bamboo fence, against which two *ron-davels* were constructed. I was shown a latrine, a basin of warm water, a comfortable place to sit.

"You are my daughter," said the old woman as she embraced me. She was Mama Jane, 'Mè Jane's mother. She seemed to me no older than 'Mè Jane, but her eyes were clouded and her back hunched. As I sipped my tea, she gently held my hand and told a broken story of her ancestors. Father, grandfathers, aunts and the mother of all people were intertwined in a single episode that seemed to hinge on a well that produced too much water. The well overflowed and the ancestral mother drowned.

Mama Jane left me alone and toddled in to see to the others. I stepped outside the bamboo enclosure. The sun reflected brilliantly on the rocks. The compound was tucked into a rocky col at the base of the high pass they call Do Not See Me. The pass rose almost vertically to a place where streamers of mist or snow were driven from the ridge by mountain winds. Immediately against that was the top of the sky. Below, the lowlands spread out like a thin scattering of dust upon a sandstone and clay planet. I searched the ribbon of road but saw no movement, no soldiers. We had escaped, it seemed, along one of Deadkumar's plans.

I HAULED MY FATHER'S VALISE out of the car and up to a rocky perch where I sat on it, satisfied to be alone for a moment to watch the road and trails below. There was some comfort in having that much of my father with me. In the clarity offered by the cold mountain air, I saw that we would not be going home.

"Do not look so worry, Girl. Hey, we got away, didn't we?" Deadkumar Uncle squinted up at me, his teeth glinting in the sharp light. He held his flute high in one hand as he climbed up to my perch. Then he released a few soft notes into the air. The notes floated in the stillness.

"God, god, god...," sighed Deadkumar. A great dip in the land at the very edge of the world was all we could see of our home. "They thought nobody find them there. Hanh..."

"Who thought..."

"Your ma. Shiv Patel Sahib. I warn them many times. I said 'I don't think you are safe here.' But, you know, they never listen to man such as me."

"Does that mean they will find us here?"

"In time, yes. If we stay, they find. If we go, no one catch. We need some luck."

"It is you they are after," I said quietly.

"Hanh. That is what you and every somebody say. You maybe think it was those Durban men who came to our place last night..."

"I saw them with the soldiers. I heard them speak."

"And you believe every sight and sound, Child? In this place of mountains, witches and magic things?" He brought his flute to his mouth and played off his teeth a sharp string of notes that rose like a startled pigeon.

"What I saw wasn't real?"

Deadkumar Uncle shrugged and rubbed his teeth with his forefinger. "This place is very complicate. Who knows anything?"

I shifted on the smooth surface of my father's valise. One of the latches popped under my thigh. Deadkumar looked at it and a bead of sweat appeared on his forehead. "Very complicate place...," he murmured.

"How did you know about this valise? How did you know where to find it?"

"Simple, Child. I was one who brought it, that is all." He shrugged as though that were a sufficient explanation. I glared at him until he looked away. "Okay, I tell you what I know, Koko. It is your right to know things. Look how big you are and everybody still hide the truth from you as though you are still a baby girl. Anyway, you already know the worst part. Your pa dead a long time ago and he is never coming back..."

"You came back..."

Deadkumar looked startled for a moment, then he recovered. "Yes," he chuckled. "I did come back. I did."

"I want the whole true story. All."

DEADKUMAR TOLD HIS STORY. He said it was a long time ago and he did not remember everything, but he told of details as though they were etched into the bones of his skull and he was forced to think about them every day of his life. It was a story of Deadkumar and my mother and along the way, it was finally a story of my father. I listened and filled the gaps. I wanted to fill in enough of the missing images that I could close my eyes and see it all, in spite of my intuition that what he told me was not all true either. I sniffed the weaknesses and the deceptions, the scent of a certain fungus rot set into this offering of Deadkumar

Uncle. I closed my eyes and other pictures, perhaps ones my dead father chose to send me, filled my head.

Deadkumar said he had once had a relative whose name was Ramesh and who lived in Durban, South Africa. Now this Ramesh sent a message to his family in India, and this message travelled from one branch of the family to another. It told of the fortune to be made in South Africa, and beseeched any young, courageous and trustworthy member of the clan to step forward and claim a new life and a share in the fortune. This message did not say anything about the way things were in Durban, with Indians and Zulus and Xhosa all struggling under the rule of the Boer government.

"What did I think? I was young then. I had no idea of the big world. And I was having trouble at my home. Nothing big. You know, in the villages in those days, there was not much luck for a young man such as myself. Everything was according to our tradition. Our family, our caste, was of small merchants. We would always stay small, and we would always live according to the law of the Brahmins in our community. And you know, those Brahmins are like our friends the Boers. They like any dark people to be their servant, but they hate them all at the same time. This has been the way for thousands of years in India. The Boers must have learned a thing or two from them..."

In some ways Devkumar's place was like our valley, a small village on a small river. But India is a place of temples to whole nations of gods, all of them vying for attention, and jungles rich with ancient mysteries, wandering *sadhus*, winged monkeys, elephant-headed humans, and women with snakes for hair. When I thought of that place, the land of my forefathers, I saw no place for myself.

But it is easy to imagine the young live Devkumar spending his youthful days relaxing on the banks of the river, playing his flute and troubling girls as they bathed, just like the young and blue Lord Krishna. Every day an ancient and holy *sadhu* with his bowl and walking stick and dusty beard would come to the river to admonish Devkumar and try to teach him principles by which to live in this world. The waters of the river swirled by, catching the reflections of the rich green trees and the bright birds. That is how I imagine that place.

One day an important man, a Brahmin landlord, came down to the riverbank. He was this short, potbellied man with thin, white skin and a parasol. This important Brahmin asked Devkumar why he was playing flute instead of working with his father. Then he bade Devkumar to follow him because there were things that needed to be carried from the market and no able-bodied servant was about.

Devkumar should have said nothing. He should have gone on playing the flute so that his mouth was too occupied to speak. He should have used his musical skill to charm the Brahmin and make him sleepy and thick-minded. But instead he spoke from his young man's proud heart and from his young ideas of fairness and justice. He told the Brahmin that he was not his servant, nor would he ever be. He said that the Brahmin should carry his things himself instead of pestering other people, and he told the Brahmin to go fetch his *goondas* and, that if they would not do his bidding, he should make his lazy and fat wife help him.

That Brahmin said nothing, but went away with terrible red eyes and the vein in his bald, old forehead beating with the unspoken things he wanted to say and do to Devkumar. He said nothing, and that made Devkumar think. In his young and naïve and stupid head he knew he was in terrible trouble, since indeed the Brahmin did have very ruthless *goondas* at his disposal. They protected the honour of the Brahmin and had somehow made a whole clan vanish some years before, but no one made a fuss about it because the family were lowly people who stripped the hides from dead animals.

"I never have seen my old ma and pa since that day. I took my flutes and I went. How I got from the village to Natal is too long a story and it took a long time. First I go to Madras, then Calcutta, then I work as a sailor man for a few years before I came to Durban. I learn how to watch out for my own life and survive. I learn how to behave like a man. I learn everything about machines. One day the boat came to Durban harbour and that's when Devkumar made up mind to stop that life, so Devkumar jump and Devkumar swim."

So here is this photo of the real living Devkumar, with the sea swelling up in the background, with the cap of a sailor man on his head, and sails billowing above him. This photo is bleached from the ocean sun and Devkumar is large and muscular and his teeth are perfect.

IT WAS NOT DIFFICULT for him to find his way in Durban. He found there a welcome fit for a lost brother, and the bustling and rich business of Ramesh.

"Ramesh, oh he was a smart man. His father had come from India years before and made that store called Quality Goods. They were not those indentured people who came to South Africa long time ago. They were smart merchants who saw a chance in all that danger and European and African people and all. The store was in good place, near the African and European areas. He was a very rich man already. Money, he had that. At home, four fat kids and a smiling pregnant wife and a Mercedes car. But the whole family had to live in a flat on top of his old ma and pa because he was not allowed to buy a big property and house. But you know, his store was famous all over Durban. All kinds of people come there to buy watches, furniture, food...everything. One day he would have two hundred Japanese radios, another day a big stock of medicine. Everything good quality but cheap prices. Somehow everyone, Indian, African and white, they all knew that Ramesh sell cheap. More and more people coming all the time. It get so busy that some days there is lineups to get into door. Once people wait for a thing like that they got to buy. They feel they waited just to have chance to buy! So it was true, he need help bad. He tell me, 'Devkumar, you watch over employees and keep customers moving through.' Ramesh trust me right off just because of blood tie. I trust him too, you know. Trust him and like him more and more. I saw what a good man he is. Always say something good about others. Never complain. Never make gossip. He help lots other store owners less lucky. With me there watching over things he took more time to make purchase and keep accounts. Business even better. More customer come down. Maybe too good..."

DEVKUMAR SLEPT in a little room at the back of the store, amid newly arrived sewing machines and dolls and *pangas*, blankets and chains and dried fruit, watches and tennis racquets and dishes, the local newspapers and, best of all, the secretly imported books and science magazines that Ramesh collected and stored outside the city in a hole in the ground, along with ripening bananas. Ramesh paid wages in cash and Devkumar imagined himself staying in that place until he had difficulties, then taking his large collection of cash money and his leave. He was vaguely aware of the weight of the expanse of the continent of Africa stretching endlessly northward to fabulous and uncharted horizons. As he waited for the difficulties to arrive, he worked in the store and he read the forbidden science and technology books and magazines. He bought nothing but the bare essentials and, despite the rules that governed where everyone lived and worked, Devkumar felt as free as any man on this earth. He was not attached. His heart was whole. He understood his work and his role and there were people around him. Devkumar was a man who needed people lest he transform into a lost dog with begging eyes. He found his way among the easygoing African men his age, and he found favour and humour among the young women clerks who swayed to some interior music as they worked, until finally Devkumar set up a music system in the store and played the African hits loudly enough that the store resembled a dancing party that also happened to be a business. According to Devkumar, he never yearned for his family or his home. He knew they missed him. That was enough.

With Devkumar beside him, Ramesh's store did even better. They changed the name to Ramesh-arama to give it the air of a modern place where, as you bought, you could dance, and you could go out the door laughing and singing. The store became busier than ever, and the money flowed into the tills from morning until late at night. Ramesh bought a new Mercedes 500 car. Big wheels for a big man.

Perhaps Ramesh imagined that he was so successful and so big that he was more important than the Republic of Race Laws. Amid the full money tills and the dancing African customers and rich white customers and bartering Indians, he forgot who he was. He looked for a new place for his growing family to live. It would no longer do to live in their cramped quarters. What good was a Mercedes Benz car and the best store in South Africa if his family could not grow up amid the fragrances of a family garden, bathe themselves in the family pool, and entertain their friends beneath the family pavilion?

"But you know, those white people who made up apartheid, they did not do it for fun or games. They will not let a fat and rich Coolie-man buy just anything or move just anywhere. All the place he want to move in, they say, 'no Sir, that is not Indian area and we got this Group Area Act. And not only that but you better not walk on the sidewalk either.'

"He said, 'You know Devkumar-bhai, if this was Amer-iki, I would not face this problem...'

"Ramesh try and try. He think of ways he can bribe the officials. He is nice to people. But nothing...and that made Ramesh blood start to curdle and turn to yoghurt. He should not have complained, but he did.

"Next thing is Ramesh get this government letter. Says his store is not allowed where he got it.

"You know, Ramesh was not some stupid bloke. He knew a few things. He took the letter to a barrister of law, a white friend of his. Ramesh said he was good, this barrister man, and he like to fight the government. So that barrister took the case and get a day in front a judge. The word of this hearing went spread around the town like smoke. Everybody wanted to see the government be told off by the judge. People like me, we know the things that happen in the real world. Court is on the side of Brahmins. Court is on the side of Boers. Court is always on the side of the Powerfuls because they friends and brothers. Same family, see? Politicians and government and courts. I just close my eyes and wait. When something really bad is going to happen, you know my feet start to sweat...you ever get that? So I went around slipping and sliding, waiting for the bad thing to happen.

"One night these men came to Ramesh store after it was closed for the day. We had an old *chowkidar* who was hired to watch over that place. He was an old *madulla* and would just go around tapping his stick on the ground in the dark and keeping the thieves away. That man work there for thirty years, I think. Well, those men who came, they use their knobkerries to beat his head like it was some kind of fruit, then they bust open the locks and went in Ramesh store. Oh, they were not afraid of anything, those boys. Not of police or anybody. They just took their time and smash and bust up some parts of the place. Did not steal a thing. They left most of the stuff in the store in good shape, but they made it look bad, like a big chaos, just like the universe when it got going. Heh, if they were smarter, really, they would have used some kind of thing blow up that place instead. Amateurs!

"Me, I was all ready for the bad news, of course, so I thought to myself, 'finally...,' but when Ramesh found out he call the police. The police wait till morning, then they take a quick look around and close the store down. 'Security reason,' said the police. Ha!"

DEVKUMAR'S FEET remained soaked in sweat. His shoes rotted and burst and he had to wear sandals.

Injustice was in the air of that place, even when nothing much happened. But some people are never prepared for it. 'Mè Jane said this was because they are people with faith, and when faith does not help, the disappointment is worse.

Poor, faithful Ramesh could not bring himself to go out of the house for days on end. He gave up speaking. His wife became subdued, her parents frightened. His children cried and hugged his legs, and Dekumar waited, sweating, thinking what would happen when he was discovered not to have proper papers to live in this Republic of Injustice. He was ready to move on, maybe to the open and endless free Africa to the north.

But after a time Ramesh shook himself out of it. He came out one day and walked around his house looking at it, rubbing his chin. Everyone thought he was going to do something important. He called Devkumar to take tea on the rooftop. Ramesh kissed and hugged his children.

Just then a clerk arrived from the shop with news. White men with papers had come. They had ordered the place cleaned up.

"Come, Kumar," said Ramesh. "Come and we will see. These people are finally coming to their senses. They are trying to make things right after all."

Devkumar strapped on his sandals and came.

"WE DROVE DOWN in Ramesh new Mercedes car, very grand, except for me. I did not feel grand. First thing I see when we get down to store is the white cross of policemen. That made me

want to go home, but I came along with Ramesh. When we get
to the door of his shop there is two white young men blocking
us from going in. Men with nasty, looking-down smiles. 'Where
you think you going, you two?' says one of those boys. And
Ramesh he say nothing, but I can feel the air going out of him
right then, just like he was a balloon too filled with air. Suddenly
it leaks.

"'We don't allow you people in this store, man. It's a European
establishment.'

"I look at Ramesh and wait for the air to finish going. I knew
I was going to have to get him home all deflate, you know, and I
wondered if that would be hard. Just then this older *Angrezi*
white man came out, and he takes us into the office and offers us
our own tea in our own cups, served by our own tea girl. Then
he smiles like he was our best white man friend and he tells us
very polite and gentleman that what happened was not his personal human decision. He was a businessman and he felt very
sick and terrible about the way things happened to be. But it was
the way things were and every folk had to...what was the
word...*abide*. Ramesh, he stare. He did not look to be a man who
abide. That white man kept talking and drinking our tea. Oh, he
said some fancy what-all thing like *this is a terrible complicate society
with so many folks try to live together but still be in their own right place.*
The more he talking, the more I sicking. The more I hearing
same old thing from my own village. It was then I first saw that
this Republic of South Africa was just Republic of Old Village
Caste System.

"Hoo, boy, how that man could talk. Make your stomach
dance just to hear. Like someone important, maybe Queen of
England. He call the store *victim of reorganization*. I thought that
was funny, so I laugh a little, and he stop talking and look at me
like I was some stupid dark-skinned bloke. I still remember that
way he look. Then he get out a nice white envelope and hand it
to Ramesh and Ramesh just fold it and put it away as if someone

hand him a dirty hanky. He knew it was money. He knew it was not much and not enough. Not enough for his store. Not enough for the sour-bad taste in our mouth. Not enough for the ugly government rules that make Ramesh and the Indians go where the Whites decide they should go. He stood up and walk out, very saggy balloon and very old too. He walk out of that place for the last time...

"So what happened next? Nothing. For a long time Ramesh shut himself in his room and go silent again. His wife told me to sell his new Mercedes car. Then Ramesh took up playing with whisky and listening to old Bombay gramophone songs. A few months later he was dead as a fish. Something happen to his inside parts, they said. What doctors call it does not matter...

"I stay around for a while, try look after Ramesh family. But too much misery in that too-small flat. I thought maybe I go back to India and take my chance. Got a job fixing car engine, thinking I could still make some last money. I guess God had other plan for me..."

Tall Woman

If there were a photo to look at here, it would be one of my mother during her first days in South Africa. It would be a picture of a very tall woman, perhaps the tallest woman anyone had ever seen. Everyone would be looking up at her, but she would not be looking back because that was how she was. She would not know she was something to look at, not be aware of people watching her, not know or care. Her young mind would already be out of her time and place, dreaming of a world without hatred or a sun without heat. My mother, in those days, was something like a giraffe: elegant, her head floating above the fear and pettiness that was South Africa. Around her the people would be asking *who is that girl who is unafraid in this place of fear? Who is this giraffe?*

"JAH, MAYBE BECAUSE she was so tall," said Deadkumar, wondering. He went quiet for a minute, either remembering, or maybe *selecting* how the truth should be presented to me.

"What I can say? You never know what going to come up in life and change everything with one kick in the bum. The thing that kicked me was Zara. Ha, she kicking me ever since. Maybe if she was not so tall, and different, maybe I would not have seen her. But she was, and I did. I did...

"I never saw any woman look like she. Every bloke stop to watch her. Even women watch her. Even the dogs and cats watch her. Even police and street sweepers and kids. She was what you would call an *obvious woman*. I do not know how she get *obvious* like that. Maybe that was how they make people where she come from overseas in England or Canada, wherever came from. Zara never talked about that to me. She got to tell you about that herself...

"She moved in right in my street, so I saw her every day. First time I saw her go by, I got nervous, and I start to think, and then what, my feet start to sweat and I don't know what the hell happen. Next time I see her it was worse. This little part of myself just bust away and take off and follow her. 'Where the hell you taking off?' I said to myself. See, this was a new thing. I never knew a man could lose some bad-welded piece of himself to a woman just because she look like some outer-space-tall, temple-dancer beauty walking on this poor bloody South Africa earth. I thought, 'Oh my Gord, what I am going to do now. I got to get my parts back together.' See, in those days I had not much experience with *love* and *nature* and all those movie thing. I mean, I knew how to play with ladies a little bit, but this was different and I had no idea what did it mean..."

DEVKUMAR WAS WORRIED about himself. He thought that he had lost his soul to my mother. Maybe he was right. I can see how he should have worried. If he had known what it would mean in his life, he should have worried. Maybe the part that he lost was his future, or his chance for peace. He wondered if he was weak, and that is a terrible thing for a young man to consider. He decided he should talk to this giraffe who was my mother and he should get his parts back together.

She was a fast walker. Devkumar, even young and alive Devkumar, would have struggled to catch her on his stumpy legs. I can imagine him scrambling along the streets behind her, ducking and bobbing and unsure. He finally caught her up that day, caught her by the elbow so that she had to stop and face him. He intended to announce his presence, since she was so oblivious, and find out how it was that a woman had taken possession of his soul.

The conversation did not go far. He opened his mouth, but the words and ideas crowded forward in his throat, disordered and complicated, then suddenly he seemed to freeze even though it was a sunny South African day in November. What could he do? From that moment he was plunged into my mother's disregard, her distant attention, her preoccupation and her insensitivity. He said, "Well, hokay, I went up to her but I could not speak. I got what you call *shy*. Also, I could see she had seen me before and had no inclination for friendship with a bloke such as myself..."

Deadkumar looked at me from some deep place in his head, his ratty teeth wet and shining. I knew what he meant, but I carefully kept aloof, the way mother had so many years before. You have to be skeptical of the Dead. If you are not, they will steal your dreams and your money in short order. Yet I wanted to know more about that part of him my mother possessed. How had she done that? This was yet another secret of the sisterhood of women.

"So there I was, a man with a piece missing, feeling like a dog run away from one dog disaster right into another worse one. Or some floating piece of junk that come off a boat and is just floating around because the wind and the water current. First Ramesh, now this. I had no direction. No home, no job. I thought if I could just talk to her things would be fine and I would stop floating. I would show her I was a man who knew something about motors and real things. Then she would see and I would be fine. But no, that could not be. It was not part of the Big Plan.

"One day I sat down on a little patch of dusty grass in front of the house to play my flute. Some kids came around like they always do. A couple of them start to dance and some others start to play games by me. Kids always love that flute music. And more kids around, the better I play.

"Then I look up and there is The Great Magnificent – your Mother. She is standing looking at those children and listening to my flute, and, you know, finally I know how I could speak to that woman and talk some sense into her brain. With flute! So I play and play and play – more difficult songs, and songs I never played before, and then songs I never knew I knew, and ones I knew I did not know. I played for a long time. All the while your ma she is with those children and playing and talking to them and listening to every my note and being told that she needs to give up the piece of something she stole from my soul. I never played flute like that ever in my life. I thought my problems were over and I was going to be a complete normal man again. Then that Zara smile at me in a way I don't know what the hell she means, and she went off on her way. So I stop playing then, stand up and watch her go and all the little kids stand there with me too..."

He had no choice. He collected his flutes and followed her, thinking to charm her with his music, or perhaps not properly thinking and letting his feet go their way. Maybe he knew already, even on that day, that he would be needed to help her in her life. It seems impossible that he knew nothing about the jumbled future he would have with her. He floated after her. He drifted, his brain wrecked, his mind a tangle. He had not slept in days, it seemed. He wanted to lie down but he did not. She went on to the university, into a building, down a hall and down a flight of stairs. At the bottom of the stairs there was a door.

"You know, sometimes you will come to important doors in your life and you got to decide to open them or leave them and go on your way. But I did not think of any of that. I open and walk in, my brain-nerves bug-jumpy and working bad, my flute held in my hand in front like I was some holy man. In that room there was a small crowd, less than it sounded like. They were sitting in a big circle arguing. Some people were shouting loud. And your ma was already sitting like she was part of the group in there. But I was not. They all went quiet when I came in. I felt like some kind of *goonda* – thief. But that did not matter to Devkumar. Devkumar intrude on lots of things through his life. It is part of my *dharm*.

"And there was this one bloke who was sitting at a desk and he was trying to make some order in that place. And that was your real pa, Kuku-girl. That was Hari Patel."

Deadkumar looked at me, expecting some reaction, but I kept myself straight and frozen and flat and acted as though this story was an old one. Nothing could touch my heart where it beat quietly in my chest. Locked safe, in a box made of metal and stone. One day I would unlock the box and my heart would go free, but not on a day when it could betray me.

"Yes, Girl, that day I first saw your pa his face was calm and full of understanding of people and I knew he was a good man and meant for a good life. Beside him sat his brother and that brother is Patel-doctor sahib."

My heart was still and closed, locked away. *Uncle Dr. Patel...Dr. Uncle Shiv Patel...*

"Those people stare at me, but I just found a chair and sat like a real top professional *goonda*-thief might do. Nobody in that place says one word for a whole minute. They were all young as I was, but they were students in jeans and T-shirts and spectacle eyeglasses. Not one of them could change rings on a Land Rover without my help. I could see that right away.

"Your father, he look at me and he look at my flute with his understanding look and he ask me who the hell am I. And I answer, all smart and clever, 'John Vorster,' and maybe I must have laughed, but, you know, I knew my brain wiring really starting to act up. It is like when you got short circuit – things connecting that should not be, electricity going in places it got no business. So everyone in that place laughed. Then I said my real name.

"And your dad says something like, 'And why you come barge in here, Brother?'

"And I say something like I heard about all these important somebodies having this important sort of meeting about things. And I call him *Brother* just like he did, but everyone find that funny.

"Your pa, he doesn't mind this smart-alecky laughing. He smiles very kindly at me even though I am making some fun to take the attention off why I was really there. Instead of asking more question or try to show off how big and smart he was, he just say nothing and wait. So I wait too. It is hard to do that waiting game in front a whole room full of people you don't know. The only reason I could do it was because I try to show off to your ma that I am a man.

"No one in that room moved. They all wait for something to happen, for someone to lose the waiting game. Then someone say, 'Throw him out, Hari,' but your Papa say, 'Hey, time to adjourn,' and he stand up."

Everything about my father would have been large. His feet were boats, his head a boulder, his shoulders mountainous. He would have peered down at Devkumar and Devkumar must have peered back with his beady eyes red-rimmed and sore, the veins bulging a little the way they did when he was afraid, ready for a fight or chasing Flori's frock. Devkumar thought he was among a family of giants, or an ancient and obscure race of *pathans*.

He was aware of my mother's eyes upon him, with a bad little smile dancing on her lips, and with that piece of him dangling from an invisible string around her waist.

Tell them who I am, Devkumar's eyes said to my mother.

And what should I say? she might have answered.

My father stood by, waiting.

"He lives in my street," my mother finally said. "He's a musician."

Hari and Shiv crowded around and over him, blocking the light. She sat in the background with her curious and bad smile that made his heart beat stronger and made him bold. When she looked upon him, his way in the world seemed clear. Even if he was a small child amid the forest of limbs of my father and uncle.

"A musician? Where did you hear about this meeting?" my father asked gently.

AND THIS, PERHAPS, is the point at which Devkumar really went from being a normal lying man to being a fabricator of motivation and a sower of confusion.

He said, "Look here, somebody got to do something about this bloody place. I heard someone talking about changing that-all thing..." His voice would have become stronger as the lies were spawned, fed and grew. An understanding came to him finally, even as the words were leaving his mouth. Everything became clear; the fog dissipated. "I got this cousin, Ramesh his name..." He told them of Ramesh and the store and how he had to do something about it. About the *injustice.* He actually said this word for the first time since he had come to South Africa.

And who told you about us? they wanted to know.

He looked at my mother, wanting to draw closer to her by saying *it was she who told me,* but she read his mind and shook her head, one deft move to the side that said *don't you dare.*

He continued to lie. He had heard someone talking in the street. And as he said this she laughed to see how badly he fabricated. She saw through his steadiness and stupid shortness. Then he realised that she knew exactly his flotsam state. That was why she smiled. She found him amusing! A bug! A walking spatter of juice! A pair of balls and a prick!

Hari and Shiv left Devkumar alone without further comment. My father, in his deliberate way, collected his papers and moved with elephantine grace through the too-small doorway. Zara, after a moment of further twitching, bemused and mocking smirks, went on behind them.

Devkumar stayed on in the room to collect himself. Steady ground was what he needed. And there was a more obvious problem. He was inflamed, as impassioned as the big-balled he-dogs of Ntate Lekhlaba. He could not stand properly, even if he wished to, without displaying his ardour to all. He endeavored to suppress it with thoughts of a child found in the ditch, drowned in a freak runoff from the hills. He remembered the detail of the rotted, maggoty little corpse, and tried to recall the horrible smell. But none of this discouraged his rampant emotions. It was ten minutes before his passion subsided enough that he could venture into the streets and find his way home.

Then later that night he lay awake, trapped within the confines of her smile and her mockery. Alone, his night was endless, or perhaps time warped because of some cosmic disturbance caused by my mother's power over him. His senses twitched abnormally, each moment bending and twisting upon itself. His mind preyed upon details he had inadvertently learned: my mother's scent, the precise shading and texture of her skin, the way her rib cage shifted slightly with each breath. As he lay in his room, adrift among the deserted and undulating hours of the night, he attempted to analyze her scent into components, each component originating from another part of her. But it caused his blood to rage and the little blood vessels around his eyes to pulsate. His eyes were rimmed with red worse than usual. It is a wonder how the heart can endure the ravages of blood like Devkumar's, as it surged back and forth through him at ridiculous pressures, driven by passions.

He's a musician, she had said. A musician! Devkumar had never thought of himself as such a thing. Amid the unsteady currents of night, the truth was stark; he was nothing but a poorly educated village Indian far from home trying in vain to recall his pride, and his dignity. *Musician!* The truth was that he was nothing but a speck among the masses of humanity. A walking, talking ridiculous stain!

His blood boiling through him, he stumbled out into the streets, fleeing the hot pit of his bed.

The night was still. A jacaranda tree dripped blood on the grass. Under the dripping branches, tormented by the cool breeze on his skin, he paced for a moment before moving toward her flat, afraid of what he might do in this inflamed state. Nasty imaginings of push games swaggered through him. But another part of him laughed at this: he sensed quite clearly that Zara would shake him off as easily as a dog shrugs off a flea.

The lights in her flat were off. The moon stood guard over her building. He made his feet move, one, two, in concentrated sequence, and then he was moving again, past her place, and on through the streets.

Devkumar found himself in front of the store that had once belonged to Ramesh. As the moon sank away behind him it reflected for a moment on a high window like a flickering flame, then dissipated the way a dream shrinks from the mind of the newly awakened. He walked on stiff legs to a refuse bin and dug in there until he found plastic bags. Oddly, a length of hose came into his hand. Nearby was a parked van with a full tank. The fuel cap fell into his hands. The hose went in and he drew upon it, took the stuff into his mouth and spat, then a steady stream flowed into the bags. One bag filled as the moon vanished entirely, then two bags, and three. By the fourth bag, petrol spilled into the gutter. It spilled over the steps and the walk as he lugged the bags to the doorway of the store and dumped them so that a stream ran under the locked door.

"New management," he told himself. "They need new management."

The air was thick and sweet with gas. He sniffed at it, felt the stuff on his feet and hands, a wet and poisonous richness. Time suspended itself once again, amid petrol fumes and the rich secrecy of a night still and black. Almost as an afterthought, he moved away and lit his remaining cigarette. In the immense realm of dark space and freedom it was down to one cigarette and one small man.

He tossed the lit cigarette at the doorway and was gone half a block and running as the realm of darkness broke gently apart. By the time he reached his flat, Ramesh's store blazed smartly against the sky, a store under new management.

THE FOLLOWING MORNING Devkumar awoke late after a heavy sleep. At the corner where he bought his tiffin, someone said the word *arson* in hushed tones. He heard it, but it was distant and strange news. He had not seen or heard a fire. He had no interest in it. No impulse to see for himself the smoldering ruins. He felt vaguely ill, aching from the bones outward, physical proof to himself that he had become deranged, a man with a piece of his anatomy missing. A dirty stain on the surface of the real world. The real fire lighter was not he; the real arsonist would never realize what she had done.

He shuffled up the street, limbs leaden, repressing the urge to walk past her flat, and hid himself in his place, pacing and fretting there like a wild and uncomprehending creature trapped in a pit.

Then the air changed and brought heat. Within a few minutes his flat became an oven, driving him out. But there was no relief in the street, as if the heat of the fire pursued him, caught him and dwelled in and around him. He had put on his last clean shirt but it was drenched with sweat in moments. A grey ash collected on his hair and shoulders. He bought a pack of cigarettes and the smoke hazed around his head, burning his eyes.

He headed to the seashore, hoping to catch the breeze, and came out at the main European beach, but he stood at the edge of their area anyway, his heart simmering in his chest as the waves swept back and forth. He had to escape this place. Without ancestors, a family or friends, he was loose and drifting and dangerous. For a moment he saw that he would leave this Republic of Bad Fate, or he would follow another way that led to difficulties. There were no spirits to guide him, no ancestors nearby to speak to him in his sleep.

A policeman appeared and forced him with his hostile eyes to move along. Devkumar did not challenge this, but followed the shoreline to the port, where the ships lay loading and where once he had come ashore.

The pier was quiet. The heat seemed to have gathered and concentrated and sat upon the town like a heavy-bellied Buddha, stifling the great engines of trade and commerce. In the shadows the longshoremen shifted about, heavy-limbed and reluctant. Nearby, two hapless workers struggled to control a white horse with zebra stripes along its hindquarters. These men were sick with the heat, but the animal kept dragging them into the sun.

He moved through the port, searching for clues to his destiny. There were Indian ships in the port, floating like fat dead fish upon the swells. They were not the great things he had ridden to come to this continent. He wondered how he could reverse his route, track backwards, board and be away without anyone noticing.

It was then that he became aware that he was being watched. Devkumar turned and looked directly at my father, for Hari was too large and distinct to blend with a crowd, slide behind a screen, or cover himself in shadows. He stood back though, half hidden in a doorway. Even as Devkumar felt his own powerless state, he was alert to Hari-out-of-place, Hari-searching,

Hari-trying-to-be-secret perhaps. Hari hesitated. He was quizzical and glum to be so easily spotted, but then he came out of the shade to lean his forearms on the rail so he could overlook the wharf. He was not standing near enough to Devkumar that an onlooker would have thought they were together, but neither was he so far away that the two could not converse. They appeared as two strangers remarking on the size and shape of the ships, perhaps speculating on the odd spectacle of the zebra-horse which, despite the heat, had summoned new energy, and was intent on either knocking the men into the water or dragging them off the pier and into the streets of the town.

"Why have you come here?" My father spoke toward the oily waters.

Devkumar started at hearing this question. Why was he anywhere? Why did he move from place to place, work, argue, chase women, breath air? Why? Did he mean here at the wharf? Here in Durban? Here in the Republic of Trouble? The question sounded significant, even profound. He looked upon the furious war between the horse and the men. The horse was winning and knew it. It managed to land a hoof on one of the men, sending him sprawling on the concrete deck.

Why had he come here? He said nothing, his mind turning like an engine that refused to ignite.

Hari was not alone. A stranger had joined him. This stranger was somewhat older than Hari. He was dressed in a badly wrinkled suit and sunglasses, but this was a poor effort to disguise a person who was nothing more than an irritated and exposed nerve.

"This is...my friend," said Hari. "And this is...:"

"Nagarajah," Devkumar said softly. "...it's a Tamil name."

The man took off his glasses. "Tamil? What is it?"

"Oh, we are an old people. India, you know."

"Will you come with us?"

"Come where?"

They walked as the dusk settled prettily over the port. Blue lights came on. The zebra-horse stood alone near a railway track, like a blue statue under the lights. Some distance away the two handlers squatted by the curb sharing a bottle of beer, discussing their next move.

As the dusk progressed, the three men moved heavily through pools of darkness, through the thick and hot atmosphere. Devkumar's smoke clouded around his head, and he thought, *I am a speck. A lost and burning speck.*

They came to a car, got in, closed the doors. The man took the driver's seat, while Hari and Devkumar sat side by side in the back. They did not go anywhere for a while, just sat breathing in the stifling interior air of the car.

"We knew about your cousin, Ramesh, and what became of his store," said Hari. "But we don't understand who sent you to the pier."

"Only I sent myself," said Devkumar with surprise. "You think I was sent, that I am someone important to be sent for some reason." Part of him was ready to laugh at this; another part of him was sick. Still another part of him understood clearly the situation. *They are afraid of me. Afraid of a mere speck of dirt.*

"How did you know my cousin Ramesh?" he asked.

"Many people knew about what happened to him. His place was very popular. You see, we take a special interest in matters that affect our communities," said Hari. Then he added. "We know who burned the store too. We know that."

Devkumar's eyes smarted. He desperately wanted another cigarette but the thought of pulling a match from his pocket and lighting it at this very moment was so ludicrous he had to suppress a giggle. Instead he said, "Well, whoever that was who did it, he must have thought he was important, don't you think so? That person must have thought he could do something really big. You people have been following me, nah?"

Neither of the men said anything. Then the man started the engine and they drove along slowly through the dark streets.

"You have been watching for some days, nah? How long? Since I came to that meeting?"

"Before that," said Hari finally. He turned sideways and looked at Devkumar. "It was necessary. You will understand. It is all necessary."

The sweat that had poured from Devkumar all day began to collect in puddles along his shirt, at his crotch and in his shoes. Distantly he wondered how he could contain so much water, then thought that the sweat must be petrol that he had absorbed through his clothes and skin. Around his head floated a halo of smoke. If someone touched him at that moment they would know everything. He was volatile, ready to go off at any time.

He lit another cigarette and feigned ease. Gassy sweat ran from the inside of his shirt into his pants and dripped steadily down his legs. His shoes were oily.

They were in the township now, driving slowly along a wide dirt road, through rows of low houses, some with weak yellow lights shining through tiny, barred windows. They pulled off the road and sat waiting. A car passed them and they watched it go, then they drove again for a while, then stopped and waited. Hari sighed and said, "Do you love this country?"

Devkumar shrugged in the dark, "It is not a good place for me. I would never live here. Even if they let me."

"Yet, you do live here, my friend, along with the rest of South Africa's unfortunates," said the man. "But terrible things happen here, it is true."

"And wonderful things happen as well, right in the midst of hopelessness," said Hari. "Every day a child is born, full of love and hope. Every day someone does something kind. Every day someone shows extraordinary courage, just as you did. There was injustice, so you had to act. We need people like you. People with courage."

"You are probably thinking of some other bloke," said Devkumar.

They had been driving again, passing down a narrow street. Now the car stopped at what looked like a small, concrete cubicle but was, in fact, a new house.

Hari and the white man went into the house and returned five minutes later. They carried packages that could have been groceries or mail. Devkumar was not surprised when Hari put one of the packages in his hands.

"This one is for you. But don't open it until you receive the word. Promise, jah?"

"Promise, sure," said Devkumar. The thing was heavy and he held it gingerly all the way back to the city. They let him out near his home.

"Go straight to your place and keep it concealed," Hari urged. "When the time comes, you will receive instructions..."

And with that they were gone and he was left to make his way to his flat. He lay the package on the bed, then moved it to a corner, then behind the toilet. There was nowhere to hide this thing. And what was it? He knew but did not want to know. And at the same time, there was a sense that he was meant to have it, that now he was more than a mere stain or speck.

HE LAY IN HIS BED, closed his eyes and replayed the previous night. This was not difficult; petrol still perfumed his hands despite the litres of sweat that should by then have washed away all traces of it. He could hear the gasp of the petrol igniting behind him, and see the flickering reflection in the windows as he sprinted away between the shops.

One small man. One tall woman.

Stain

"That is why those soldiers came to our place last night? That is the real reason that Sohrab is locked away?"

"Well, maybe," answered Devkumar thoughtfully "At least that is how I get to meet Zara and Hari. It was back in that time of fighting and sneaking around. We got to be friends together. You know, your pa was not one of those puffed-up kind of Indians. He like people and people like him back. No matter how short or not-important was that person. He make friends with street sweepers and drivers, teenagers and old folk. Tea-wallahs and watchman and mendicants. Sometime I think Hari like those little people better than he like his university-talking smart-heart crowd. But more than anyone, he like your ma..."

Deadkumar sighed and looked away across the lowlands. Smoke from cooking fires drifted into the sky and billowed into vague forms of large women and small men. It was a perfect winter morning beneath the sun, perfect for people with safe homes and clear futures.

"Is that all?"

He kept his eyes on the morning vista and tightened his crossed arms. "I am very dry," he said. "Dry as dirt. Hungry too.

I wonder if your ma is going be okay in this place. It is not a good place to rest and get strength, no. Too much dry and hunger about..."

As he spoke I felt the air soaking away precious moisture from my skin and nose. I had listened to Deadkumar enough. My mother waited in her suffering for someone to rescue her. "You have explained nothing," I said to Deadkumar as I stood up. "You have made up some and left out some. Besides I knew all these things. I have heard it all before from my mother."

But Deadkumar grinned like a big dog. It was not an unkind grin, but it told me I was being silly. "Of course what you say, Dear," he said quietly. "Only trouble is, half what I told you is thing your mother never knew. See, after she came to Lesotho she never want to talk about that whole thing ever. She like to pretend South Africa never exist and nothing ever happen there. She even get mad if someone bring it up. So I never did. We went on our way and made the life we could make, until people start to notice where we hid..."

I picked up my father's valise and went into the compound to hide my embarrassment. My insides were churning. I felt diarrhea coming on. It felt as though it would be bad.

There was *baap* and sour milk and tea ready to be taken to Mother. She looked at me, sniffed at the food and turned away with her eyes alert.

"You have been listening to Devkumar..."

"You heard what he told?"

My mother did not answer, but said, "And you have found something that doesn't belong to you."

"It does belong to me. I rescued it and brought it with me." I hugged the valise to myself like a small girl with her doll. I wanted to grow up and be a woman, but this valise, this dying woman who was my mother, were standing in my way. I would be a woman when I became free, and I could not be free until I knew the truth.

"Tell me what is inside," said my mother.

"Things that belong to him. My father, Hari Patel. My father you could never name and about whom you told me nothing."

My mother sighed. "I told you plenty. You must have forgotten..."

"You never even told me his name."

"A name is not that important. A name is just a collection of sounds if there is no person attached to it...

"People don't exist after they die," whispered Mother. "They become empty space on a canvas, a vacuum, a theory, a collection of thoughts, fiction. They cannot hold you in their arms, cannot father your children, cannot hear your laments..."

But the Ancestors, the Old People, the Dead. They are part of us. They are our guides and mentors and our best hopes. I have felt him near me, nameless and faceless because he was denied a daughter who knew him. Silent and invisible to me, without name or face. Now he would speak. Now he would come to me and my heart would open to him.

I tucked the blanket around my mother's thin shoulders. Her life should have been a grand adventure, filled with romance, but instead her path had led to this hovel in Do Not See Me Pass. Now I could feel her remaining time dissolving into a fine dust to be blown across the Republic of Wasted Lives.

"You must have patience, Aousi," muttered 'Mè Jane as she bustled past.

I waited. The sun came and peered over our scene for a few hours, then seemed to become discouraged and went elsewhere. Dr. Patel and Bushman had gone up one of the steep and scattered trails and would not return until late. I knew they were thinking of food and escape routes and soldiers and plans. I could only wait patiently and tend to my mother.

The reward for my patience was my mother scrutinizing my face and biting her lips in thought. I was, finally, fully in focus. There were things to say, so many things. Perhaps she did not know where to begin.

"There may come a time when I leave you behind..."

If my heart had not been safely protected, I might have betrayed myself and wept to hear her break. As it was, I shrugged and managed to appear too distracted with the task of adjusting her blankets to listen further. She began to say more, but I went outside pretending to need something. There I stood, and breathed in great volumes of silent air, as I studied the small movements at the top of the pass. Suddenly, now that Mother was ready to talk, I was afraid. How could it be? Perhaps she had been right to keep things from me because she knew more than I about my state of readiness. Or maybe there were things in that past that, if disturbed would lead to confusion and trouble. I searched out 'Mè Jane and brought her by the hand to sit with me, to listen for me, lest the pieces of what my mother revealed were too large or too jagged for my limited brain.

As soon as we entered the room again she began afresh to tell me the things that Deadkumar had left out. It was her instinct to show Deadkumar to be misguided, shallow and wrong in all he did and understood. But it was also time to bare the truth. She had hardly spoken over the last days, had collected the words and the stories. Her throat was weak and as she talked her voice grew small. 'Mè Jane plied her with rugged root tea that she kept boiling over the fire, whispering, "Now, now, Madam. Now, now."

Mother said to me, "You are changing into a woman with each passing day. Soon you will undergo the metamorphosis of your insect kin." She laughed softly.

I looked down at my muscular lower half. I could see no change and felt very little like the goggle-eyed, segmented creatures that had learned to avoid our straggly gardens.

"You will cross the threshold as I did long ago. Then you will wonder if womanhood is everything you had hoped. But once you pass from the place of children, you can never return..."

My mother closed her eyes, opened them and focused.

"THERE IS A DANGER for girls who have fathers. Fathers become lost in the innocent dreams of their daughters. They glimpse the inner heart-soul of women, and may even believe they can know things that are not in a man's nature to know. It is this, more than love, that makes them envelope their daughters in confident and unquestioning love. Then those daughters must face the real world...."

In the beginning, my mother was plagued with an overconfidence that comes from having a loving father. Perhaps it was made worse by something embedded in her spirit, or, as my mother would say, *in the genes* (although if this is so, then the spirits or genes failed to be passed down the line to me).

She was sent to the best schools and universities in rich and modern places that we had only heard about: *London, Geneva, Montreal.* Her people were wealthy, her father a busy physician.

"I had every advantage, and that was my undoing. Because I commanded the respect of my family, I misunderstood the world. I thought I could go anywhere and do anything."

I could see her at my age. She would have been like me only in her height, but a girl loved and confident, *overconfident,* walks with the warm sun upon her hair and an unassailable shine in her eyes.

Her family, obstinate people who had fought against the British a hundred years before, had taken that defiance and sense of destiny with them when India became free. The family flourished, the sons dispersing across the globe. And my mother grew up full of this grandness and destiny as she studied and graduated and graduated further, until she was ready to challenge greedy spirits, cruel policemen, and evil republics.

"Then my parents brought me home, suddenly. They had arranged a suitor for me, a young man with a carefully selected name and education, from the right caste and class and location. The right-coloured eyes, the right hobbies..."

"You were lucky, Madam," 'Mè Jane put in.

But my mother was appalled. Her preparations for life were suddenly a mockery.

"I was reduced to a specially prepared dish, ready to serve to any suitable young man. Naturally, I refused..."

Those loving, rich and grand people had made a mistake. They thought that, because they had given so much, their beloved daughter would do their bidding, believe in their beliefs, reward their efforts. I could have told them that my mother was capable of stopping up her love. I could have told them that once she had it all she would craftily horde what she had been given and return nothing.

So she left her family, cast them out of her heart and into the place of unforgiveness. She took a job, saved her money, wandered far. She learned about the Republic of Anger, and all the people who were trodden down, and about the people who had done the treading. And she found her work and her love.

SHE SAW HIM IN LONDON. It was a *demonstration of protest*, a gathering of disaffected, belligerent and overconfident people who thought that by standing outside in the rain in London they could cause the Republic of Power to let go the dream of White and Black, and take up another dream of Sharing and Fairness. He was there, my father, his head wet and cold in the London winter, with less clothing than he needed for the coldness of the place, but his body, young, strong and knowing no better, steaming the rainwater out of his thin jacket.

"I noticed him because his head stuck up above the others, his hair hanging in his eyes. I pretended not to notice, but he was there like a nail that stuck out, unhammered. I saw the way he watched others, with an expression too honest and too open. I thought, 'Now there is a youth who creates problems with his handsome face and too-trusting air.' I saw right away that he could easily make men open their wallets and women open their..."

"But Madam...," 'Mè Jane cut in.

"How was it that we came together? Reflections in a mirror were your father and I. Two unnaturally tall children of our diaspora in London in winter. A mutual attraction based on height, curiosity, narcissism. A sense that we deserved a certain regard, a certain loving attention."

My father left London to return to the Republic of Destiny and my mother was left to look into herself and to endure the cold rain of London.

"He wrote letters..."

Love letters, of a kind. I was starting to know my father. His letters, honest and clear, told of the struggle for freedom. He was in an organization and he sent messages through others he trusted, making her privy to things she imagined were important secrets. He pulled her in, but it was honest and clear and she wanted to be pulled. And so, within a few months, she joined him. But she came for love, my mother. All her dreams of defending the oppressed were made small in the shadow of her personal love. In the glow of their love-fire, it became the Republic of Romance. The Struggle for Freedom was the Struggle for Happy Talk and the Struggle for Bliss.

"How could anything terrible happen to us when we were in love and we were tall and strong and handsome. Youth is so stupid, intoxicated by hormones and conceits. We thought we were doing the things that must be done. We thought we were more significant than we actually were..."

"It was a mistake, Madam?" blurted 'Mè Jane.

My mother closed her eyes.

She came to a Durban that was divided and tense, yet it was a city of thick and resinous air, perfumed by flowers and the pungent, chlorous sea. And it was a city desperate in the overcrowded sections where Africans, Indians and Coloureds were packed too closely into their areas. She reached out her hands and started working. She would banish the evil spirits of that place, care for the homeless children, create trust and respect by her example.

I can only think that my mother was kinder in those young days, before Devkumar and the rest of us ruined everything.

'MÈ JANE SAID, "But where is Mastah Devkumar, Aousi?"

We knew that Deadkumar would be listening by the wall, straining to hear my mother's voice telling us these things she had not told him. "Let him be punished in this way and kept outside," I thought. Nonetheless, I thrust my head out of the doorway. He was there by the wall nearest her bed, but he did not try to conceal his eavesdropping, and he glared at me in a small fury that reminded me of the times before he died.

"You think Devkumar never knew these things, hanh?"

"I must have laughed out loud the first time I saw that man in the street," Mother was saying to 'Mè Jane.

Deadkumar pushed by me and came inside to my mother. "Really," he said, "you really laughed when you first see me?"

But Mother surprised us right then. She suddenly broke along new seams. She shook her head gently and kindly and took his hand.

We might never know all of what had passed between Deadkumar and my mother. There had been times when she pitied him, was amused by him, found him useful (so that she might escape her responsibilities), found his skills indispensable, or was, in some deep place that she hid from us, sentimental about him. But now, as he sat by her, we saw more. We saw other complicated bonds that resembled that of a sister to a brother, and then of a mistress to her dog. We saw two people who must have known something the first moment they were together, and no matter how much they tried to ignore it, they must have felt the hot and dry breezes of the future burning their eyes.

"You always tried. I cannot fault you for that," she said. "You would deserve an 'A' if we were marking for effort."

"You would give me 'A'?" bubbled Deadkumar.

'Mè Jane put her hand on his arm now, but it was meant to restrain his enthusiasm.

"Mastah, maybe that is enough talk for Madam. She must be really, really tired to give an 'A' like that..." And, of course, 'Mè Jane was right. Mother had never given out an 'A' easily in her years of teaching. We went out of the hut and she fell instantly into an exhausted sleep. We were dazed by her change of mood toward Deadkumar. In our hearts we were afraid that it would embolden Deadkumar, and that he would lead us into rash schemes.

"I think she meant a 'B,' don't you?" murmured 'Mè Jane.

"I ALWAYS HAVE the highest love for Zara," said Deadkumar quietly. It was some time later and dark. We sat together by the wall, hoping to find the heat left behind by the sun, but there was none. We sat together in a row, 'Mè Jane, then me, then Deadkumar. The cold was drawing away our energy and our thoughts, but at least I could feel the warmth of the little oven burning in 'Mè Jane's round belly. Deadkumar's flesh was cold as stone.

"I never heard that Hari and Zara love each other in London and all. I never knew that stuff. She never told. I always hoped we three just bump into each other all at the same time and place. Now, you know, it make a bloke feel he missed some things. Well, I had that gift your father gave me..."

DEVKUMAR BROKE HIS WORD to my father. He opened the package and did not keep the contents well concealed either, because there seemed to be no place where he could conceal them in the simple flat that he shared with a family of mice.

The package contained a small and ineffectual-looking revolver and a small quantity of plastic explosives. He wrapped the things again separately, making use of a roll of Christmas gift paper left over from Ramesh-arama. The paper was glossy red and decorated with gay drawings of Christmas trees, sleighs and a white-bearded gnome with red cheeks. As he wrapped he giggled at the picture of the gnome. He hid the gifts behind a rough panel he made in the wall beneath his bed, knowing they would be found if anyone cared to look.

Later he went to a meeting in a modern building near the campus. The meetings were irregular, but every few days someone would be sent along to him to inform him where and when the group would convene. He always attended.

It was a wonder that the small Christmas papery gifts could make a stain on the world feel suddenly important. As he went through the streets he drew himself up tall. He now had messages to give the group. He would position himself where he could catch Zara's eye.

For my mother's part, she would have enjoyed these extra attentions as confident women usually do. She might have found them exciting. She had her love, her Creator of Bliss, and now she had her little Shiva of Lust and Violence. She had her handsome giant, and she had her gnome of frustrated longing and twisted words.

"WHEN THE POLICE made their move they did not try to conceal themselves."

They came during the height of day, white-crossed, large, stone-eyed men who were expert at breaking down doors. It seems there were several meetings going on across the campus, all of them concerning the immorality and illegality of the state. The University of Durban had become a nest of fledgling revolutionaries. The meetings ceased.

And so it was that one evening Devkumar happened along the street just as one of the members of that meeting was accompanied by two officers into a waiting car.

He fled to his rooms and packed his worn-out box, then unpacked it and threw his essentials into the canvas sailor's sack that he had brought ashore when he had jumped ship. After that he might have lit a cigarette and sat still in the falling dusk, looking at the place where the packages were and wondering how to go on.

A car moved slowly along the street, then stopped somewhere nearby. He hopped out the back window onto a low roof, then down, to land on an stack of old tires. He ran away in the twilight, through back lanes saturated with the scent of curries. He saw a widow in her white sari leaning from a window, lowering a bucket to a Zulu housemaid. Further on, a boy with eyes that bulged white in the semi-darkness plodded stonily along, pushing a rolling wheel rim at the end of a long stick.

It had come to this: he was in the street. He had no direction, no people. No job and no home. He had never thought that he would ever be more than a stain that the police might walk over without noticing. Now, with Zara, Hari, the meetings, the packet, the fire, he was suddenly too much more than a stain. Perhaps it was he that they sought. Perhaps they would question the others in order to find him out. In his home, the packages lay heavily in their too obvious hiding place, scenting the flat with gunpowder and gun metal. His identification papers were shabbily produced fakes. He had never had a proper passport. How did the police deal with stains? Laundering perhaps?

He had no home, no money. In fact, the starkness of his lack of anything was sinking rapidly into his thoughts as he fled. "Even rats have families. I wonder if I am as good as a rat..."

Then, suddenly, he saw a looming shape on the walk before him. Hari drew him aside into the shadow of a stone wall.

"Our meetings are cancelled," Hari told him with his eyes shining. "Indefinitely. But nothing to worry about, Brother. It's the regular sort of police sweep. They like to keep a check on who is doing what. In due course we will meet again." He proffered a hand, which Devkumar shook. Hari looked at Devkumar's sack. "It looks like you're off for a ramble. The Drakensbergs perhaps. Lesotho is nice this time of year..."

"Oh, moving here and there," answered Devkumar quietly. "It is not safe for me here..."

Hari looked at him for a moment. "No, of course not. We know nothing of you, Nagarajah. And you know nothing of us, you understand. And...it would be a good idea to get rid of...you know." Then he took Devkumar's hand again, warmly, firmly, huge hand smothering the smaller one.

"That was the last I saw of your pa."

Devkumar waited for my father to move away in the darkness. He considered his chances. The packages were in the flat, waiting to be found. Yet he was too afraid to go back, retrieve them and dispose of them.

"I should not have stood that way. I should have moved."

They came on him quickly, as they always do in the Republic of Security. The car slid up beside him, doors open. He was surrounded by uniforms and white faces and badges and caps. "Come with us," someone insisted, and to press the point they took him by the arms and bundled him into the back seat, the car lurching forward before he had an opportunity to protest or even think about how a stain should protest to the South African police. In another few minutes the car was stopping in a dark place which he knew was not the police building. He was shoved along. They passed a broken wooden gate and went through a wooden door with the marks of a furious entry gouged into it. They pushed him into a room empty but for a bench and a chair. A uniformed officer came and sat in the chair. "Sit," someone said, and Devkumar sank slowly to the bench.

"I will be direct," said the officer. His hair was a kind of yellowy white, his eyes pale, expressionless. "You are either my friend or my foe. If you are my friend, I will treat you with respect. But if you are my foe, then we must fight. If we fight, you will lose everything you have, perhaps even your life."

Devkumar shook his head and smiled. "I do not understand, Sir."

"Understand," said the officer slowly. "We know everything about you. We see everyone you see. We know where you sleep and where you eat and where you shit. We know when and why. We know everything and have eyes everywhere..."

"Of course, I never believe him. They push me and shove me, knock me on the face and head. I even went knockout, but none of that hurt. This old head hard as rock, you know. They lock me up in a room with a mattress full of bedbug, so I just walk and walk all night. Sore head. Little bit blood here and there. I was okay. I guess they check through all my fake papers but they never notice anything wrong. They thought they were smart guys, but no. Next day, they let me go..."

Deadkumar stopped and 'Mè Jane and I looked at him. He looked off in that way dogs look off when they know something is wrong. We waited for the rest of the story as he dodged here and there, weighing the option of the truth against some other things.

"So...when I got out I heard about Hari and Shiv. They got detain too..." He looked away again, unwilling to meet our gaze. "Well, they got detain but Hari never get out of it..."

"What happened?"

"Don't know. Maybe he fought with those police. Maybe he run. They took him away and he never come back. That is all I know about that. It happened to other Indians the same way. It was what happen when you fight the Boer police..."

Deadkumar climbed down and sat the rest of that day near my mother. For the next few days he stayed close to her, with a crease of sorrow and apology stamped across his dark brow.

The Places of 'Mè Jane

Our refuge, in one of the places of 'Mè Jane, was at the end of a meandering row of dwellings that formed the village. Anyone travelling through the pass into the highlands had to cross the centre of the village, or scramble along steep walls to avoid it. But no one actually stopped in that place. This was because they found nothing in the way of welcome: no gabbling, singing women patiently hawking their tomatoes, oranges or cabbages in the sun, no bright bags dangling from sticks to signify that a *shabeen* was here and a bucket of *jouala* awaited a parched throat. The villagers were suspicious and closed, for they regarded themselves as the sentries of the pass. They examined sidelong every living creature that moved through it. On a massive slab of black basalt, someone had represented a few of the more notable travellers as a warning; a man with three heads; a winged, flying wildcat, and a creature that consisted only of glowing, multiple eyes.

It was not a place to approach in the night, as we had done. Our presence had disturbed the brittle and cold atmosphere. The air rustled with the shifting and gossiping of things we could not see. 'Mè Jane's mother and father smiled cheerfully, but there was caution in their eyes as they watched the strange associates their daughter had brought to their home.

"At least we dodged those army bastards, nah?" murmured Deadkumar. No one was in the mood to congratulate him on our escape. He kept looking carefully over the unpromising village and the humble compound, but tried to reassure us with a fake grin that was full of teeth. I could see that Deadkumar was working over a plan.

The thing was, I was afraid and had too many questions even to begin to ask. My urge was to return home and resume our quiet and small lives there. I had known nothing else. In my slow-moving brain I tried to decipher the future as I tucked blankets around my mother. She was cold all the time, yet did not complain.

Well, there was another thing, and it was strange. Even though I was afraid, I was also excited. I felt, even during this time of the world around us shuddering and cracking like an old-fashioned clay pot, that something big was about to present itself. Something especially important for me. Deep inside, beneath my brain, beneath my heart, womanhood waited, suspended, for a signal to burst forth. There were times when it was good to be almost a woman, and ready to be a woman, but not a woman. But now my state of between-ness had become tiresome. The future swarmed around me, just out of sight.

As I took my place beside 'Mè Jane and Flori, caring for my mother, I found myself daydreaming. I pictured myself as a tall and angelic woman, my eyes blazing with knowledge and insight. But then my mind did a slow loop and I remembered the *muti* that was meant for Sohrab but had ended where it should not.

I had never said anything about this to 'Mè Jane, but it was clear she knew everything. It worried both her and me almost as much as Mother's illness, Sohrab's detention and the truth about my father. I sometimes caught her looking my way, her face in a lingering contemplation, but her mouth firmly set. She knew too much. She had her ideas of where problems came from and where they went, and she must have wondered about all the ways that a girl can be diverted, distracted and set upon a fateful course. Some time before, back through the years strewn with sweat and dust, 'Mè Jane had been a young woman like me.

ON THAT VERY FIRST DAY at Do Not See Me, our 'Mè Jane went away up the paths with her faded and worn travelling blanket bunched up around her shoulders. She said nothing to us, and slipped away before we could interfere. She moved slowly up the steep grade on her stumpy legs, but she did not look hesitant or tired. Her pace was that of a woman raised in the mountains who knew how to walk long distances, and a woman who has worked and hidden her strengths and her talents in order to satisfy the illusions of others. My 'Mè Jane was a person full of wisdom and love, and as I watched her grow small against the immense wall of granite and broken stone, I was torn between following to see that she was safe and staying by my mother. 'Mè Jane had lately become old, or perhaps suddenly I had noticed that she had always been that way.

I turned to attend to some task, and when I looked back she was a tiny speck high in the pass, the mists swirling around her. After some hours she would reach the top, then go into the blankness and mystery of the place they call Mamahau.

'Mè Jane's absence always unbalanced our family. Shortly after she left I heard Flori weeping in the corner. My mother had knocked over her teacup, saying it did not taste like tea at all, but like sweaty socks. Deadkumar suddenly seemed unsure of his planning and calculations. Patel Uncle made comments about the shortage of food in the village.

Mama Jane told us that 'Mè Jane had gone up to the house of her husband. "Maybe she wants to take you there...just for visiting purpose. It is her own house too," she added helpfully.

We had known this, but over the years the idea that 'Mè Jane had a husband and a house of her own had become abstract. Her trips away had become infrequent and short. She said little about her husband, except that he was old, had never given her children and never left his place in the highlands. "He is one of the Basotho," 'Mè Jane told us. "The real type."

We waited for a day, then another day, not wanting to make a move without 'Mè Jane. Mother slept or sometimes sat up staring at everyone. We kept our minds occupied trying to sort through what had happened. We made ourselves useful by helping 'Mè Jane's old people repair their fences and walls, buying up the small amount of mealies available, watching the road for soldiers and waiting for the familiar round and waddling form to descend from Do Not See Me Pass.

It was difficult to keep from lapsing into desperate trains of thought. Remotely, I wondered how I would go on if Mother died and 'Mè Jane never came back. I would be burdened with the care of our men. Eventually Flori would run off and it would be only a matter of time before the remains of Deadkumar finally disintegrated. Army soldiers would come and question me, and I would tell them everything I knew of the lies and stories I had collected over the years. These fabrications were what I believed. The soldiers would become frustrated and put me in the cold water behind the dam...

AFTER TWO DAYS 'Mè Jane came back to us. With her was a young woman of the highlands.

What happened was this: she had indeed entertained thoughts of bringing our whole family to the place of her husband, Ntate Mohapi, but she was disappointed. Ntate Mohapi had not aged, despite years of tough and spare mountain living. In fact, not only had he remarried while 'Mè Jane was away toiling and sending him money, but he had forgotten to ask her permission. When we heard this, we thought it very impolite, but 'Mè Jane took this news with the great grace and forbearance that could only come from a woman who knew well her ancestors and her gods. In fact, she was kind to the new, young wife, telling her she was her sister and not to worry. She remained respectful to her husband, despite his betrayal. She prepared his favourite dish of tripe as she had planned, and gave him half of her saved money, as she had always done.

After two days of this, Mohapi became disturbed. 'Mè Jane, as always, had risen above envy, pettiness. She had risen above him and he knew it. It was not for a woman to have such a great and generous spirit. He became embarrassed as he thought about it, and he realized he had to do something big to show that he was still master of his house. So he decided to order his new young bride to go along with his old wife, so that she would see the lowlands and the encampment and learn how to cook a proper meal of tripe and *moroho* and *baap*. He gave her some of the money 'Mè Jane had earned, and told her to purchase a blanket appropriate for a married woman, with sheaves of ripe corn imprinted on it. 'Mè Jane would assist her in the purchase, as she was a shrewd bargainer.

'Mè Jane agreed, of course. She did not bother to mention our family problems and the soldiers. She neglected to say that we could not go anywhere near the encampment. Late in the day the two women appeared, one old and bunched up and short and wizened, and the other as young and supple and fearful as a prized calf led to the slaughter.

The new bride of 'Mè Jane's husband was called Lebohang. She sported a perfectly woven Basotho hat atop a head of thick and wild hair. Her teeth were strong and white. Because she was young and beautiful, she carried herself proudly, with her head held up high for all to admire. But it was her breasts that impressed us. Those breasts were like no other breasts we had seen. Not only were they proud, prominent and strong, but they seemed to have individual personalities. When one moved north, the other shifted south. While one slept, the other stayed alert. As one danced, the other kept time. It was impossible not to be interested in those breasts. In amazement Bushman exclaimed that they were sisters and would be his friends. He told me those breasts had names: *Fantu* and *Coku*.

WHEN WE WERE FIRST TOLD that this was the new bride of 'Mè Jane's husband, we were confused. We looked upon her hat and her breasts and wondered how 'Mè Jane felt. But it was plain that Lebohang was afraid. She watched 'Mè Jane with eyes like moons and her backbone tensed. She was ready to run, thinking that 'Mè Jane meant to kill her. She had not wanted to leave her home. Her husband had insisted.

This Lebohang slept hardly at all, and kept her arms crossed over her chest and her hands on her breasts. She sat quietly in a corner and watched 'Mè Jane with eyes that expected an attack. She said little and ignored Bushman when he approached her, singing, *Coku and Fantu, come out to play...*

It had never been easy managing Bushman, but now that we had fled our home he was more trouble than ever. Perhaps the knowledge that he was homeless and would shortly have no food and no bed affected his mind badly. I saw sparks flying from him as he cast about from my mother to me, from 'Mè Jane to Flori. We watched these sparks from the sides of our eyes and hoped Deadkumar or Patel Uncle would notice and do something other-worldly, or maybe manly, about it. Now and again I tried to grab him, thinking to pin him to the ground and beat him into shutting his mouth, but he was faster than flies, and much faster than locusts.

Instead, as the day went on, Bushman attempted to make Lebohang, or at least Fantu and Coku, take him seriously. First he pretended he was a cobra, slithering on the floor with his head raised and his hood spread. Then he suddenly struck my leg, which made me jump up and look for the marks of his fangs. When this received no comment, he reverted to a gecko, making sudden dashes with his legs and arms stuck out, freezing in odd positions, flicking his tongue and swivelling his eyes without blinking. Lebohang kept her eyes on the comings and goings of old 'Mè Jane, or covered her eyes with her hands rather than look at Bushman. She clenched her teeth to keep herself from weeping.

But Bushman was not done. He made himself into one of those special dogs with three legs. He did this so realistically that we rubbed our heads to make sure our brains would not think he had become a real dog. Lebohang looked at something in the distance. Finally he came close and snuffled at her feet, then proceeded along her leg to the hem of her frock. His tongue lolled out and he drooled on her knee. Just as he was about to stick his snout up her dress, 'Mè Jane grabbed him by the scruff and dragged him outside. He stayed there but set about howling and barking with such imagination and enthusiasm that all the villagers came out of their houses.

AS MY MOTHER SLEPT, I was left alone with the new bride. From outside came the sound of Bushman whining and scratching and singing praise songs about Fantu. He had changed his tactic and was trying to soften them up, one at a time. 'Mè Jane was berating him, saying, "God will strike you dead, Abuti, and when you wake up you will truly be a dog! Stop your evil dog ways, Abuti. Stop now!"

"Is it true that 'Mè Jane gave her old husband to you, Aousi Lebohang?"

Lebohang looked at me helplessly for moment, but recovered, saying, "Maybe he gave himself." After a while she added, "I am a Missus now. You must call me 'Mè, not Aousi. I am not a sister of young unmarried women now."

"Ah, yes 'Mè," I said with a snort. "Married."

"Why do you laugh?"

"No, only to be happy..."

My mother awoke and listened to this exchange. She smiled at something we said, the first time in many days. Bushman had switched his praise to Coku and had taken up a wholly different, mournful tune.

"There are strange things in this lowlands," said Lebohang suddenly.

Instead of looking her in the eyes, I looked at Coku and Fantu, despite my best intentions. One breast was still and attentive, while the other seemed to play some game.

"What things, 'Mè?"

"*Strange* unholy things."

"Are you a holy person?" I asked.

"Only as I believe in God," she answered with an irritating air of confidence.

"Tell the strange things," I said after a while.

"I cannot. They are too unholy and strange," sniffed Lebohang. "I am telling you just that and no more. I do not like this danger place. No one does."

"Why did you say *danger*, if you won't tell?"

"I tell you so you will beware. Young women need to beware, more than others. You know, if I tell, Things will hear. That is why it is not so good to talk, only listen..."

"Listening is fine. Secrets are fine. You are fine. *Hantlay*."

"Yes, *hantlay*."

"But tell the secrets so I will know. How can I beware if I do not know?"

"I cannot say much. It is medicine from the Republic. Very powerful."

"You say. The Republic of Powerful Medicine..."

"Yes, and people pay for it..."

"No!"

"First they need a young, eager girl who has been initiated. Maybe a girl like you. They watch her for a long time. They take from that girl her unborn children, then leave her with nothing, only to be empty and wander in the mountains..."

I noticed that my mother was still smiling and I laughed a little, just to see her so. Lebohang could not see why I laughed.

"Who are these sorcerers?" asked my mother.

"Ah, they have no proper names. But there is one called *One Eye*..."

"He only sees things in halves?" I asked.

"He is often seen with one they call *Bad Smell*..."

"Sorcerers never bathe...," I suggested.

"and *Too Much To Eat*..."

My mother giggled, but it was restrained and tentative, as though humour was painful. "Those are terrible names," she managed to say.

"And what would those people do with unborn babies?" I asked after a long quiet.

Lebohang gave me a look as though she wished I would not ask questions. But she was swollen with fear and needed to release it with talk. "Well," she said. "They say the Unborns are taken to that smiling Boer President, the one they call *The Old Crocodile*. That is why he is so famously Evil, that old man."

She stood and Fantu and Coku sat up like two trained dogs ready to guard their mistress. Well, Fantu looked stern. Coku seemed distracted by Bushman's pleading songs...

AT THAT MOMENT my mother pushed herself up to her feet. I went to steady her but she waved me off impatiently. Her face was pale and drawn. It was not comfortable for her to stand or sit or lie on the cold floor. She took a sharp breath, then walked unsteadily out to the latrine.

I had stopped encouraging Lebohang to talk, so she gave forth freely, fearing to lose my attention.

"Young women used to walk freely in the pass, but now they cannot. If they do, they will disappear..."

A part of my mind went elsewhere. I thought about my father and how things would be if he were alive with us now. He would know what to do better than Deadkumar. I was aware that Bushman had fallen silent. Another part of my mind wondered where he had gone.

"There was a young beautiful woman named Lucy. Her mother was blind and poor..."

For Bushman to break off a pleasurable activity like singing wild dog songs to irritate people, there must have been something important and interesting to him.

"It was not more than eight years ago, when the rains were steadiful and plentiful and rich. All through the mountains that year people were finding diamonds that were just like teeth. Same size as teeth. They even looked just like teeth..."

Perhaps a creature or smell had attracted him away.

"...people wondered what sort of creature had diamonds for teeth...maybe one creature from some other Place..."

If I opened my mind to everything that was happening, I would be flooded, drowned, bloated and washed ashore to rot. My mind would go mad and no one would know what to do with me because I would be huge and impossible to control. Part of my mind was on *muti* and sorcery, while another part was full of waiting soldiers and their guns.

"...then the childless man went out and found Lucy wandering, and he told her there was a wedding at night and she should come with him. He was nice and his eyes were bright so that Lucy thought, 'I will go with this Handsome.'"

My mother was outside the compound at the flimsy latrine, struggling perhaps. I stood up to go outside, but my brain was snagged by what Lebohang was telling me.

"...but at the party he made close talk to young Aousi Lucy and told her he wanted to touch her and be her husband. So she finally agreed because no man had ever asked that and she was lonely wandering with her goats all the days. They went away from the party and the fire and went behind a *kopje* and in some rocks and he made her to do sex with him..."

I rushed outside. Bushman was nowhere to be seen, nor was Mother. I checked the latrine, listened for sounds, searched the rocks and boulders up the trails that led to the pass. Lebohang came behind me and followed my searching gaze.

"...and then they did Evil Things," she said. "The childless wife of the childless man came and together they cut that Lucy and removed her Unborn Babies. Ai! They killed her..."

I went off at a trot down the path toward the car and the road, suddenly sure of where Mother was. She was tired. She had had enough of the long journey to death and wanted to go home, soldiers or no. I sensed her frustration with this process of weakness and death.

I ran along the shadowy path, seeing strange flitting forms at the edges of my vision. Then Lebohang floundered past me in a panic, one hand holding Fantu, the other gripping Coku, restraining them from surging exuberantly out of her frock. She had terrified herself with her own story. Her eyes were wild. She grunted with fear and exertion.

"Where, Aousi, where do we run?" she gasped.

We came to the small place where Deadkumar's papery and unbalanced-looking car was hidden. Mother lay in the back. Bushman was in the driving seat looking for the way to ignite the motor. He had his hands on the wheel but seemed puzzled. He knew something was amiss; it was too quiet. This was a peculiar thing about Bushman: he treated motors and machines as though they were live creatures, not mechanical objects. At this moment he knew the car creature was not making the growling sound it made when it moved. But he had no idea how to make the sound happen. He turned the wheel back and forth in his hands, stopped, pulled on the gear lever, frowned. Then he noticed Lebohang and abandoned his efforts so that he could sing dreamy praises for Coku and Fantu.

I opened the door to my mother's hiding place. "I need to go home," she pleaded.

"Ah, we can't go back there. Soldiers. Paramilitary police," I told her gently.

"No, not there. West Vancouver. British Properties. My mother needs me. And I've had enough of this unhealthy life we lead. I don't know why we stand for it. It's unhealthy and rough and dry and...I should just go home..."

"Properties," nodded Bushman. "She needs British Properties."

I looked at Lebohang for help, but she was heaving with fright as she eyed the dark shadows cast by the stony walls. She still had her grip on Fantu and Coku. I was on my own.

"Well, that will be fine." I managed a sympathetic purr. "We should all be able to go to British Properties. But first we need to tell 'Mè Jane and Devkumar and Patel Uncle. They will need to prepare, no?"

My mother came to my lie easily. She nodded and said we could all live there quite well, even Flori would like it. She came out of the car and let me lead and carry her back to our place of refuge. "And when can we go?" she asked.

I shrugged easily. "Right away, of course. After a rest."

"Good idea...after a rest."

"But how far is this place?" asked Lebohang. Her words came in short gasps; however, she had released her breasts and had given up the project of ignoring Bushman. Now he lead her along the path by the hand as he sang his praise songs.

"It is far," I said. "But not difficult."

"Oh," said Lebohang. "Then I will come too. Just to see..."

Mother and I looked at her.

I RESTED ON THE MAT near my mother as she slept. She was dreaming of her place of *British Properties*. I could not picture it though. It was yet another piece of her story she had not told me. The photo of British Properties and West Vancouver would be completely dark.

'Mè Jane sat by my side while Lebohang worried the edges of her old blanket. She was in need of a bright new blanket that would offset the loveliness of her face and the rest of her, but she showed no urgency to go to the Seanamorena store in the encampment.

'Mè Jane said to me, "You know, we must be kind to Aousi Lebohang..."

"Yes, 'Mè. But has she not taken something of yours?"

Lebohang looked up at us with eyes wide and breasts quivering.

"Perhaps she has. Perhaps. But you know, sometimes a husband is not good. Sometimes he has only bad seed and his sex is weak like overboiled cabbage..."

"'Mè?"

"Well, look at poor young Lebohang. Very nice and beautiful she is. Like a young woman should be...or *could* be...," she corrected.

"Is he not nice, that husband?"

"Ach. You see, she will not have any baby with Ntate Mohapi. She will never be a woman with that old man either. All of that niceness and beauty will just be as air. You know, long ago, I was also a young bride..."

"Were you beautiful, 'Mè?" broke in Lebohang, her voice cracking.

'Mè Jane chuckled. "Maybe, maybe, but not as you."

"And no babies came?" asked Lebohang, her hands going to her breasts.

"None. Then, after a time I went away to the Republic to become a nurse and help others where I could..."

"And did you go to a wedding? Did a young man meet you there? Did he want to be your husband outside on the rocks? Did you agree because he was so handsome...?" I blurted.

"What wedding? What young man?" 'Mè Jane frowned at me and turned back to Lebohang. "After you buy a new blanket in the encampment, I think you will have to find your own way back home through the pass..."

LATER THAT NIGHT Bushman and I slipped out the gate and waited in the shadows, hoping to see the Things that move in and out of the pass. We climbed atop some large boulders outside the high-fenced kraals. When the moon rose and filled the notch in the high ridge, the stone all up the pass glowed. In that moon glow, we detected movement. It was so dim we had to avert our eyes to see it, and even then it was the stealthiest Thing we had ever seen.

"It has the Night Eyes," commented Bushman.

'Mè Jane and Dr. Patel came and looked at us but said nothing.

"A Thing came," Bushman told them in a whisper, which made 'Mè Jane scuttle away and return a moment later with pieces of wood and dried grass. She lit a fire where we sat. The Thing was no longer visible.

I said knowledgeably, "I heard this was a good place before. But now girls wander the hills, searching for unborn babies."

"People should not misplace babies, especially unborn ones...," commented Patel drily.

"Many devils come down the pass," said 'Mè Jane. "After a time they become mixed with the Normals."

"Your people are Normals." Bushman squinted at her through the smoke. "Aren't they?"

She squinted back at him.

"Are we Normals full, or Normals part?" he inquired. When she snorted at him he added, "I wonder."

We looked away from the fire at the dark mountainside. A hundred shadows cast about, sniffing the ground. We shuddered and stoked the fire and pressed our backs to the fence, but Dr. Patel yawned and strode into the maw of the darkness. A moment later we heard him making water in the rocks. It was long and plentiful, his water, and at the end Bushman exclaimed, "Ha-ow!"

"Did you see anything?" I asked casually when he returned.

Dr. Patel looked at me blankly. "Go to sleep," he said. "Maybe tomorrow we will find a way out of this place."

Highlands

ere is a photo of a Basotho pony. This pony has large furry ears like a donkey, but it is brave and strong and well-loved, if underfed. Upon the pony sits my ailing and thin mother. Behind them are the vague and huge forms of the rocks of the highlands.

For two more days we waited at the foot of the pass for Mother's strength to improve, even though we secretly knew that she would not improve any time soon. Then came the time for difficult decisions. Mother expected to go to Canada, to the place called British Properties, but she had failed to connect her worries over Sohrab with her urge to leave Lesotho. It was as though she now had two, or perhaps more, brains, each with it's own memories, worries and emotions. We waited for a sign. Patel Uncle and Deadkumar conducted quiet discussions, Deadkumar hissing and waving his arms despite his efforts to appear calm. And each time my mother awoke, she asked me when we would be setting out for British Properties.

Our sign came one morning. When we awoke we found that outside the compound a band of small children had gathered.

They were the first children we had seen in the village. Now 'Mè Jane came and looked at them and muttered that they were unclaimed and rootless things. She shooed them away beyond a large clump of rocks. They stayed throughout the morning, observing us with hollow eyes.

"Why do they wait? Have they no homes?" 'Mè Jane fretted. At lunch she relented, and cooked and handed out the last meager portions of mealies. The last child to receive the food was a girl with a dusty face. In return for the mealies she presented a live lizard with two tails, which made 'Mè Jane squawk and flap her blanket and retreat into the house. Bushman stepped up and accepted the lizard, calmly tucking it down the front of his trousers. He went away down the path after that, limp trotting, with little cries of glee.

Those mealies were the last food in the house. We had exhausted the provisions of our hosts and now they apologized for the misfortune. When we heard this we were sorry for them and were immediately assailed with a burning hunger. Each of us retreated into private thoughts of roasted meats, *roti*, gourds of soured milk.

"It is time to take ourselves along to the road," said Deadkumar Uncle.

Dr. Patel held him back. "Impossible," he said.

"Eh, Morena," croaked 'Mè Jane's old father. "The roads are not safe now, especially at night."

Patel and Deadkumar fell to arguing, their confusion laid bare for all to see.

I turned to 'Mè Jane to ask for her wisdom, but she looked suddenly tired. "Eh, Aousi, go and find your brother. We don't want trouble with trouble..."

I wondered what she meant as I followed the path to where the car was kept. At that time of morning the car was not hidden well. The sun angled down between two rocks and fell into the rear window, warming and illuminating the seats inside. I could see that Lebohang was there, in the back. I stopped in the shadows.

Before her was the naked and sunlit magnificence of Fantu and Coku. The tips of those breasts were dark and beautifully shaped, the nipples upturned like the faces of children. And then I saw that those faces were asking questions and that the questions were being answered by someone sitting very still at the other end of the seat. That someone was Bushman. He wore an adoring and reverent expression as he admired his friends Fantu and Coku. He sang his song in gentle tones. As I watched, he reached out to touch one, then the other. He patted and stroked them, felt their weight in his palms, sniffed their scent as Lebohang closed her eyes and turned her face away. He suckled at them lovingly and when that was done he jumped out of the car and jigged away, high stepped, raising a warbling, triumphal song.

I retreated up the path alone, my blood bubbling through my veins, my skin and flesh sensitive and joyous.

When 'Mè Jane saw me she stopped and said, "What did you see?"

"Nothing, 'Mè," I replied, but my blood bubbled exuberantly through my cheeks.

"Eh-eh. You saw something that made you laugh..."

IT WAS AFTER THAT that 'Mè Lebohang changed. She lost her caution of 'Mè Jane, perhaps realizing that if 'Mè Jane really hated her she would not kindly provide her with an extra mat to sleep on, ensure she had a fair portion of food, while we still had food, and encourage Lebohang and me to be friends. So Lebohang went to 'Mè Jane and said she could never be her sister but only wanted to be her daughter, "Like Aousi Koko...," she said. "And Mama," she went on, "why do you not want these lost people to come and stay at that house that is yours and mine.

There is food at that place, and warm beds to sleep. It is your place that you made with your money. Then, when they are ready, they can journey to Mamahau. You can live in the mountains, breathe the mountain air and be well. It is these lowlands that makes people to be troubled..."

She told me she could not go back to that old man, Mohapi, by herself."He never touches me," she shuddered."But you know, as a wife, I have to be touched." She knew she would be childless forever if she stayed with him, and eventually she would have to seek Evil Ways. But I knew other things that she did not say, about how her Fantu and Coku wanted to ask questions of Bushman and learn the answers in his praise songs, and respectful and soft lips.

THE IDEA of going to Mamahau stirred everyone and the next thing was that Deadkumar showed up with a skinny little pony. "Basotho pony," he said."Cannot go down, only up."

We set about putting our few belongings together for our climb up the pass. Then we began our journey with our stomachs wondering about food.

In the pass, the air carried the biting chill of snow. Above us the mountainside was an endless, upswept terrain of broken stone upon slabs of basalt rock. Only a few scraggly tufts of brown grass stood here and there, like the whiskers on an old man's face. A pair of eagles with shaggy plumages and prominent crowns hung in the air, watching our progress as though they weighed our chances. Once they came close enough that Bushman skittered away under a rock. The eagles had yellow penetrating stares.

After only an hour of climbing, Mother began to shift in her saddle, her shoulders hunched forward under her blanket. After a few more minutes she leaned over and collapsed into my arms, whispering that she was not sure this was the correct way to

British Properties. 'Mè Jane and Flori fluttered, batlike, around her, while Deadkumar placed one foot upon a rock and gazed down over the thin ribbon of road and the line of toy huts below us. He said, "Ho boy, they never give us trouble up here..."

We knew that Mother was too weak to climb the pass. I cradled her head but I did not give myself up to tears, despite the small voice inside of me that suggested the grand nature of our tragedy. I could not weep. I was far away and cool. My heart was shut and locked against such tragedies and disasters. Nothing could touch me. I was not a woman, perhaps not even a human anymore, only a large walking thing, the daughter of locusts or some other mystery.

I carried her as far as I could, cradling her head against my shoulder. She slept like that, warm against my working muscles, soothed by the rhythms of her child's breaths. After that she went back onto the pony more comfortably, and that pony seemed to understand very well the way things were. It picked the smoothest and most delicate path through the stones, and sometimes waited for a moment listening to its rider to make sure she rode well. Flori watched the pony and after a time began to speak and sing to her with praise and encouragement. After a while we all joined in and the pony perked up its ears and eyes. We loved that humble creature that carried our mother. As we sang and praised and watched the scant muscles of the little horse working, we fell into reveries that some god from the great Mount Khailash, or from British Properties or maybe from the realm of our Ancestors, looked over our problems and assisted us to bear our burdens.

It was that small horse from God that led the climb up the steep skirts of Do Not See Me Pass. Often we rested and looked down upon the troubles of the Kingdom of Lesotho, spread below us like an ant colony upon a fissured and ancient stone. Beyond, in the red and hazy distance, the River Caledon snaked along the edge of those troubles, and marked the border with the Transvaal.

And as we reached the top of the pass the winds came on us, devoid of moisture or comfort, and caused the benevolent gods to flee back to where they lived. Our reveries were broken by scudding clouds and the hunger in our bellies. We heard things shifting about in the stormy winds, howling in the distance to distract us and make us lose our footing. We stumbled and might have stopped if that small horse had not flattened her ears and doubled her careful steps. We thought we heard the spirits of young girls moaning for their unborn. But the light of day kept those things back, and we went on through wind and worry.

The storm became worse as we trekked across the rock and moss and thin grasses of the plateau. In the highlands the air was cold and harsh, but our heads cleared there, just as Lebohang had claimed. Late in the day, as lines of grey geese sailed past, we came to a few *rondavels* clumped in a shallow dell. Here, shielded from the storms and driving winds, were the gardens of Ntate Mohapi. Here we got Mother off of her pony while 'Mè Jane and Lebohang delved into the wealthy food stores that belonged to Mohapi, had been paid for by 'Mè Jane, and were now the domain of young Lebohang. That old man appeared after a time, wizened and light on his feet and surprisingly fierce in the defence of his possessions. But neither woman deferred to him now. They knew well his limitations and ignored his complaints. 'Mè Jane said, "Be kind, Ntate, so that someday you are not the traveller who is unwelcome in a rich house..." After that he was still.

We filled our bellies with *baap* mixed with soured milk, then we slept and woke, and with each waking the sharpness of our minds became less uncomfortable, until we lapsed into an attitude of suspension. In the early morning we woke, but kept our breaths small so we could count the number in our company to ensure that the old souls of the mountains were not sleeping among us. And I waited to know whether or not the Ancestors would be merciful and come and take my mother by the hand and help her cross the abyss to her final destination.

Outside, the wind subsided to the wail of a wild thing pining for a lost mate. We smelled rain that was released to blow about in the wind, knowing, without having to look, that the rain would not find its way to earth but would only dry in midair. Through the doorway I saw that the flock of geese had settled on the ridge of bare rock in order to observe us. Behind them a lone hooded figure ran stumbling across the plateau. Mother moaned and settled in her sleep. She had slept through our tumultuous arrival, missed Mohapi's reaction to our invasion of his house and stores. Now she stayed asleep, unable to countenance our jagged reality of storms and dry wind. Only later, when the fire was well-lit and had burned for some time, and the sun had banished all the doubtful beings from the mountaintop, did my mother awaken so that I could accompany her to the latrine.

"Is death painful?" I asked her as we walked out in the thin air.

"I don't know. Is it?" she answered sincerely. Her hair was streaked with new grey and the flowing of her hands had ceased.

For a moment we stayed there, captured by the sight of a flock of geese that waited for something in the wind.

Patel

This photo is old and faded, like the memories adults have of childhood. In this photo we see two boys with thick hair that grows low down their foreheads. They stand against something that looks like a strange wall with a corded, complex structure. On closer inspection, we would see that they are standing against the trunk of an immense tree.

THIS IS ABOUT how my father died. It was difficult for me to know this at last – no made-up story could be this bad. But I know this part of the story is true because it was painful to tell, and it came from a man who I now realized had never really lied to me: Dr. Patel.

Dr. Uncle Patel. Uncle Dr. Patel. Shiv Uncle. Who was he? He had always been in our lives, down the hill, silent and brooding in his stone-walled house of the principal. He was familiar, but we knew nothing about him. We did not know we knew nothing because we rarely thought of that. I now knew that he was the brother of Hari, my father. His name was Shiv. It took a long time for this idea to settle, and there was not enough time. Events were cascading one against another, and we were being shoved forward into an unpredicted future.

Now Dr. Patel sat by my mother, watching over her sleep as her eyelids fluttered. We could see that he had a great affection for my mother, even as she lay mired in her dream world of cages that capture light, of a remembered childhood in distant lands, and of our return to the valley of dust, snakes and farting soldiers.

"Is death painful?" I asked him.

After a moment he said quietly, "Death can be many things." Then he added, "Yes, it can be hard..."

"We must take care that it is not hard for her. She cannot tolerate pain. She is more afraid of pain than most people..." I gulped.

Dr. Patel coughed and looked at my mother, perhaps wishing for her to awaken and reassure him that she would not find a painful death too hard.

I said, "No one knows whether my father died painfully. But I sometimes wonder..."

Patel glanced at me across my mother. I do not know what it was that went between us, but it was some new thing. Perhaps it was blood, for he was my real uncle, not like Deadkumar. "No, that is not actually correct," he said. "I was with your father when he died..."

My mother's eyes were open. She had been listening all along. I saw the questions in her eyes and saw that she too had wondered.

"I was incapable of speaking of these things, especially to a child or a grieving widow. Now I find I must," said Patel leadenly. "For the sake of the two of you. For the sake of myself perhaps..."

He gathered himself for a moment, and my mother and I stopped breathing lest that process be disturbed. Then he said, "I will tell you all I know. But I want to go back so that you will also understand better who he was and why he died."

"OUR PLACE – our first home – was in a place called Cato
Manor. You don't know Durban, Child – maybe in some better
times you might go there. Well, our times were not so terrible,
but then things happened that were not supposed to happen; the
fire came and burned away part of our childhood forever. I have
only two clear memories from my early childhood: one of the fire
and one of a tree, but the tree, it was such a tree, bigger than any
tree you can imagine, and fire, that was from hell itself..."

Uncle Patel looked off into his past. I could see that he was
blessed with memories of a mother and father who cared, of
brothers and sisters who were ordinary and did not have strange
odours and bad eating habits. *Ordinary* memories slid languidly in
his eyes, of a small boy named Iqbal, his best friend, now lost somewhere, and of a small orange kitten that never seemed to grow.

They imposed Pass Laws in those days, the rules that controlled the movements of people according to race. There was
great turmoil, and people protested against these laws. Then the
communities turned on each other. The Zulu community
attacked the Indian community in that place of Durban.

My uncle remembered people running through the streets.
Playing, he thought, but then a van crashed by the road and he
saw a group of youths beating a man. My uncle grew frightened
and clung to his kitten as it fought to be free. He knew that if he
let go, it would run and be lost. Perhaps he clung too tightly.

He was a small boy, alone, in a house on fire. That was what he
remembered for us: sparks showering down from the ceiling, his
inability to find the cat, then everyone suddenly moving quickly
through the room and, finally, scooping him out the back door.

They never returned to Cato Manor. It was burned, their
home misplaced in that violent history.

Sometime soon after that Hari, my father, was born. Shiv
forgot, finally, his lost kitten. Or perhaps he thought my father
was the cat returned, reincarnated. A thing like that is never
completely knowable...

THEY WERE CLOSE, small Hari and Shiv. They never argued or fought. It was as if they knew they had only a short time together. At least that is what Shiv Uncle remembered. Hari was always by his side, learning the necessities from his older brother. How to ride a bicycle. How to climb trees without looking down, collect insects, win a fight by not giving up. How to be kind and care for those smaller, weaker, poorer...

Those people moved away to the country, where a relative owned a farm that had on it a great, rare baobab tree. This baobab was thicker and taller than ten normal big trees, and it was old, a great-grandmother of trees. It was vast enough that a dozen children could hide from each other in its trunk, all of them on the ground. Like a great-grandmother, it nurtured and provided a haven for every sort of young life. For the children, it was nest and refuge, a place of dreams. Under the boughs of the great tree my father and Patel Uncle Shiv drew their breaths, grew.

It bore a strange, gourdlike fruit, which would turn brown and drop, and the animals would gather to eat it. Shiv and Hari ate that fruit too. It was powerfully sweet and bitter and enticed them to eat even more until they were ill, and then they would stop.

Perhaps it was this strange baobab fruit medicine that made them grow.

They lived in an old house at one end of the property, while their uncle, who owned that land, lived at the other. The great tree was in the middle. It was at that place that my grandmother bore the other children, one baby after another for many years. In time there were too many children, even for the great tree. But the uncle and aunt had no children at all.

To solve this inequity of fortune, these people did not seek out young virgins or *muti*. That was not their way. Instead they shared the children. The two eldest were taken to the other end of the farm and told they had a new ma and pa.

God needed help with some things. It was a weak spirit, there in the middle of the farm, in the shadow of the enormous tree. That god had not noticed that those people were without children. This was how it was explained to Patel Uncle, who was eight, and my father Hari, who was five.

The boys took this in stride. They had each other. And their real mother was nearby if she were needed, although by then she was so busy with the younger children that she had no time for big boys.

In their new home they were treated with great affection, for those old people, the uncle and aunt, felt those two boys were a great blessing. The old man took care to treat the boys with the respect accorded to adults. He had collections of coins and tools, village antiques, books, sculptures and natural oddities. One corner contained only the skulls of horned animals and an assortment of eggs, while another contained shells of every colour from the sea. Another room held an assortment of assagais and knobkerries and knives and bows and arrows and ceremonial masks. At the end of every week, the old man and the boys would wander through the villages in the hills on terrific searches for these curious objects.

They loved these rambles. They had a real taste of adventure and freedom. Sometimes they found things. Sometimes their *Pa-ji* would pay or barter for found treasures. They learned the vernacular languages, Zulu and Sotho. And wherever they went, Hari made friends with a local child. Everyone liked him because he was truthful and his heart was trustful...

That was my father. Trusting and large. A man who could be loved for his generous nature and true heart.

Of course, there was school. They were sent to Durban town for that. There was only one school open to them. They were Indian boys and so needed an Indian school.

Each day they travelled far from the farm to attend school. One day, as they waited for the bus, they noticed some boys nearby playing football. They wore blue school uniforms but they were not from the same school. They were White, those boys. English, or perhaps Africaaner.

Now, my father loved sports. Football and cricket and tennis. When he saw a game, it drew him. He always wanted to join in the fray. But this day in the town of Durban, he watched those other boys until the ball came his way, then Hari played it to Shiv and Shiv to Hari and in that way they showed, in the international language of children and football, that they wished to play. One of those boys came to get the ball and not only took it, but came and slapped Shiv as though he were a small child. And when that happened, Hari spun that white boy around and slapped him back. He slapped him hard, my father, so that this boy's nose ran with blood. Then the other boys came and there was a brawl. At the end of it there were police, then Shiv and Hari were kept in a room. For seven days. Shiv was fourteen, Hari eleven.

"After that we knew more, and that was when we began to study with *Pa-ji* about Marx and Gandhi. Well, let us say that those men were great thinkers. You will need to learn about that..."

The brothers began to understand their place in the world. Now boys take time to accept that they are something less than free and magnificent presences in this world. The hard part for a boy with brown or black skin is to realize that he is not free and that he is considered less than others. It is something a boy will fight and rage against until he is old enough to know what his sister already accepts. Then he stops fighting, but sometimes this does not happen until he is old, like Ntate Mohapi.

But Patel Uncle and my father were in the Republic of Unfairness to Children, and it did not feel natural or free or good. They saw that they would never play football with the white-skinned boys even if they were better players, even if they were trusting and kind.

"Then came the first time Hari and I were apart. I went to the university while he finished school. For those two years I saw him very little. I steered clear of trouble, as is my natural tendency. I studied things that were untouched by the corrupt wishes of humans: chemistry, physics and math. Of course, when Hari came to varsity he registered in humanities and plunged into literature and philosophy, politics and history, those things I suspected of being false. Later, I realized that I was afraid these things were the foundations of the unjust society in which we lived. But your papa burned with these ideas and I saw that he had learned some things that I had not, and that he understood some things that I did not. He went fearlessly on with big questions of morality, justice, free will and determinism, and was fascinated, not in some abstract way, but in a useful, immediate way. He wanted to know how he could solve our problems. And as we studied, history unfolded before us. In those days, you see, Africans and Indians and all the other people who were not "white" were starting to fight the government. There were protests and marches, and the ongoing preparation for a real war to be waged..."

These were the times in which my father and his brother were young men, times much as the times we know now. The fight had been taken up. The organization known as the African National Congress had been banned. Their leaders – Mandela, Sisulu, Mbeki – were locked away on an island in the cold ocean.

Shiv and Hari heard that people were beaten and tortured by the police and soldiers of the government. Everyone knew. But my father would not let these things pass. He had been placed on the earth to fight. Not to be the father of an overgrown girl. Not to live to be an old and aching man.

But Dr. Patel Uncle knew the dangers. He tried to steer my father in other directions. My father would not be steered, of course. The opposite happened: he convinced Patel Uncle of the inevitability of history and the necessity of doing one's utmost. He invoked the lessons of the Mahabharata. He invoked the lessons of Gandhi. But in all of this he harboured no hatred or resentment toward anyone, only a great sense of optimism and hope...

Hari Patel attracted friends, and followers. The great issues of the Republic of South Africa were discussed, analyzed. Why this injustice and cruelty? What was the root of it and who had the strength to dig it out and stop it. When they talked that way, it must have been like looking into the eyes of deadly Shiva or the Ancestors, telling them that they were mistaken and that the way they had made things needed correcting.

In due course, David appeared. This David never attended these discussion meetings. He was a man who did not like to talk. Someone knew David enough to know that he was an outdoorsman and a mountain climber of some repute. He had been the first to find his way up a number of South African ascents, but he was never recognised by the South African mountaineering associations because he was "coloured." The pictures of his face, which Shiv and Hari thought was very white, were never permitted to ruin the pages of the climbing books and periodicals.

There were many stories like David's in the Republic of Colour. Injustices that left a lingering bitterness. Over time, the bitterness grew and blew and billowed about the country, never settling. It had the same flavour as red dust on the tongue, so bitter it is sharp.

These are the things that make people suffer.

So this David, who was wronged during his short life, made a pact with my father. The two of them would change South Africa, or die trying. That was the pact. They used the discussion group to recruit others into the organization that they themselves joined: the *African National Congress*. With such an important and grand name, it was not hard for my father to attract students to the group. Then they would get to know him, and, in time, they trusted him. To trust was to follow. The discussion group grew.

Young men always think they know of risks and dangers. But they never understand fully until it is too late. So it was that Hari and Shiv heard about people being picked up and beaten, but it did not make them stop the meetings, or take precautions. In their imaginations, being beaten by the police would test their mettle. It would be an adventure that would turn them into men. They would stand up to the worst abuses, hold their heads up, laugh at their captors. If the police beat them, they would fight back! They would win!

It was only later that Shiv recalled the members of their group who either spoke too vociferously, or who said nothing.

"In retrospect, we did not know enough..."

MY FATHER was given an opportunity to go to London to meet others in the movement. And this was where my mother came in. Unplanned and unpredictable, she. My father may have had a sense that this was not supposed to happen to him. It complicated his life. It led to other mistakes, because a man in love is a man blind. A man smitten has fuzzy instincts, weak reflexes and cannot smell the trouble under his nose. She was a foreigner. How could she be expected to understand the Republic of Black and Brown and Colour and White? So, confused, doubtful, worried perhaps, he told Shiv nothing.

DR. PATEL SHIV UNCLE gazed upon my mother. She had drifted into something like sleep and looked vulnerable, her eyelashes fluttering in her sleep like those of a small child.

"She was so beautiful," he said quietly. "Tall and dignified. She is still."

I could not remember my mother as beautiful. At that moment it seemed she had always been shrunken and weak. The beautiful, strong woman of Shiv Uncle's memory was another person entirely.

She came to them with more than beauty. She brought an outsider's perspective on their struggle and their country. When she spoke, her accent oddly sustained and relaxed, they listened with fascination. But they did not take her seriously because young men must always challenge or dismiss a young woman. Perhaps they think that because she is beautiful she must not be intelligent or deep of soul. Young men are not wise. But Shiv Uncle saw that my mother knew much about the Republic of Struggles. He could see that she was impatient. Haughty, well-educated and determined. She had little patience for the ways of arrogant young men.

"I HAD MY FEARS, but I kept them to myself. A habit from childhood. I was never as trusting or confident about life and people as Hari was. But it was my *kharm* to love my brother, so I endorsed his bold approach to life..."

He might have stopped my father. But then, who was right? When a person burns with passion, when their beliefs create a fire, we become captivated. Who was he to be water to my father's brave fire? Shiv Patel Uncle explained that suffering too is only *maya*, and *maya* is the illusion that distracts from enlightenment. But even he could not know what would happen. Even he must have looked back after the fog of the future had receded, and questioned whether he could have saved my father.

"Who understands the cycle of life and death? It is beyond us, out of our hands. We are mere toys in the hands of the Creator. Nothing we think or do affects the ultimate outcome..."

ONE DAY the brothers took a ball into an open area near their flat, sent it back and forth the way they had so many years before, that day when they had not been allowed to join in the game. The sun was bright. My father picked up the ball and came to his brother, but he would not look at him. He was embarrassed, almost shy. Instead he looked at the football, so that Shiv Uncle said something like, "Hari, you want to say something to that ball." They might have laughed a little, to find themselves, two brothers, suddenly awkward with each other. Then my father told Shiv Uncle his secret.

"Zara is in trouble," he said.

Shiv had no idea what he meant at first. He had no idea that Hari was talking about the beginning of life. "I had no idea that he was talking about you, Koko..."

Yes, me. The secret, and their trouble, was me. Zara was pregnant and they were not married. There was nothing but trouble about the beginning of me.

Uncle Shiv Patel patted my arm and chuckled softly. I was aware that he had not often ventured to touch me these last years, now that I was big and grown. I remember, though, one day when I was a small child, I fell and lay crying in the dirt and Uncle Patel came and picked me up and held me in his arms with such gentleness that I fell asleep on his chest. It is strange that a memory can be lost and found again, triggered by the look on a worn, old face.

Poor Shiv Uncle. The brother whom he always thought had told him all, the brother who was his closest confidant and best friend, had not told him this one most important thing. He had not been able to tell him about his lover, and now it was late, the situation troubling. He was angry and hurt for a moment, but a big man like Patel Uncle sees further than his feelings. He shook those feelings away and told Hari to marry my mother. He cuffed him on the head, shoved him with both hands, embraced him.

My father told his brother everything then, about how the love had evolved, how he had been the one to bring her to South Africa, about London. There was the matter of safety. He had thought to keep her as much as possible out of the eye of the authorities because of her foreign passport. Hari seemed to know that he was on a security list. So was Shiv, even the others. But Zara, despite being seen by all, noticed by all, or perhaps because of it, had escaped notice, and he wanted to preserve that. He had seen the Security Branch men watching their flat from a car. Sometimes he was aware of being followed.

"Hari had no doubt as to what should be done. He simply wanted my blessing, it seems. Told me he wanted my permission, if you can imagine such a thing."

They jogged home in the late sun, passing the ball back and forth. My father would have been relieved at that moment. He must have been happy, blundering forward in time, unaware, innocent and truthful beneath the skein of principles, passion and secret strategies.

When they reached their flat he phoned Zara, then they both took turns bathing. They sang the old movie songs, the "Lata Mangeshkar" and "Kishore Kumar" that their *Pa-ji* loved to play, and the hits from *My Fair Lady*. The sun glowed red, pouring in the window like an indecent spill of blood. They were two blundering, singing youths, innocently bathing in the bloody light, dreaming that they controlled fate.

But then fate came to them without knocking, with only a ten-second warning ring of their phone. The door came down and in came the Security Branch men of the Republic, men of rough accents, as pink as flowers. They brought my father out of the bathroom. They let him dress, but refused him shoes to make him vulnerable. They wanted to make him shorter too. These police and security men hate people who are taller than they. It makes them afraid, and when they are afraid they are dangerous. My father, being young and in love and a man about to father a daughter, would not cower, would not slink. He looked at those men as though they were unimportant functionaries. He showed little interest in their individual identies, characters, personalities, family ties, aspirations and hopes. They were white men in uniforms, and he was not surprised at anything they did.

But then the man in charge appeared, a man called Viljoen. *Captain Viljoen.* This man mocked my father, trying to bring him low. "Where are your shoes, mon? You must try to wear shoes when you come to the city..." and he laughed a hollow and false laugh.

"Barefooted Hindoo. Just like what is his name, yeh. Your little bloody bald chap..."

Patel Uncle said, "I found myself despising Viljoen and his men and their cruel sense of humour. But strangely, over time, even after all that has happened, I have come to understand those people. Someday I would like to learn to forgive even the most evil of men, for they too are agents of their own destinies. We are all companions in that way. We grow old and we think. When we are alone we think too much. I did not understand then, that they were cruel because they knew that Hari was pure. It was their task to destroy that purity. It has always been their task. It always will be. It is a principle of *kharm*, the way the universe was formed."

SHIV AND HARI were taken on a long trip through the night in a van with no windows, then were taken out into a tall blue building, up the stairs to the tenth floor of that place. *John Vorster Square.* Johannesburg.

They put the brothers in separate rooms.

There is no way of knowing exactly what they did to my father. Shiv Uncle would only vaguely refer to what they did to him. He guessed that it was the same for Hari. He heard his brother bellow in indignation once or twice, but the tone never conveyed fear, exhaustion or panic.

They showed Shiv Uncle a written statement made by David, the ANC man. There were names and places in the statement and Uncle knew that David must have been put under terrible pressure to sign something like that. The Security men knew all about the discussion groups, and they played that out, using it as both a threat and a source of yet more names. But Shiv Uncle would say nothing to the interrogator, that man Viljoen. Then Viljoen would stop and a Major Swanepoel would take over. Sometimes neither man was present and there were the rude and crude tactics of the subordinate men to contend with. These small men were worse in a way, because they seemed to harbour an impersonal and unfocused hatred. Shiv had a clear sense of that hatred in the middle of one rough session. He saw that it came out of deep wounds that provided a kind of fount of endless cruelty. He saw that cruelty was a contagion that spread and infected through the generations, across borders, through countless torture chambers and interrogation rooms.

They tried to break my Uncle's bones, but anyone could see how difficult that would be. And there was relentless verbal humiliation, which had little effect on him once he had glimpsed the nature of the hatred.

The interrogators came, became frustrated and left. There were no windows in that first place. It was not possible to sleep and so he lost track of time. Without sleep, even the hardiest mind can lose its balance.

"THEN, AT SOME POINT, the interrogators seemed less frustrated, as though they were going through prelimaries to the real stuff. They asked questions about MK, the military wing. They had another source of information, someone other than David. They would say, 'our information' and I began to hallucinate almost, that some shadow person named 'our information' was out there. It was an infiltrator, perhaps. But my mind was losing clarity at that point..."

My uncle endured. He kept himself lucid by making up names and places in the way they had been shown by David.

When he was finally taken from that room two or three days later, he came face to face with my father. Hari smiled and winked to encourage his brother and show that he had stood up well. Now they were both taken to a room with a window over-looking the street, ten floors below. It was a clear Transvaal night, but the stars were extinguished by the orb of city lights, as if the stars and sky had no right to exist in that world of cruelty. Swanepoel presented a long statement to each of the brothers. They were supposed to sign, admitting that they were members of the militant society known as MK. They were supposed to admit they had broken the Terrorism Law and Security Law. Shiv Uncle and my father looked at each other then, only a glance, but it was enough to give them strength and courage. My father asked why he must sign incriminating statements without having gone before a judge, or having had the advice of a barrister.

"We have chosen to fight the injustices in this land. But we will not sign an admission that we are guilty of crimes."

But this major did not want to play word games. "'You have been arrested under the Terrorism Act,' he told us. 'We have information about acts of sabotage, arson. If you deny it, you will never again see the light of day. I guarantee that.'

The men became very rough. They beat my father and my uncle again, more violently now. The brothers fought back, when they could, as they had always promised each other they would, even with hands bound and bones aching. Uncle Shiv was knocked on the head and went out for a moment or two. When he revived he found that the men had brought a device that looked like an old crank telephone with exposed wires into the room. He knew what it was.

But those soldiers of the Republic of Torture could not make that device work. Like schoolboys, they argued among themselves about the principles of the thing, and about the cause of the malfunction. Someone brought a car battery and other wires and the argument continued along new lines as they hooked it up. Hari and Shiv waited patiently to be tortured. At one point the men asked Shiv to explain about voltage and currents. Shiv explained and the men went quiet, listening with the respectfulness of students, then set about hooking the thing up according to Shiv's instructions. One of the men bragged that someone had died recently, his heart stopping while under the care of the one of the electrical shock devices. They had had some trouble to cover it up, someone else said. "Created a bit of a problem, ja?"

Finally they were ready.

They had the idea of torturing my father first, in front of Shiv Uncle, hoping that one of them would break, talk and sign the confession. They placed wet cloths at the ends of the wires so they would not leave marks. The brothers almost wanted to laugh at how particular those torturers were. They started brushing the ends of the wire across my father's chest. But he got one strong and angry leg free and kicked out so that someone fell into the battery, which spilled acid. One guard ran out, his hands burning. More men came in. They had knobkerries and sjamboks. It looked as though they were getting set to beat the prisoners to death. They gathered around my father saying nothing. Then they pinned him down, and when there were two men on each leg and two on each of his arms, they lifted him and opened the window and thrust him up on the sill. One of them turned to Shiv and said, "You ever heard of a sammy named Timol? We tried to teach him to fly, ja? But he was a slow learner. Nothing you wish to tell us?"

"I told them to stop and call Swanepoel, but they were too far gone. They said, 'We can't hear you, mon,' and they thrust Hari further out so that only his legs were inside."

But my father's legs were very hard and strong. His shin struck the sill. His nerves were taut and tired and he was a young man. So the pain in the shin of his leg sent a message to his spine, and his spine sent a message back to his leg, and his leg kicked back like the leg of a great hare. His heel caught one of the men in the groin and he went down.

"I saw it all unfold, milliseconds before it happened. I leaped up and shook my captors away. I leaped for all I was worth to catch my brother. My hand actually touched his foot, but he was gone. I could not reach him. I could not. He fell..."

Shiv Uncle stopped for a moment. He looked at his hands.

"As he went down he called to me, 'Shiv...,' but it was not in alarm. He called out as if to say goodbye. He wanted my blessing again, or maybe he was asking me if death would be all right..."

Patel held out his right hand. "This is the spot that last knew Hari alive. Just this spot. It is all that I had left. A moment of contact and to this day I have no understanding of the wherefore or the why."

I looked at his hand, the last place that had touched my father, but I felt nothing.

I tried to imagine my father's thoughts as he spilled through the night air. He would have been worried about Mother. Perhaps he even worried about the unborn me. Perhaps he died burdened by a lost future. How much can a mind think during a short fall through the darkness? Is it enough time to understand the future?

"After that there was confusion..."

The window broke apart. A policeman went through it to his death, although Shiv Uncle could not say precisely how. He knew he fought. He fought in a way he had never fought, fighting for his brother as though he could bring him back through the open window. Men kept coming forward and he tossed them about as though they were made of rags. Blood filled his mouth, his eyes. He saw through a haze of blood. Then, somehow, he got through the door and found stairs. The place was filled with shouting soldiers. Shots were fired. He flew down the stairs into the street and ran screaming my father's name, searching for him. But he never found the spot where Hari died. The soldiers were after him, and he had to run, finally, into the narrow lane behind the place, and then into a maze of streets and lanes. A big moon came out. Shiv Uncle thought that he could run toward that moon and find his way out of his nightmare. He ran in a stupor and his sight was fractured into blood-hazed visions. He was offered a glimpse of South Africa, not as a country or a home to people, but as a prison and a battleground. He saw it as a *kraal* for cattle, a bloody and overcrowded death-*kraal*. He had a vision of the sickness and death and pain and torture and suffering as no more than the contortions of a herd of starved and infected cattle.

Eventually he had to stop running.

There was nowhere to go but the other side of the *kraal*. Once at the other side he would have to turn back. Escape was an illusion. He would always be a prisoner. So he walked. Above him a ghostly death-moon floated toward the sky and a group of prostitutes found him. They took his broken hands, gently held his ripped and bloodied fingers and led him in a procession through the crowds and police and through streets filled with violence. *Babu,* they said, *you need us. Babu, you will not forget...* They led him through the night, through unlit places. It was as though, with their straightened hair and polished faces and spike-heeled walks, and strangely formal manners, they were special angels sent to protect him in his woe. They paraded him through the night until the streets came to an end and the ground became rough. There were no stars in the sky, only the strange moon that darted this way and that like a ruptured balloon. They stuffed money into his pockets and kissed his torn cheeks and left him...

At this point my mother opened her eyes to watch Patel. There was fear in her eyes. She had been listening to the story for some time and I saw that Patel knew that.

"THE SUN CAME and a new dawn. A ray of light came over the horizon. It poked my good eye as though it too were a torturer. I preferred darkness. I wished for endless night. But the light came on, the first morning of a new life for me. I was reborn into an empty box, in which I was without my brother, and haunted by rage and fear."

The blood on his face had dried. He did not wait at the edge of the city, but went on in the first red rays of dawn, striding across Transvaal's farms with their rich waterworks. Across the slag heaps and around the great scars in the land made by mines. Across open and empty veldt. Along the beds of rivers, down through rolling hills. Across wild lands where no human had set foot and where animals reigned. Bands of baboons challenged him, then charged, only to give up when he did not flinch or flee. Perhaps he no longer cared about his own death. Hyenas arrived to follow him, their jaws clicking and their drool spilling, awaiting the moment he would lie down. But he did not stop. He stumbled on through bush and past a pride of lions and past a leopard in a tree. On into a mixed herd of *boks* and zebras that was drawn along with him for some miles.

"The sun rose and fell and rose again. But I walked..."

He came to a *dorp*. Africaaner people stopped their cars to stare at my uncle as he went by with his stunned and grieving and bloodied steps. They saw his shredded clothes and torn and bloodied fingers and head and they thought of calling the police, but then they looked at him and they saw what they knew but did not want to remember, that there was trouble in the Republic of Bring and Braai. They let my uncle pass through their *dorp*.

He went on, gave other towns a wide berth. Maybe he walked for a week. Maybe two. Starving children took his hands when he came to poor villages. Others brought water. But he said nothing to anyone, for he could not. He neither wept nor bled any longer.

The land sloped away and down to the coast. Then he turned to follow the highway and, when the landscape became familiar at a place called Umhlanga Rocks, he turned inland. He found his way back to familiar ground. By the time he could see the top of the grand old baobab, his feet began to drag in the dust, no longer capable of rising. He shuffled under the tree and lay down.

For a long time he drifted in and out of sleep and dreams. Sometimes he heard the echo of voices in the boughs of the tree. He heard two voices, optimistic voices that went together easily, playing off each other well, one voice questioning, the other friendly, comforting and happy. There were memories of Shiv and my father caught in the branches. He imagined the tree was sorrowing for past childhoods, or the death of Hari, or the brother who was left behind.

He found the fruit that he had once loved, ripe on the boughs of the tree. He ate some of this and finally summoned enough strength to move along to his mother's house.

Over the years, first his father and then his uncle had died. The aunt who had raised him had left the place and moved to Durban, leaving his mother alone on the farm with the youngest of the children. It seemed to Shiv that he had not been home in an age. In a short time, the world had been transformed.

His mother was standing in the doorway of the kitchen as he came across the compound. The house was unnaturally quiet. A rusted car was wedged fast along one wall of the house, as though it had collided with the wall and stuck. The gardens were overgrown. His mother, my grandmother, wore a look of madness.

"What is it you want?" she cried out. "Who are you? Leave me alone or I will send my dogs out." She closed the door and bolted and locked it. Shiv Uncle could hear his mother calling the dogs. Years later he wondered how it was that at that moment he had been cut loose from his past, from his humanity.

As he stood there before the house, his mother went around to each window, closing and shuttering each one against the stranger on the property.

So he returned to the tree and lay beneath it and waited for death. He waited through the night, but death did not come and he could not rest. The voices in the boughs called him back to memories, and the memories of Hari and of childhood made the blood flow in his veins.

He rose with the dawn and went down past the house a last time and on out the drive. As he went he heard a window open and he turned to see a small girl watching him. It would have been his youngest sister. She looked at him as he went and, when he turned a last time, she suddenly waved and he waved back.

Now he walked straight west, inland towards the Drakensberg. His feet moved automatically again, the same force of the spirits or gods that had brought him home now taking him to an unknown destination. Around him the air swirled and sunlight fell on the surfaces. All these things were full of thought and choice, but he was not. The grasses thought as they wavered before him. The crowned eagle that floated over his head wondered about the world. The lizard and the mamba drew conclusions. But he did not think. He was the vessel of an unwordly force that pulled him toward the distant mountains.

He walked until his shoes disintegrated and he felt the thorns and stones tearing his feet. When it was too bad he had to stop and lie under the open sky, under the scrutiny of the entire cosmos. He wondered if he would be permitted to die now. But nothing happened and the numbness of his feet spread through him. His body floated and fluttered and it seemed after a time that perhaps he had actually died without noticing it and that he was now in another dimension. But then, after a time, even death did not seem to matter. Life, existence – it all seemed highly improbable. Hari's life was a freak of nature, a blip in the universe.

He slept. For days or weeks – it was impossible to know. When Shiv awoke he found an old man squatting on his haunches nearby, watching him. The old man was almost naked but for a few tattered shreds of goat hide. His old legs were gnarly and toughened by sun and dirt and his face was as wrinkled and as bruised as Shiv's. But there was something familiar about him and Shiv Uncle was not alarmed. After a time the old man stood and waited, looking at him in such a way that my uncle brought his feet beneath him. Together they began to walk. Like my Uncle Shiv, the old man's feet were ruined and bleeding. Like Uncle Shiv his hands had been smashed.

They went on over stubbled yellow grass and soft green grass, through handsome woods and cool streams and eventually up into the Drakensberg. The old man killed a large monitor and dragged it for miles until they camped and then he roasted the thing. After Shiv Uncle ate, the pain in his hands, his eye, his cracked rib and his ruined feet began to throb. The meat tasted of flowers and nuts.

They walked through the high ranges after that, and came to snowfields and trekked across. They forded high and icy streams, then descended steep paths into the lowlands. They came to a *rondavel* with a writhing puff adder impaled on a stick at the peak of the roof, and here the old man vanished inside and did not come out again. It was the end of the journey. Nearby, my uncle found the college and the villages of the valley. That was how he came to that place.

"I never saw that man or his *rondavel* again. I asked a local farmer once but he ran away whining."

"Perhaps it was a spirit from my father," I suggested.

Patel Uncle Shiv looked at me from under bushy eyebrows. Then he shrugged his great winglike shoulders, rose and went out of the hut to stand alone in the twilight.

monnesepula

Monnesepula

I dreamed of my father falling through unlit spaces. Without wings, without magic to break his fall. Then these dreams were interrupted by the sound of gunshots, and I and each one of us woke up privately in the dark to listen and be afraid. The shooting was far enough away that, as the air shifted, the sound became faint. But it was unmistakable. Short bursts followed by long silences, then it would begin again. I slept, dreaming my terrible dreams of people contorted and shot.

Late in the morning I roused myself to discover that during the night a ragged visitor, one of Mohapi's old associates, had appeared, seeking refuge. We could see that he had been places and had experienced much.

The country, he told us, had been invaded by the South Africans. They had arrived with guns blazing, helicopters whirring. Fear had spread across the land. There were rumours that the king was dead and the government toppled.

Mohapi brought out his shortwave radio so that we could listen to the African Service of the BBC. It was not long before we were able to verify most of what the visitor said, even the part about helicopters. Those South Africans had moved in their efficient and treacherous ways, smoothly taking control of our small country in a few hours.

But this was not the worst of the news. With the invasion came paid raiders from outside the country and inside, men without countries or families or allegiances who roamed freely across the night. They attacked the rich and poor, and dedicated special attention to the unforgotten enemies of the Republic who had arrived earlier. And there were others too. Bad Elements had been unleashed amid the confusion and the fear: those who opposed the government, criminal gangs, bad sorcerers, murderers, the insane, all of them aroused by the rich scent of opportunity and vengeance and malice. Ordinary people had been disappearing into the night, only to be found later in the sewage fields of the towns or at the bottom of high cliffs. The encampment, our town, had become a battleground.

We listened to the developments on the shortwave radio all that day. The South African soldiers had invaded other neighbouring countries as well, Zambia and Botswana. Then we heard that the UN was stepping in to negotiate safe passage for refugees.

It was this news that caught the attention of Patel Uncle Shiv. He and Deadkumar went into a long and private discussion on the ridges, just out of earshot.

I could not help, as I watched them, wondering if I had made both of them drag out the things they wanted to forget. But I knew I did not control the truth or memory. There were larger forces at play. Patel Uncle and my mother may have wished to forget, pretend and lie, but the truth is not so changeable.

After their discussion was completed, Patel Uncle quietly collected a few things into a small satchel and strode away toward Do Not See Me Pass and the trail to the lowlands.

THE REST OF US were left to watch over my mother. We watched her every gesture, her every breath. We listened to each utterance she made, and leapt when she requested any small thing. Deadkumar hovered outside the doorway ready and anxious.

But for all of this attention, or perhaps because of it, Mother did not ask for much. She had been eating and drinking less with each passing day, becoming skeletal, her nose and cheekbones taut and hard, her eyes staring as though from beyond the world. Every few hours 'Mè Jane prayed over her, beseeching *Modimo* and Jesus to join forces and come to this place and release 'Mè Zara, please, as a special great favour. My mother finally asked her to stop.

Then one night Mother rose from her pallet as if propelled by an otherworldly strength. "Why, why do we stay here?" she cried out.

We milled around her. "They have much to offer," I lied quietly.

"What? Who offers? What do they offer? Why aren't we going home?"

"Well..." My attempts to lie faltered in my mouth.

Mother sank back with a knowing look. She ventured over to the Other Place, the world beyond our world, seeing what it was like. She remained there for hours, exploring, her body tossing about on the tumult of that place. She muttered about what she was seeing there, and whom she was meeting. Then she returned and had a normal sleep. She would tell me nothing after she woke, leaving us to our speculations.

After that she went to the Other Place more often, now that she had beaten a path there. We could only watch our future loom and vanish like a ghost.

After two days of this she became a spectral visitor who made Deadkumar seem as alive as a newborn. She lay with eyes half rolled back, her mouth hanging and dry. Periodically 'Mè Jane placed her cheek against Mother's bosom to listen to the writhing of her heart.

"Is it strong?" I asked once, and immediately regretted asking.

"She has the heartbeat of death," 'Mè Jane said quietly.

But Mother surprised us all, as only she knew how to do. She sat up straight and spoke in a clear voice. "Rain," she said. When Deadkumar came to her she seized his shirt. "Rain," she whispered. "Make it rain." Her hair hung in wisps around her fleshless skull. She reminded us of the Head that had haunted us years before. "Rain," she repeated, and released him.

Deadkumar smiled down at her as though she were the most beautiful woman on earth. "Of course, Zara. Of course. Devkumar asked means Devkumar does." He looked proudly at me and 'Mè Jane and patted Mother's hand. Then he straightened himself and went out of the room, a man with a mission.

I ran out after him. "What are you doing?"

"Rain," he smiled. "Your ma is a smart woman. She wants rain so who she ask? She ask Devkumar, that is who. She know that Devkumar can do, which is why," he said, stopping, "all those years back, your ma love me..." He pinched my cheek. He took up a sack into which he threw a blanket and sweater. He put on a worn-out vest.

"But how will you make it rain in this time of drought?"

"*Monnesepula*, Girl. I know some things about Rain Doctor."

That was how my mother made the *monnesepula* come to the evil village at the foot of Do Not See Me Pass. Mother's request; Deadkumar's mission.

Now a dead person like Deadkumar would not really know much about *monnesepula*, but he seemed to remember the things he had heard over the years when he was alive. Highlander stories about mountain magic. So he set out into that highland place of large outcroppings of stone and fleeting figures in the distant and cold air, knowing that the remote reaches of the high Maluti were the places where such things exist. He went off knowing and glad too, feeling that if he never returned it would be fine and we would always know that it was him, Deadkumar, to whom she had turned for help in the end.

His quest took him into high trails that he cursed for their strange lack of direction, not knowing that the trails were made by wild animals. For the first hours he met no one. Then, as nightfall approached, he came to a remote *rondavel* and *kraal*, where a family gave him mealies with tripe stew and a sheltered place to sleep. In the morning they led him to the entrance of a steep-sided canyon in the high plateau. This was where the *monnesepula* lived, the people told him. This was where all *monnesepula* came from. They left Deadkumar alone.

He went down into the canyon, finding only the leavings of eagles and the odd footprints of monkeys in the dust. Faint trails led nowhere. Water holes were dry. Rock slides had encroached along one side of the canyon. As the sun dove toward the ridge above, he saw a thin, wavering flag of smoke in the distance.

By the time he found the place it was dark. The home of the *monnesepula* was a hump of reeds and mud. When the magician emerged it was as though he erupted from a fissure in the earth. His face was of sun-scorched rock, his limbs gnarled, his aspect ancient and tired. On his back he wore tattered jackal hides and thick fibrous grasses. About his neck hung a shrivelled human hand and a whistle made of bleached bone. He looked Deadkumar over, then squatted and urinated in the style of women. From beneath his cape a rivulet of urine soaked into the ground at first, but then ran in a small wave towards where Deadkumar stood.

Deadkumar became unnerved and began to speak. He stammered out his story of Mother's request for rain, that she was about to die and that soldiers were about to find us.

The *monnesepula* said nothing. With an expression of great contemplation, he continued to relieve himself.

Deadkumar's eyes locked on the yellowish stream that glistened under the dark sky. He went back, his confessions bubbling, gushing forth. He spoke for an hour, stopping only when the *monnesepula* had thoroughly soaked the terrain around the hut.

The *monnesepula* said, "I will come to that place where you stay. But there are conditions. You must not let the Bush-boy come near...and then there is the matter of compensation..."

After this he gave Deadkumar careful instructions and released him to find his way home in the dark.

DEADKUMAR did not return directly, but went instead to the village near Ntate Mohapi's place. He spoke to the Headman and the Headman called a big meeting. Everyone was excited. No one had convinced a *monnesepula* to come out of the canyon and perform his miracle in some years. A *letsolo*, a special hunt, would be needed. The hunters took up their traditional weapons and the villagers followed them to Mohapi's place, where they gathered along the stony ridge and waited for the miracle to begin. When we came out to see what the excitement was about, the villagers cheered and called Mohapi and Deadkumar some old praise names.

After some hours the *monnesepula* approached. From far off he blew his bone whistle so that it echoed all the way to the pass. It was a parched sound, like a mountain wind. But as we watched the *monnesepula* arrive our hopes faded. We noticed that his youth and vigour had long evaporated and we felt discouraged.

THE *monnesepula* STOOD before us and held the whistle for all to see. "This," he announced, "belonged to the father of the *monnesepula* people." He blew a long scratching note that made a few people cough. Then he held up the shrivelled human hand and muttered words from an ancient language no one remembered. He shuffled his feet to the incantation and the scant flesh on his flanks flapped like empty water skins.

But there was another sound too – the patter of a small drum, the sound of our Bushman.

The *monnesepula* missed a beat, then two. His words hesitated. His eyes rolled up and down. "What," he demanded, "is that?"

We saw Bushman dancing between the huts, laughing, paying no respect. He scampered onto a high rock and beat his drum in an unsteady and irritating patter.

Some people laughed. Others drifted away. Such a wizard! Such a rain man! Brought down by a half-grown Bushman!

But the *monnesepula* was not done. His eyes became red. He placed his whistle between his lips and drew in air through nostrils flared like those of a mating donkey. Then he blew a note that dried our eyes. The sound grew like a dust cloud. We smacked our lips and drew no spittle. Men turned away dreaming of beer, green grass, insect larvae and urine. Women saw their own breasts shrink. We sat down because our blood became sluggish in our veins. And when everyone was sitting and every itchy eye was upon the *monnesepula*, he let the whistle drop from his lips.

He told us that the cost of rain was high. He would be risking his life. All the power of the Ancestors would have to be marshalled. The price would be paid by everyone, even the smallest child and the poorest elder. It would include cattle, goats, chickens, maize and the kill from the *letsolo*.

We listened with hearts choking on dust. It was hard to remember what rain was like. On behalf of everyone the Headman signalled his agreement. He waved to the hunters and they readied themselves with bows, arrows and killing spears. They marked their faces with red dust and ash. They threw upon their backs the dullest of blankets and the hides of animals from other *letsolos*. Then, with a few parched croaks, they set out. Not one of them had enough spit to manage a hunting song.

After they were gone the villagers dispersed, leaving Deadkumar and I and Bushman to cast around behind them. When he saw it was safe, Bushman came down from his perch to announce that he too was a hunter. "I even have a spear," he hissed, and he ran away and returned with a thin, bent sort of spear, a sack and a blanket.

"Already you irritate everybody enough," Deadkumar told him, but his heart was not in this chiding. He had no confidence in the hunters to carry out a proper *letsolo*. "Those guys catch nothing but potatoes, I know it," he said. He took up his jacket and wandered out after the hunters. At the time we thought he meant to supervise the hunt himself. It was only later we thought that he had another purpose in mind.

Bushman quietly watched him go, then took up his sack and spear, went a short way up the goat path and stopped, waiting patiently. After a while I shrugged and fetched a sweater and my own blanket. I did not want to leave Mother by herself, but could not let Bushman go into the mountains alone.

WE DID NOT TRY to catch the other hunters, since we knew that a girl and a Bushman would not be welcome in their company. So we wandered a safe distance behind and stopped often to survey the blasted and rocky terrain of the highlands. The spine of this ancient Africa was laid bare here, curving away to the north. The high Maluti seemed to cut through the older hills like new weeds in a garden. And amid this grandeur was the smallness of our country, with its perpetual cloud of dust. It seemed as though all the red soil of Lesotho had risen up to take flight across the Caledon to the land of green. The Boers were winning the Battle of the Soil, just as they had won the Battle of the Farm Vegetables and the Battle of the Border. Why was it that they held such power over our world? They controlled the plants, the water, the rain in ways we did not understand.

We cut away from the goat paths and climbed a pile of rocks. Above us and in the distance was the yellow glow of the hunters' fire, already blazing though they had trekked for no more than three hours. We knew they would have set their camp in an auspicious spot and probably were trying to unclog their throats enough to sing. Deadkumar was nowhere to be seen.

The air became cold, the sky clear and dark. As the stars were unshrouded we lay on our backs and were forced to clutch the ground as the universe spun around us. We wrapped ourselves in our blankets and lay back to back, taking turns facing our own small fire. For a time I slept. When I awoke, cold and thirsty, Bushman was stoking the fire.

"Listen..."

I listened and heard the crackle of twigs and grass. I listened harder and heard Bushman's breath, my heart beating, my dry eyelids scratching my eyeballs, the whisper of wind in the wings of an owl. I heard narrow rivers of air pouring over the highland peaks and the rocks cracking as they cooled. I heard the mountains surging from beneath but crumbling under the weight of the ages. And I heard more. I heard the drone of the spirit world, the dripping of live blood. I heard the delicate touch of a leopard's paws...

Above, the moon emerged from its *kraal* and rode out across the veld on its pony.

"You hear all that?"

"I hear."

Bushman's eye gleamed orange in the firelight. He sniffed at the dark shadows at the edge of our fire circle.

"Come," he said. "We see better away from the fire."

We dropped our blankets and moved through the cold. The moon threw a pale luminosity upon the rocks, but Bushman made himself a mere shadow, a moving darkness in the other darkness. I closed my eyes and could see him better. I opened my eyes and took my own path up the slope at angles until, when I turned about, I saw our own little fire as a strange orb in a sea of moving shadows.

I pushed on higher, until I heard the hoots of small creatures and the patter of a drum. Bushman crept along in front of me, guided by the special eye he claimed was in his big toe. We came around a hulking rock, and then the ground flattened. The world righted itself, yet we were among the regiments of mountains, and heard their sleepless moans.

"What is this place?" I mouthed and Bushman answered only with a touch.

Columns of stones stretched over the plateau, poised, marching to the songs of war. Beyond was the glow of the fire at the hunters' camp. We moved toward it until we noticed a figure to one side of the fire. As we watched, it leapt into the darkness, reappeared, leapt, crouched. The fire flared and flattened in the wind. We crept closer until we saw that the hunters were on the ground in the trance of the figure.

We first took it to be a spirit-dancer. Then we saw the horns that grew from its head. We saw the knowing, fateful eyes of a wild creature. Long lines, like the twitching antennae of an insect hung in the space above it as it dove, crawled, spat and twisted. Its fur-covered snout dripped blood. Its hair stood on end. It was the thing Mother had called *therianthrope*, half-antelope, half-human figure from wall paintings and the stories of the ancients. Now it sprang high on powerful buck legs. Now it rolled and kicked on the ground making a strange white dust. Now it brayed to the stones and mountains of the country as they prepared for war. As we watched, the antennae grew longer, the blood flowed from the snout.

Then the fire flared and went out.

In the stillness that followed we were dizzy, our breathing stopped in our chests. We gawked at the thick darkness and wondered if we were actually awake, or at home in our beds. And we were not alone. For some time I had been aware of the smell of seaweed and cigarette smoke. Somehow, Deadkumar had found us.

"Ho God, what a place, this," he whispered.

Bushman swallowed audibly and touched my hand for me to follow him back to our fire. Close behind me came Deadkumar, his breathing as agitated as mine. When we had gone a short way, he whispered quietly, "I did not tell you all of the truth, Girl. About your pa."

He spoke so quietly I thought for a moment I had imagined his words.

"You know that story I told about how those police come and get Devkumar and beat me up and all, nah? Well, I did not tell you everything about that...

"See, when they let me go I went back to find Zara. I want to warn her about the cops, warn her to get away before they came to get her..." He stopped. "I am going to tell you the whole truth here, Girl, so you will know forever I tell you the truth. You will not remember everything about Devkumar in a few years, but you will remember that I told you the truth in the end." He had seized my arm, squeezing it hard and hissing through the dark at me. I caught the glint of his eye in the starlight and I thought for a moment he was the *therianthrope* and this was *therianthrope* magic.

"See, those police, those security men, they beat me worse than I told you. They tell me they know everything and they think nothing about getting rid of me for good because I was nothing. I had no papers. I was less than a piece of dog kaka to them. Well, they break some of my fingers, one at a time, just for fun. I thought I would never play flute again. Then they burn me with cigarettes. They kick me in all the bad places. Laugh at me when I lose control and scream. Then they say, 'We might not kill you right away. You tell us what you know' and I say, 'I know nothing' and they say, 'You better find out something for us' and they tell me what they want to know. Then they keep me there for long time. More shock and kicking and beating. Blood coming out of me from different place in my head. I got ready for the next life. I close my eyes. Sometime I even thought I dead. Next thing they drag me back into car, then throw me in the street near my place. I thought I was finish. I was in big pain, could not walk or talk much. I just crawl into a bush and hide and wait to die. But nothing happened. So after I rest awhile I get up and I could walk a little. I was walking bust-up nothing-man. Only thing that was left in me was Zara. I could not think of anything else. Everything got beat out me. Self-respect, self-honour...

"I thought to run away. I thought to get that gun and find those men and kill them. I thought of ending my nothingness proper. But all I could do was crawl back to my flat. I rest there until finally I think I better get a doctor to help me. Then I wait until it was late in the night so nobody see the condition I was in, limpy and all bust. Every step I think of those police.

"So I go a few footsteps from my place when I see Zara go down the street the other way with that long, floating walk. Of course, I follow on behind to catch up and warn her and to show myself to her. To tell her I did not give in to the police. I want to tell her about how I feel and ask her to forgive. But then I see, even the bad way I was in, that she was different, that Zara. Her walk was different. She was *higher* and *floatier* than before. Something in her was *up*, something big happen to her and that girl was high, and I was beat and down low, and I felt the big space between us and that make my pain worse than ever. And I could not catch her, I was so sick and bust-up. I try to follow but I drop back and back, then I see Hari come along, and then they meet and there is this electric spark between them and they look at each other and look around and then he puts his hand in her hair like I want to do, and he caress her like I want to do, and finally I see the things good and clear in front of me. I see in one moment the things I do not want to see."

In the darkness I heard Deadkumar swallow hard. "I follow them back to Hari's house. I spy on those two. Even I watch them love each other..."

It was perfectly still. We noticed on one edge of the sky a strange streak of light. It was an arc, growing brighter and longer by the moment.

"That is that thing they call Halley," murmured Deadkumar Uncle. "There the damn thing is after all this time.

"I went back home, I think. No. That's not right. What really happen is like this: I stand out there in the darkness and I cry like I was a small boy, that is what happen really. I cry because your ma is so beautiful and I cry hate of what I knew. And when I finish crying, I go to my flat and stay there for good long time until the cops come and get me again. And then, what I did, Koko...I tell those cops to let me live. I tell them Hari and Shiv were members of ANC army and to let me live. Next thing I knew, Hari is dead, Shiv disappear. Everybody disappear..."

I moved carefully away from Deadkumar Uncle, my heart closed and safely locked, my heart safe and calm. I could not hate or love this Deadkumar who had betrayed my father. He was already dead, the odour of seawater wafting off him.

"Kuku, that is why I always try to take care of you and your ma and all. That is why later, I got to go back in the Republic and fight more until it got too hot. It was for Hari. For your pa and the wrong thing I did..."

He stood motionless in the dark, watching the intruder in our sky. It was a stranger, a button of light pushing before it a shimmering flare. Somewhere nearby the *therianthrope* was dancing in the air, conjuring this strange light, and this confession.

We stood for hours, motionless, until the darkness, the comet, the night was overcome by the new dawn. Then we retreated back to the cold ashes of our fire and slept there huddled together, Bushman and I.

In the morning we made our way back to the village and the bedside of my mother. Everyone awaited the return of the hunters and the *monnesepula*. Mother held an empty cup in her hand and told us, "I will drink when it rains." Then she stopped talking and lay watching us with eyes like planets.

Some hours later we heard singing and the hunters appeared waving their weapons. They had killed three large hares, a mountain goat and a kind of *bok* that only the old people could name. The entrails were carried coiled and sticky inside the goatskin and the skin pinned together with thorns. The meat had been wrapped in the skin of the little *bok*.

The *letsolo* was declared a success by the headman. The people followed the hunters to the edge of the gorge where the *monnesepula* waited. The gorge, once charged with torrents of meltwaters, now bore only the trickle in the shadows. The people joined in singing the ancient songs, but fell silent in the presence of the *monnesepula*. Everyone carefully avoided his eyes. The hunters cast the entrails into the gorge. The *monnesepula* slung the meat-laden hide of the *bok* onto his shoulder. He strode rapidly away into the highlands, leaving us behind in the dusty breeze, our empty bellies growling for meat.

Pula (Rain)

Two days after Patel Uncle left us, he came back. He came up the path quickly, waving at me, his eyes full of hope.

"Look." He showed me a bundle of papers and tickets. "We're getting out of here."

Patel had papers stamped by UN officials that he had met near the town. The papers would allow us to take special UN flights that were evacuating political refugees from Lesotho.

"Tanzania," he said to me. "We will be safe there."

I shrugged. "We will miss that flight. Mother is too weak. And we can't leave without Sohrab."

"Yes, that is why I will stay. You, Amreek and the others will go. I will stay behind until we get Sohrab out. Nagarajah and I will do it somehow."

"Oh, I wouldn't depend on him," I commented.

"And where is Nagarajah? Why isn't he here?"

I could only shrug.

BUT WE FORGOT about that plan for a time.

My mother was now taken up in a great wave of burning, the

last fires of her life providing heat for all her family as we lay awake listening to her laboured breath. She shook and sweated and tossed and moaned in this new phase of her dying.

Patel tried to speak to her about the UN and the planes and Tanzania. But my mother did not hear. She was journeying back to the places where her life began. She went back to her ancestors, to make her excuses and learn the mysteries of death. She was requesting their acceptance of her errors in life. She might even have been pleading that she had been untruthful, in the hope that she would be excused. She showed them her children and those she had cared for. We can only hope those people were sympathetic.

By noon of the next day we wondered how such a thin, sick woman could burn so hot for so long. When Flori went to place a damp cloth on her head, 'Mè Jane waved her away saying, *Le felile. It is finished.*

Bushman pulled me outside. He looked at the sky with an implacable, calm expression. Strange clouds were boiling across the sky, making monstrous shapes. The wind reversed direction, lifting dust and litter in a curtain across the lowlands. Then I remembered what we had not seen in years – rain. It moved up from the lowlands in great windy sprays, then came on with a bombardment of fist-sized drops that we saw and heard when it was still hundreds of metres in the air, hissing towards us like bullets. We opened our mouths and found the rain was as sweet and good as roasted corn. Around Mohapi's place villagers were gathering to sing and stand with hands outstretched and mouths open. Bushman began to run like a crazed dog. He threw off his clothes and performed clumsy leaps and dives. Even 'Mè Jane stood under the clouds, letting her old blanket soak up the rain.

In the midst of the excitement we did not notice my mother awaken. She came out into the rain muttering words in a language we did not know, her eyes wild. The rain bullets became entangled in her hair. Her blanket had fallen away to reveal her large, fleshless bones. When she collapsed, the villagers gathered around her.

We took her back to her bed and removed her wet clothes. She was cool so we swathed her in blankets. She looked at us clearly. In her eyes there was hope. It was the hopefulness of someone whose mind has gone back to childhood and can no longer recognize her fate. She smiled for the first time in days.

The villagers stayed to dance to the music of the deluge. It was already filling the streambeds and sluicing down the mountainsides. Below, the rivers would begin to fill. Fields and gardens that women had planted out of stubbornness or hope or habit were dark and full of promise. Children raced through mud puddles and sang rain songs.

I FOUND A ROUND CLAY BOWL that 'Mè Jane had lovingly crafted when she was young. The bowl was round and deep and smoothed by years of use. I placed it outside on a rock, to later peer in at the dark surface of pure rain, to see my own rippled and tired face. I brought the bowl to my mother and offered her a drink.

She came out of a delirium and took the bowl and drank. We saw her face relax, her thirst satisfied. Then she lay back, and with open eyes still upon me, she died. We held our breaths and stood over her, not willing to let life detach from her, but then 'Mè Jane made us stand back and let her go free.

OUTSIDE THE GEESE were aligned on the ridge, letting the rain wash the dust from their plumage. They watched me approach them, and, with no great urgency, singly or in twos, beat their wings, and rose into the rainy sky. They formed a flying arrow, pointed at their destination. British Properties, or other far-off lands.

Curer of Minds

Once Mother was properly over on the Other Side, she must have considered what she could do to help me. So, only hours after those rains came and my mother died, my womb issued forth and I became a woman. I let go and wept until there were no tears left.

PATEL BROUGHT US to Maseru. In our numb grief, we were unable to resist. Leaving our home country in a plane was too fantastic an idea for us to grasp properly. On the appointed day we took the long trip south to the international airport in Deadkumar's car. There we found the UNHCR planes and, in the small airport building, a crowd of desperate refugees. Here were all the motley and many-hued fighters of the Republic who had collected in Lesotho over the decades. We watched in dazed wonder as a plane roared and suddenly bounded unsteadily into the gusts. It began to rain again, and the smell of wet earth and wet dung mixed with the sharp smell of airplane exhaust.

As our papers were being checked at the gate, Bushman skipped away to vanish in the crowd. We should have known that he would never leave. Perhaps it was because he was from the beginning of that place. Perhaps it was the magic power of his mother. We should have known that Bushman would not tolerate airplanes, technologies and foreign places.

'Mè Jane and Flori went after him. And Patel Uncle and I were left. Patel Uncle shoved me into the queue.

"Go," he said. "I have arranged for people to meet you in Dar es Salaam – they are waiting for you..." He propelled me forward with a big hand, but I balked.

Behind us a woman was trying to manage a crowd of five small children. She sized up Patel and me, and without a word, placed the hand of the smallest, squalling child in mine. The child looked at me with big eyes, stopped crying and let me take it up in my arms. I climbed the steps onto the plane.

IF THERE HAD BEEN PEOPLE waiting for me in Dar es Salaam I never found them, only a few bored-looking government officials in rumpled uniforms.

Leila and her children became my family. They made it easier for me to avoid thinking of my real family. I had no idea where they were or how to contact them. Could families suddenly end, leaving behind scattered individuals with bad dreams?

Those first days in Tanzania were unsettled, and there were days of squalling, hungry children. The man of that family had died, one of the victims of the Bad Elements unleashed across Lesotho. I watched this Leila push her grieving to one side as she struggled to provide food and shelter for her brood, determination stamped across her face. She had little money, but she had me to help her. At first I thought often of going back, but there was always someone pulling at my hand or clutching my leg – a little one with the runs, with croup, with an infected cut or an insect bite, a small one lost and found again, toddlers wet and stinking and fallen in the dirt.

But at night, awake and in dreams, my family and home would not leave me in peace. Then I would curl up next to one of the children and let their dreams of friendly dogs, sweet foods and playmates chase my sorrows away. I would sleep until they woke me.

THE ANCESTORS, or my mother and father, must have been watching over me. Perhaps they arranged that I should fall in with that young family so that I could know that my personal sorrows would drown in the sea of human tragedies. In my care were small children who had known their father, then lost him. I could see that this was worse than not knowing your father at all.

And there were Tanzanians and the steamy heat, the congestion and mildewy dilapidation, the big-leafed palms and the dazzling hot-water sea of Dar es Salaam. There were homeless orphans trying to survive in the streets, the starving, the crippled, the blind, the lepers and the fevered, any of them prepared to share their sorrows and their needs with me.

Polay-sana, polay, polay...so sorry. Sorry for us all.

In that heat it was not possible to cover and conceal. Lives were exposed, hearts unlocked.

My own sorrows dwindled to a small thing, a stub of the toe, even as we struggled to find a way to survive amid the millions of overheated existences in Dar.

Then that first difficult period passed and things improved. We settled, found a way to live, began to learn the *jambo* and the *mambo* of that place. With me helping with the children, Leila found work at an international organization. In short order, she was made manager, the children were placed in a crèche and I was given a place to be tutored while I helped in the offices. I began to read and ask questions. I wandered freely through the various neighbourhood projects, talking to people and learning the workings of the micromarket, the clinic, the crèche and the orphans' centre.

I wrote letters home, to the college and to 'Mè Jane, care of Mohapi. And Leila, in her quiet, efficient way, made inquiries as to the whereabouts of Patel and the others. Finally, a letter arrived from 'Mè Jane.

In her solemn and formal style she explained what had happened. Patel had left them some money with instructions to return to the college. But the college had changed. A new principal had arrived to replace Patel, and the place was being restaffed. Our old compound was occupied by strangers. So 'Mè Jane and Bushman moved, with Flori, into an old place at the opposite end of the valley. It was simple, with a dirt floor. "Very difficult to sweep and very cold in these winter months..." 'Mè Jane wrote. Of Sohrab, Patel and Deadkumar they knew nothing. Of Bushman, 'Mè wrote, "He is strange, and we hear him talking to Aousi Koko, as if you were there with him. He seems to think you will hear him across the miles. That boy knew he could not fly with you in the air."

I listened for Bushman's voice after that, and sometimes thought I could hear him. But it was very distant and I could not hear what he said. I could barely remember Sohrab's voice.

After I read that first letter, I became uncomfortable with my safe life in Tanzania. I was surrounded by caring people who needed me, I was learning, I was even making money of my own. I said nothing of my feelings to Leila or the children. I sent letters and waited for letters and tried to hear the voice of Bushman at night when it was still.

We moved into a bigger house and Leila hired people to help. Her children shed their sorrows and grew.

I took to wandering farther and farther into the town. The thieves in the market, the rich men with their shady sunglasses and gestures and comments, the street gangs and their knives, the prostitutes – none of them impressed me. I walked freely and watched and listened. Some evenings I passed through smoky lanes, seeing shadows. Sometimes I would glimpse a face in a crowd, someone familiar and alert to my presence. This was always at twilight, at the moment the sun rolled past the edge of the sky, leaving the dust that hung in the air to assume dark shapes.

A LETTER ARRIVED from Shiv Uncle Patel. He explained that he had been moving across the land, avoiding the new authorities and trying to solve our problems. There was one success, he wrote. When Zara's people in British Properties heard of her death and the plight of the children, they wired money for me to join them. I needed only to present myself at the Canadian High Commission, buy my air ticket and go. I was instructed to travel to Dar es Salaam immediately.

British Properties. It was as much a blank photo as ever. It was two words that sounded nasty, like old history and hidden scars.

I put down the letter and went out into the hot and brilliant late afternoon. I could not think properly so I walked, through the community projects, on toward the centre of town, the harbour and the narrow streets of the market. The future was beckoning me, but it was like the rich men near the market who looked for young and stupid girls. The future was promising, yet dishonest. It would lead me away from those I loved.

I walked aimlessly, passing into obscure alleys and streets hour by hour until the sunlight softened and the jittery, hot air began to settle. Then I distinctly saw a face I would never forget. At first I thought this was a trick of light, but the face was solid, and attached to it was a whole person dressed in the red and purple garments of the Masai. Her hair was knotted and filled with dust, her face streaked with coal soot, a tangle of amulets around her neck. I knew she had been waiting. She blinked rapidly and sucked in her breath at being caught in the full glare of my recognition.

It was the *mathuela*, the witch-mother of Bushman, the spirit of the head in the glade, the matron of my dreams, come back to find me. Her face was younger than it had been, as though Bushman's birth, her own death, her months of watchfulness from the branch of a tree and the search through the world had recharged her with youthful vigour.

At any moment I expected her to transform into a spirit and float away. Instead she regarded me with a twist of her mouth, tried to slip past me. I seized her garment. She muttered in the language of the Masai but allowed herself to be held.

"Are you disappointed?" I whispered.

She chuckled and examined my hand on her shroud. Her face became a blank, absorbed, the wrinkles a myriad of past decisions and wrong and right thoughts, all leading nowhere. She began to sing in the low undulating voice of a mad person. There was no structure or tune to her song, so it was easy to become lost, slip out of the moment and beyond the twilight. I clung tightly to the rough plant fibres of her garment and felt myself become a floating thing with only her shroud to anchor me, only her face to guide me. She took me into her madness, into directionless time, where there was no *pranayama*, no difference between life and death, fire and ice. I sank headlong, spun backward and forward, fell through the future into other destinies, to where the world could go other ways. Then I came back.

Her song ended. She gently tugged her garment from between my fingers and moved off into the smoky night, greeting shadows.

Sohrab

I took the money Shiv Uncle sent and I bought a ticket home. Leila cried, and the children told me the gifts they wished for, thinking that I would return. I had been with them for two years, a long time in the lives of small children.

I PAID FOR a small transport into the city centre. Patel Uncle was waiting there for me with a kiss on my brow and an apologetic expression.

He had been trying to find a way to have Sohrab released, but the contacts he made were weak, the officials jumpy under the watchful eye of Pretoria. It became clear that should he persist, he himself would be detained, or worse. Patel moved from place to place, never settling for more than a few weeks. He stayed away from our town and the college. With all that, perhaps with the loss of Mother and the strain of sending me away and worrying over Sohrab, Patel Uncle had aged. His hair was suddenly grey, his features haunted.

Now we sat together in a restaurant and I saw in his eyes and by the way he treated me, how much I had changed too.

"So you had to return to this desperate situation," he said.

"They are my brothers."

"But you could have gone to university overseas, put all these bad experiences behind you!"

"What bad experiences?"

He laughed shortly, but fell quiet when he saw that I was not joking.

"And," I said, "I came back with a plan..."

IN THE MORNING we met 'Mè Jane at the bus station, and she and I immediately went to the warden of the prison. Our plan consisted of every *lisente* we had, the money for the air trip to British Properties, the money I had saved, and the little that Patel and 'Mè Jane possessed, plus a pile of American money that Leila had forced on me. It amounted to about eight thousand Maluti in bills of every sort, stuffed into a small plastic bag. In the office of the warden we spoke to him courteously and, without explanation, placed our money bag on the floor beside his chair.

Without looking at it, he said, "And tell me again, how old did you say this boy is?"

The next day Sohrab was released. It was just as Deadkumar had said: the money game had worked.

When we retrieved Sohrab he was dirty but his eyes were clear. We led him from the prison gates, and once well away, stopped to go over him thoroughly. Sohrab went along with it, allowing himself to be sniffed over and poked and pinched in a way he never would have tolerated before. That was the first of many changes in young Sohrab. When I asked him if he was fine, he just shrugged and looked at me with bright, hard eyes. When we told him that Mother had died, he wept immediately and openly.

OVER THE MONTHS that followed, Sohrab explained what had happened.

His trouble had begun when the National Agric Police brought him and Glorius inside the Agric compound. But he would not tell me what went on in there.

"We were just boys then," was all he said.

But later he began to wander in our valley, trying to discover how to be a man. He went without home or bed. The trouble was inside of him, he said, and staying at home only seemed to make it worse.

HE NEVER INTENDED to be the leader of the *tsotsis*. He had never followed the gangs of boys who plagued the encampment with their mischief. It was enough to have the freedom to wander and to discover the thing of how-to-be-a-man.

But the boys saw him coming and going from the house of a certain girl. They trailed behind him sometimes, idly, perhaps because they recognised one of their own, a boy footloose and troublesome, or perhaps because he was indifferent.

His trousers were broken at the zipper. They dangled from his hips, flapped like flags about his legs. One of the boys mocked this style by breaking his own zipper. Soon they all took on this new busted-zipper look.

The *tsotsis* came to know Sohrab's routine. They knew when to find him in the dim rooms where he explored his manhood. They knew he lay there with the girl who called herself Mary. She was long of limb and quiet, a beauty. The boys yearned for her. They knew that when he left Mary he was unsated, prowling. They were drawn to and afraid of that, and kept their distance until he emerged from the house of the girl's aunt, his belly full of onions and meat and milk, his loins calm.

They called him Touch.

They came nearer and nearer to him to better know the thing he was after, the how-to-be-a-man. They sang his name like a praise name. *Touch, Touch. Touch that Mary.*

In the heat of an afternoon, they lolled under a shade tree and listened to the still sounds of Touch with his wife. They were different sizes and ages, the boys. Some were orphans, others were disowned, rejected, damaged. Milk often cried in his sleep for his mother. He was fifteen. Roadwork spent hours running along the sides of the roads, plodding on shoes shaped from fragments of tyre tread. His head was thick and low and he did not hear well the lorries that swirled by him.

That day they hoisted Roadwork onto their shoulders and pushed him up against the wall so that his head was thrust between the wall and the metal roof. They pushed him hard so that his head wedged into the gap. Roadwork yelped and then went quiet as he now had a full view of Sohrab and how-to-be-a-man.

"Abuti Roadwork Mon, tell us what is it."

Roadwork was making grunting sounds, and gyrating his hips, as much to communicate the sights he saw as to urge Sohrab on. He made luscious coital noises.

Sohrab looked up and saw Roadwork's head. He tried ignoring him but the grimacing knot-haired head, the deformed face, the insolent mimicking of the sounds of this slippery how-to-be-a-man thing, finally made him stop.

They had let go of Roadwork's feet so that he hung by his head and hands. When he saw Sohrab unhook himself from Mary, he kicked the wall and struggled to free himself. When Sohrab pulled his trousers on and came outside, the boys scattered and Roadwork wailed like a lost goat. Sohrab coolly registered the dusty heads, the children, the older hardened boys, then he roughly yanked Roadwork down, but did not beat him as the others expected. He examined the scraped skin on Roadwork's head with some interest, then walked away, indifferent, thinking of Mary's aunt.

He went to the river and stripped and swam in a shallow hole until the boys crowded into that swimming place. Then he went to a hiding place he sometimes used, an unfinished hydroelectric tower planted in the midst of an expanse of rock and scrubby bushes, a monument to an unattainable electrical future. The Europeans had made it.

Sohrab climbed the base, then the ladder to the first platform, then the second, then the topmost. The top place was a square metal grid that seemed to soar and sway over all of southern Africa. He could not stand on it for the vertigo and the wind. He crawled onto it and lay panting and clinging. Then below he saw the boy Roadwork, and Milk and the others. One by one they reached the ladder and, with much whooping and yelping, they climbed up. At the top Roadwork looked about and immediately shat in his pants.

From that moment Sohrab became the leader of the local *tsotsis*. It was by default, by chance, he told us. Not because he wanted it. They needed him. They were his boys. Now there were responsibilities, traditions, tasks he must fulfill. They needed food. They needed protection from police, shop owners, angry ancestral spirits. How was he to do all this? How was he to be a man?

Sohrab made them play football.

He could not explain why he led them from a raid of a chicken yard to the soccer field. Perhaps it was because he himself wanted to play, needing to sate himself in this way too, forgetting all else but the ball for a few hours.

The ball was made of rags bound tightly with string. They preferred this to the rubber thing they stole from the shop. They watched the district team, Dinare, in their practice, then took a corner of the field and, calling out the praise names of players and hunters, they shot and passed and ran until the dust and sweat streaked their scrawny legs and they were exhausted and the sun was low. After that the whole troupe, every *tsotsi* who belonged to Touch, played soccer alongside Dinare during the afternoons. Sometimes the boys were starving. Sometimes they fought. But they always leapt foward to take a pass, feint, run and shoot.

And there was the encampment, the town. As leader, Sohrab came to know the lanes behind the stores. There were places to sleep, places to hide, places to steal. They knew which doors could be opened safely and which were best left alone. Touch led the boys and the boys showed him their knowledge and their ways.

Except when they scaled the tower, they were surrounded by a shadow gang of bony, patchy dogs with the same appetite for trouble, chaos and opportunities. The dogs often singled out a weak or sick or slow boy and harassed him by running at him, yapping, then tearing away in the dust as the boy reached for a stone. They had sores on their scrawny flanks where the stones had found their marks. Like the boys, the dogs followed Sohrab.

THE DOGS were the first to pick up the scent of trouble. The dogs always knew. Trouble was a scent they loved more than the scent of food or a bitch in heat or the scorched seat of Roadwork's trousers. It came in the form of a cream Mercedes Benz car that rolled smoothly through the encampment, through trash and puddles of mud and urine, over the humped dirt that had buried the British bitumen laid down decades before, through the midst of the *tsotsis* who at that moment were watching carefully the doorway of the Spar store. The dogs elected to follow the slow-rolling Mercedes. Then Sohrab flicked his head sideways and clicked his tongue and half a dozen boys jogged along near the rotating rear wheels. The car rolled heavily to a stop and the door opened to release a breath of sweet, cool air. A woman dressed entirely in red (surely she was a queen of some sort) stepped out, shielding her eyes. Perhaps a boy, or perhaps a dog, came underfoot. She tripped, and as she fell someone got hold of her purse. It was tossed from hand to hand four times before she knew it was gone. She screamed for help, but too late. There was no one around her but a single dog that vomited a mound of worms in the dust.

SOHRAB SQUATTED behind the market butcher shop weighing the purse. Some of the boys drooled as they stared at it – they had not eaten that day. The purse was of supple lambskin polished to a leaden gleam. It opened to reveal a matching wallet containing cards, which Sohrab put aside, a sheaf of notes – Rands, Malutis and some other money they had no interest in – and, tucked beneath lip paints and eye paints, a silken crimson sachet. He eyed all these things without bringing them out. Then a pony with a rider came along and Sohrab scooped the purse into his shirt and led the boys out of the encampment to the tower. On the topmost platform, he counted out the money and distributed it evenly.

Later he slipped away alone and opened the sachet. He poured out a small pile of diamonds. Sohrab's gut contracted, as though something cold had touched it. His gut knew before his brain knew that this was trouble. His *kharm* lay nestled, sparkling in the palm of his hand, and he felt powerless. They would come after him and his boys. They would come to know that the leader was one they called Touch. They would come to know that Touch had stolen from a woman of money, Mercedes Benz and diamonds.

When he thought of the police, the memory of a smell, the sick sweet smell of alcohol and sweat, came to him. They had rattled Sohrab, those National Agric Police, with whatever cruelty they had shown him that day. They had shown him the part of men's nature that should never be shown to a child. In his dreams Sohrab relived his stay in the National Agric compound.

But it had not withered his faith or his courage. It had merely brought with it the knowledge that cruelty was inescapable.

He put the sachet in his pocket and ran. The heavy little stones slapped against his leg, unpleasant and burdensome. He saw no more of the other boys that day and no dogs ventured near him. He was alone, ear cocked for his approaching *kharm*.

He moved out of the encampment, following the deep *dongas* beside the roads. He ran toward the home he had avoided for so long, only to shun it once he neared the place. He turned towards the riverbank as the light went out of the sky. He saw Thabo Majara staggering drunkenly along the path with a large snake on his shoulder. He assumed Thabo and the snake were looking for him, which Thabo might have been had he not been sick and poisoned and bitten by Sohrab's cobra-child.

For half of that night Sohrab lay awake by the river, the sachet biting into the skin of his thigh. He might have stayed had not a sudden terrible coldness overtaken him, driving him to find a fire, a bed, any comfort. Yet he still would not go home, thinking that they would be watching for him there. Instead he went to Dr. Patel's house, unlatched the kitchen window and climbed silently inside. He found a bench with an old blanket neatly folded there, waiting for him.

IN THE MORNING Dr. Patel woke Sohrab with a gentle hand upon his shoulder. He offered a cup of hot, sweet tea and said nothing.

The sun was not yet up and Sohrab was still cold. He sipped at the tea and avoided the intent gaze of Dr. Patel. Too late he was conscious of his hand plucking the packet in his pocket. Patel glanced down at Sohrab's pocket but did not ask. He knew better.

We did not know that Patel Uncle had provided a refuge for Sohrab. Had 'Mè Jane known, she would have worried less those nights he stayed out.

It seems the woman, the mark of the *tsotsis*, was the mistress of the Minister of Information, long known as a diamond smuggler, arms dealer and collaborator with the Boers. The police searched all night. They rigorously and soberly chased down the *tsotsis* and succeeded in capturing Roadwork, upon which Roadwork described to them in detail how Sohrab had pumped his thing into the girl by the river, since he was sure that this was his crime. It took them some time to find out who Sohrab was and where his trails lay, and then, not thirty minutes after Sohrab had finished his tea, the Paramilitary Police, the soberest of them all, banged on Patel's door.

SOHRAB was put in the Police Prison on the hill in the town. The prisoners were provided with *baap* and water, and, when the circuit judge came, they were given meat and *roibos* tea. But Sohrab was not permitted food. He was left to starve the first days he was there, as part of his preparation for questioning. They did not know that Sohrab did not care very much about food any more, the relentless gorging he had embarked on years before having permanently quelled his appetite. And at night it was not hard for one of the other prisoners to bring him something small to eat.

When the officer brought him down for questioning Sohrab was sullen and would not talk. They asked him about the theft, about the diamonds, then later about Thabo Majara. They spoke to him about Deadkumar, wanting to know where he was and how he lived and where he came from. Sohrab said little and, after a time, they seemed to forget about him. But eventually they found out things, since that was their task, and afterwards he was driven to the Prison for Men in Maseru.

Sohrab would not speak of prison, saying he remembered nothing but the single visit of his family.

My Wish

A few short years after I met the *mathuela* my wish was granted, just as 'Mè Jane had predicted. My wish had been humble but grand, impossible without an intervention from powerful quarters. I wished that my father's life should not have been sacrificed in vain, and that those evil people who killed him should be defeated. The *mathuela* used her power and influence to cause the white people of the Republic of Hate to give up their project and let Deadkumar's friends take over the country. Patel Uncle wept when we heard this, thinking of my father and mother. He wept silent tears of loss, not of joy and freedom. South Africa was free but many were gone forever.

And there was another person to weep over, but none of us wept. We always thought that Deadkumar would return as he had so many times before. But he seemed to be really gone this time, perhaps back to the Other Place in pursuit of my mother. 'Mè Jane always now spoke of him as she spoke of the other Dead. She said many prayers of the kind used to wish the Dead a good journey to their Place.

"He was a good man, his heart was good, the Mastah...," she said after her praise of the many lords and gods who run this place.

Flori said Deadkumar was a hero of the new South Africa, but 'Mè Jane said, no, he was not the hero type. "He has gone to his home by now, to claim an inheritance of land and to play his flute under a tree."

I did not challenge this, knowing that it was a dream that came from 'Mè Jane's heart.

Perhaps the truth is too much for us to understand at certain times.

Perhaps the truth needs only time, simple time, before it can be exposed. This was so of the death of Thabo Majara. I learned of this from Flori.

She was at the riverbank the night he died. It was not quite dark and she was resting there because of what Thabo Majara had done to her, beating her and forcing upon her a kind of love she no longer wanted.

Flori had fled, beaten and bruised, in tears. She felt small and worthless and angry. Later by the river she watched the black mysteries in the dark water. She prayed. She thought of her ancestors and named those she remembered. In her skirt she held the big knife from the kitchen. Every time she touched it she was afraid and cold, but she brought it out finally and placed it beside her where she could watch it in the sand. She was still there, hours later, when Majara appeared with the snake hung around his neck. He swaggered and swayed along the path, but a small shadow led him straight toward her, delivering him to her. Flori did not hesitate and did not think, only took up the knife, the muscle and sinew in her arm guided by the strength of the Ancestors she had summoned. She completed what the cobra had not. Then she and Bushman watched the blood stream out of Majara's throat into the sand, the blood black. They saw the dead snake suddenly stir and take up life from the fresh blood and slide away into the night.

This is the truth. We have seen this snake, living with a crushed spine. It is enchanted and powerful, but we are not afraid.

OUR VALLEY OF BEGINNINGS never returned to normal. Many moved to South Africa with hopes for a better life or were caught in the maw of the emergency. More than ever, families were without fathers, which made all the daughters endure their lives without the confidence that a real father inspires. These girls always wonder how it is to have their father's blanket to shield them from the bad things in this world. They wonder, as their father crouches in the place below the earth, how he watches over them and how he thinks of them. They wonder what it feels like to be touched by their father's love.

THE RAINS have come and gone many times since this happened. These days the grass is high. People sing and tend their crops. Sometimes they stop their work and look about themselves and realize the enormity of their place in this world of the Living. Sometimes they engage in long greetings with their neighbours, standing amid the rows of maize in the fields, crying and laughing about the Dead.

Mwanza

Acknowledgements

Red Dust, Red Sky started its life in Lesotho, and despite being written from every geographical angle (Vancouver, Mwanza, Bic, Dhaka, Harare, Dar es Salaam and even Ottawa) remains a meditation on a period of Southern African history, written from afar, and submitted with respect by a foreigner and a guest to that part of the world.

Many thanks to many: Charis Wahl for her questions and able editorial advice; Elizabeth and David Finch for additional commentary during the final edits; Geoffrey Ursell and the people at Coteau for their encouragement.

I extend special notes of gratitude to Nyla Sunga for enabling me to search for my way through, and to Krishna Govender for his insight, courage and friendship.

I salute all the people in Lesotho and South Africa with whom we worked and played during our years there.

I salute those who fought for freedom and won.

I salute those who fought and lost.

About the Author

Paul S. Sunga wrote *Red Dust, Red Sky* after living and working in Lesotho for several years during the 1980s, the last years of apartheid in South Africa. He worked as a teacher, journalist and medical research advisor, and was also involved with the political underground. He is the author of one previous novel, *The Lions*, published in 1992.

Born in Ottawa, Sunga has a PHD in Medicine, as well as degrees in biology and philosophy. He is the Director of International Development at Langara College in Vancouver, and a consultant to the Canadian International Development Agency for public health programs in Asia and Africa.

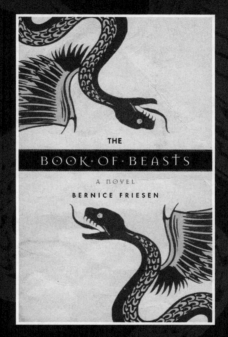